15 DAYS WITH YOU

ARA GRIGORIAN

LOVE, LAUGH, LEARN
M E D I A

Printed in the United States of America

First Edition, 2019 - Love, Laugh, Learn Media

Paperback ISBN-13: 978-1-7324621-1-3
Hardcover ISBN-13: 978-1-7324621-2-0

www.AraGrigorian.com

My wife — the hero in 'my' story. The one who alters the atmosphere.

My boys — I love how you're stepping into your destiny... but don't grow up too fast!

My parents — always and forever the heart (and the chefs) in our lives.

Above all, my Creator — thank You for Your unstoppable love.

15 Days With You

ARA GRIGORIAN

LOVE, LAUGH, LEARN
MEDIA

PART ONE

"There is nothing, nothing, sadder than a surfer who used to surf."
~Author Unknown

ONE

SHEP

THIRTY-THREE DAYS AGO, I became an orphan.

I'm holding up fine. Really. I've had time to *walk it off, become stronger,* and *not let it define me.* Those are the one-liners I've perfected during my three-day drive from Houston to L.A. Because when people ask, what they're really hoping for is a story of strength and recovery, not grief. The way I see it, if folk are decent enough to ask, then the least I can do is give them hope.

I crank down the window. The California air gushes into my mom's truck and twirls the dust in the cabin. I toss my hat on the passenger seat and run a hand through my matted hair. Gotta admit, this L.A. air is surprisingly nice. I expected smog and desert-like heat, but so far, it's pleasant. Coastal living is what Mom wanted. She wanted me to leave Texas and live with people who'd take care of me. Thankfully, the only option I had was a great one. My uncle's family in Malibu is waiting.

Although she never said it, I know she also wanted me to be at a safe distance from the court proceedings, before anyone tapped my shoulder, forcing me, like my teammates, to testify. No need to worry, Mom. I'm far from there now. My new chapter awaits.

Look, am I falling apart? No.

Do I miss Mom? Of course. Absolutely. She was my best friend, my biggest fan, my rock. But cancer—a word that had never stepped foot in our home—broke down the door and took her away. It sucks, but I can't change that.

I smile at my reflection in the rearview mirror, amazed at how convincing I sound. All that alone time, ranching and fishing after her death, seems to have paid off.

As I plop my hat back on my head, someone honks, speeds by in what looks like a bright red spaceship, and gives me the finger. *Welcome to L.A., Shep.*

I give him my best smile and tip my hat. Not sure what pissed him off: my amazing cowboy hat or the fact that my truck can't exceed fifty-seven-point-five-miles-per-hour.

In fairness, I don't know if that's the real speed. Everyone—I mean everyone—even the blue-haired octogenarian, has sped passed me. When I floor this puppy, the needle sort of hovers in between fifty-five and sixty, then drops to forty-ish. Who knows. I've learned to accept this tub of rust and steel for what she is—transportation.

Back home, my teammates drove me around. I was taken care of, because I was valuable to the team, to the school.

But that was then. Everything changed, literally over night.

I reach into my shirt pocket and pull out my cousin Carmen's "after you exit" directions.

On the day I told her I'd be moving in with them, she chewed my ear about the great weather (which so far seems amazing), and making friends with her friends (which does not sound amazing), and starting senior year together at her high school (which is definitely a win since being the new kid at the new school sucks), and meeting the football coach and my soon-to-be teammates (which I would love to delay for as long as possible). She has so many plans.

Mom and I had plans, too. The map next to me is evidence. I glance at the blinged-out, hand-decorated map splayed on the passenger seat. Over the years, Mom and I marked up a bunch of them with drawings, stars, and trails, daydreaming how one day we'd go on road trips, exploring cool places. Just me and her.

Now, these maps are just a reminder of what we can't experience together: No hiking Machu Picchu, or going up and down Pacific Coast Highway, and no visiting *La Isla*, her island of Puerto Rico. One day, I will complete all of them. On my own, because that's my new normal—a lone wolf.

What I can't do on my own is get answers to the countless questions I had about her past and the man she never spoke of... my father. Maybe my uncle will have some insight. Maybe.

There's my exit: Kanan Road. As I slow to get off the freeway, the exhaust pipe rattles so hard I think my rear bumper may fall off. The only thing holding this truck together is stubborn rust and caked-on dirt.

Dirt. I scan around then take a quick sniff of my pits. *Yup, acceptable.* This has been a long ride. My uncle wanted me to fly back with him, but I didn't want him to plop down that type of coin. Also, I didn't want to leave Mom's truck behind. One day, this pup will be a classic. In a hundred years or so.

I sputter uphill. I would push the truck, but I'm too stunned by the neighborhood. Holy home-and-garden-TV, they live here? Mom always said my uncle was a successful business owner. I thought he had a coffee shop or a hardware store. I don't think selling hammers will get you a house in these woods.

A right turn and I find their house. This ain't ranch-shed-Texas, Dorothy. Better slip on your magic boots and get ready.

Enormous eucalyptus trees surround the perimeter of their Spanish-style home. The driveway leads to gigantic front doors, then loops around, like a U, back to the street. A gleaming gun-metal, open-top Jeep is parked haphazardly in front of the four-car garage, which by the way is four times larger than the guest house we lived in. The path is made up of pavers that appear hand-chiseled. I picture my truck's nasty, five-year-old oil all over them and decide it's best to park on the street instead.

Gotta admit, the house intimidates me, but this is home now. For the time being, at least. I hop out, grab my oversized duffle bag and the picture-frame box. My uncle had a moving company pick up my other stuff—books and junk. But this one, the box with my mom's picture frame, I didn't want to leave in the hands of strangers.

My uncle took one item with him: my mom's urn. When the treatments stopped helping and the prayers by her church didn't heal her, she gave him specific instructions. Instructions that were not shared with me.

I head up the driveway, my heart hammering away to a beat that only rolling thunder would truly appreciate. Less than twenty yards from the entrance, one of the doors swings open and my cousin Carmen, in a bikini top and shorts, sprints toward me.

"Shep!" she yells, running all out, not breaking stride. Her shoulder-length pitch-black hair sways with her movement. She's petite with pronounced calves and powerful shoulders—the build of an athlete, I realize for the first time.

I drop my bag and place my box on it just as she rams into me, causing my hat to fly off. She wraps her arms around me, tight.

We hug in silence for a few moments. She has always been like a sister to me. Like clockwork, she called on Fridays to wish me luck before the games, and on Saturdays to find out how many yards and touchdowns were added to my stats. She doesn't know what's happening back home. I hope she never does.

"I am so, so stoked you're here," she whispers, then releases her hold. Her hazel eyes sparkle.

"Stoked?" I ask. "Is that English or Californian?"

She frowns. "It means glad. Happy."

I pick up my hat, plop it on my head and wink at her.

"I'm stoked to be here, too."

She smiles. Unlike me, she's all Puerto Rican. Her skin is always sun-caressed, but now, she's fully bronzed.

6

"C'mon, let's go in before Mom and Dad get even more annoying. Mom's been all neurotic over your room, your boxes—"

"I told them I don't need anything special. I have a sleeping bag and—"

"Shep, you think Mom would let you live like a homeless person?"

She reaches for my box.

"Be careful with that," I say.

"Sure," she says then tucks the elongated box under her arm and takes my free hand.

I swing the duffle bag over my shoulder and hand in hand, we head toward the house.

"Dude, did you get taller?" she asks as she looks me up and down.

"Probably. Dudette, did you get darker?" I ask.

She grins. "Yeah, summer's been all surfing all the time."

Surfing?

A cold shiver runs up my spine at a distant memory. Many years earlier, Mom had taken me to Pirates Beach in Galveston. A bunch of surfers were there pulling off amazing moves. I wanted to surf, badly. So I nagged her until she eventually allowed some guy there to take me out on one of his boards. I surfed for what felt like hours. Most of the details are fuzzy now, but I do remember him calling me a natural talent. Mom even called me her Silver Surfer after that day because I rode like a bullet.

The smell of ocean and sand rush back at me.

So does the clipped memory of the wave that slammed into me and held me down, because it wanted me.

I lost consciousness.

Then, Mom's lungs gave me air and her voice pulled me back to life. She's the one who saved me, not the lifeguard, not the surfer.

I wrote off the ocean after that day, because on that day I dodged two bullets. I nearly drowned because I froze when I saw the bloody water surrounding me. Seconds earlier, a shark had nipped a chunk off an older lady's calf. That could've been me. For years I was convinced that shark was meant for me.

Haven't been back to the water since.

Carmen is a courageous girl for willingly playing in a shark's kitchen.

I eye her again. Is that how she has that body? "I didn't know you surfed. Are you any good?" I ask.

She nods. "Yeah, decent. Not as good as your mom was, but I'm getting there."

"My mom?" I ask, chuckling, as we step into the house. She was strong and in decent shape for a mom and all, but a surfer? Hardly. "Mom was no surfer."

She studies me like I'm from Mars. "Seriously?" she asks.

"Yeah, seriously. Mom didn't surf."

Her frown deepens.

Why is she giving me that look?

Just then, my Uncle José and Aunt Rosie appear from a corner. Not sure what to focus on: the stunning home with more windows than walls, Carmen's comment about Mom, or the family that's taking me in. I decide to focus on them.

"Took you long enough," José says. His smile reaches his eyes.

My aunt hugs me. "Shepard, you must be so tired and hungry. Come on, let's feed you."

"And turn you into an overweight poodle," Carmen whispers.

"Don't listen to her," my aunt says. "It's all organic and clean. If you eat trash, you become trash."

"Oh boy," Carmen whispers. "That's so cheesy."

My uncle takes my bag and places it on the hardwood steps. I take off my hat and scan the house. Amazing. And scary. I'm almost afraid to touch anything. Not because the house isn't welcoming, but because I'm not used to new stuff.

He walks me to the kitchen—a vast, beautiful space with chrome and stainless steel and stone everywhere. I scan the rest of the space.

That's when my eyes lock in on the poster-sized framed picture behind the wet bar. I approach it slowly.

It's a picture of Mom.

Young with long wet hair. She's studying the ocean.

Nestled under her toned and deeply tanned arm is a surfboard.

TWO

SAMANTHA

THAT MUST BE Carmen's cousin. Even though I'm on the second floor, I take a small step away from the window before he sees me. I don't want him to think I'm some weirdo stalker or anything. Okay, fine, I *am* weird, just not a stalker.

After weeks of build up, he's finally here. She's been talking him up non-stop, to the point that I've been counting down his arrival too with hopes that she'll stop telling me that he's a "gifted athlete," and "a highly-recruited running back," and, "an amazing guy." Here's the thing, I know a lot about star athletes—particularly football players. And none of it is good. Carmen knows this too, from personal experience, but none of that matters. This is her cousin we're talking about. I just hope he's not like the others—a cliché.

"Your cuz is here," I yell out.

Carmen doesn't even respond. All I hear are her bare feet slapping across the hall and down the stairs.

I turn back to the window and study him as he strolls across the driveway. He's got an easy way about him. Not a strut, but a comfortable gait.

His oversized, weathered cowboy hat is impressive. The way it rides on his head, you know he and that hat have seen long days and nights together. He's wearing a blue and yellow flannel shirt, sleeves rolled up, exposing fairly developed forearms. Wide shoulders stretch his shirt tight across his chest. The shirt is untucked, over thread-worn blue jeans. They do wrap nicely around his well-developed thighs and hams. He's the real deal all right. A studio costume designer may pick up a thing or two by studying him.

I snap out of the trance. Okay, maybe I've been studying him a bit too closely. What can I tell you? He's easy on the eyes.

A text message pops up on my phone. My little sister, Nomi.

Sis: *Mom thinks I should do that scene I told you about.*

I moderate my breathing before I reply. What is Mom thinking? She's only fifteen.

Me: *If you don't feel comfortable doing it, then don't do it. Remind her that legally she is first your mom. Agent is a distant second.*

I hit send. There's nothing for a while so I add more.

Me: *I'll call her and tell her to back off.*

Sis: *No, don't. You've taken too many bullets for me already. I'll tell her.*

That industry is filled with slippery slopes. She needs to be strong now.

Me: *I'll take all the bullets in the world for you. Even real ones.*

Sis: *I love you, Sam.*

I grin and a silly tear fills my eye.

Me: *I loved you first!*

I don't ever want to see my little sister hurt. I don't want to see anyone I love in pain.

I slip my phone in my back pocket and hope she takes a stand for herself. I may have to get into it with Mom again. Hey, what's one more scar?

The voices from downstairs confirm that he's inside now. As I head down to the kitchen, I pick up his distinct voice. A deep tone, low timbre that nearly hums in the chest.

Time to officially meet him. I take a deep breath then adjust my bikini top and shorts. A thought enters my mind that I try to push away, but the thought wins. Although I'm so flat I make walls jealous, I hope his eyes don't assume my voice is coming from my breasts. I hope he's different.

THREE

SHEP

"THAT'S MOM," I whisper, staring at her image. I don't understand.

My uncle stands next to me, admiring her photo. "My favorite picture of Olivia. She was sixteen there."

"Seventeen," Rosie corrects.

I stare at him. "Mom surfed?"

He returns my stare, dumbfounded. "Well, yes. A long time ago, but that was her thing." He hesitates, interpreting my blank expression correctly. "She never mentioned it to you?"

I shake my head. "No." I don't know how I feel about this. The one time I surfed, it wasn't even Mom who took me out. Why, I wonder? Maybe because of an injury or a traumatic experience like mine?

José runs his hand through his hair and I see something drift past his eyes. Something's on his mind. "It *was* a lifetime ago," he says.

Maybe. I turn to Carmen. Now I get why she gave me that look earlier. She slides on a barstool, then taps the one next to her. "Have a seat."

I oblige, but eye the picture one more time. Mom looks amazing.

My aunt pulls the casserole out of the oven, while my uncle places a plate in front of me.

"This is unnecessary," I say, even though I'm starving.

"I hope you're not a vegetarian or a vegan," my aunt says.

"Nothing wrong with vegans, Mom," Carmen says.

"Nothing wrong with them. It's their diet I question. You're okay with prime rib?" she asks me.

"He's a Texan," José says. "'Nuff said."

My mouth waters just at the thought. Past month I've been living off of cold cuts. I gape at the plate. Man... is it wrong that I hope all our meals will be like this one?

"How was your drive up?" Carmen asks.

"Long," I start, as someone enters the kitchen.

I turn, assuming it's my younger cousin Carlo. But *she* is *not* my cousin.

"Hey, you must be Shep," she says, strolling in like sunshine.

I study her, but try not to stare. Her long light brown hair has streaks of blond. She's got legs that go on forever and shoulders that are worthy of an Olympic athlete. The rays of sunshine streaming into the kitchen must be causing an optical illusion, because her eyes are a greenish-yellow and her skin, golden.

"Shep," Carmen says, "this is my best friend, Sam."

I rise. "Good afternoon."

The Olympian grins as she strolls toward me. "Wow, so gentle-man-like. Did you see that?" she asks Carmen. "He rose for me."

"Yes, Sam, we all saw that," Carmen says with a mock tone of exasperation.

Like Carmen, Sam's also in a bikini top and boy shorts. She must be a surfer, too. Had they been surfing earlier today?

Sam plops right next to me, smelling like sunscreen and sand and salt. It's like she's bathed in nature's tonic.

"Nice hat," she says as she plucks my hat off the counter and places it on her head.

Okay, so let me say that I have this thing—not a good thing, mind you—but I have an issue with people wearing my hat. I mean seriously, who takes someone's hat without permission? And although I am tempted to say something—nothing mean, but a choice word or two—my ten-gallon hat looks awesome on her. The words that want to come out are a mix of *how dare you* and *you look amazing.*

Thankfully, she rises before I'm able to vocalize my thoughts. She saunters toward the double-door stainless steel refrigerator and pulls out a large container that has green liquid in it. It looks like the type of goo you find in sewers.

I study her as she gulps down the green mess. Her arms are toned, her back muscles, pronounced. She's a serious athlete, all right. I'd bet she's also a swimmer, not just a surfer. The slightly shifted back strap of her bikini exposes a deep tan line. I'm beginning to forgive her for the whole hat-stealing thing.

She places her cup inside the sink, then leans on the counter facing me.

Focus on her eyes. Just the eyes.

She turns to Carmen. "He's no *Boricua*," she says.

A what?

"No, he's not," Carmen agrees.

"Sorry. I'm not a what?"

"You're all white and blondish," she says.

My eyes widen. Good looks and fully-functional eyes. She's the whole package. "Yes, always have been."

She grins. "What I'm getting at is that Carmen is all dark and short and not like you. She's a true *Boricua*."

I wait for the explanation, but it's Carmen who interrupts. "*Boricua,*" Carmen says, pronouncing it differently, rolling the 'r.' "From the island—Puerto Rico."

"Oh that," I say. It's true. Carmen looks more like my mom than I do. The fact that I look nothing like my family is a stark reminder that I am my father's son. Whoever he may be. "No, I didn't win the genetic lottery," I say.

Something in Sam's eyes tells me there's a whole lot she wants to say, but won't. Are we almost flirting?

"Anyway," Carmen says, clearly trying to change the topic.

"Sam is like my second daughter," Rosie says, also trying to move on.

"She basically lives here," Carmen says. "Has her own room and everything."

"Welcome to the neighborhood," Sam says then pushes off the counter. She grabs an apple off the basket on the counter and takes a huge bite out of it. "I'm gonna shower," she says. "What time's the Dodgers game?"

"We leave in a couple of hours," my uncle says.

"Cool," she says then strides away, but stops in front of the pantry's glass door and analyzes her reflection. She turns this way, then that, adjusting the brim of the hat. "I need to get one of these." She removes it, walks over to me then plops it back on my head before she leaves the kitchen.

I follow her movement until she's out of view.

A pinch and I hop. "Sorry, what?"

Carmen is giving me that look.

"What?" I ask, feeling the flush that must be brightening my ears. Within seconds the redness will spreads to my cheeks.

"What did you do now?" Mom would ask. When I was younger, I was sure she had super powers. How else could she know I'd been up to no good? In sixth grade Sally Perkins let me in on the secret. My stupid ears.

Like Mom, Carmen gives me a knowing smirk. "Eat up," she says, "so we can get you settled in."

———

"THIS IS YOUR ROOM," Carmen says as she places my box on a desk and moves out of the way.

I step in, confused. I see the bed, a bookshelf, my boxes, and a desk with a laptop on it, but I'm sure this huge room can't be just for me. Then I notice another room. I step into what turns out to be a hallway leading to two more rooms. One is a closet which is larger than the entire living area of our home on the ranch and the other is a bathroom. I see an ocean of polished stone, a standup shower encased in glass, and a tub. It's like an indoor hot tub.

I turn to her. "This is my room?"

She studies me, her eyebrows furrowed. "Yeah. Is it okay?"

She can't be serious. "Yeah, it's okay. It's more than okay. It's too much. I don't need all this." If this is my room, I might never leave home again.

She shrugs. "That's how the rooms are. Each bedroom in Dad's homes are like master bedrooms."

José must be a contractor or a developer. That would explain this house.

"Hey," someone drawls from the door. It's Carlo. A very pale version of Carmen's brother. He's either tired, or doesn't see a lot of sun, or both.

"Hey, man, how are you?" I ask.

"Whatever."

"Wake up, ass-wipe!" Carmen says. "Our cousin is here to live with us and that's all you have to say?"

He shrugs. "What's one more freeloader?" he says.

I blink.

Carmen gasps.

FOUR

SAMANTHA

AS MUCH AS I love the ocean's salty texture on my skin, the warm shower makes me feel new and almost appropriate. Until the next time I open my mouth that is. Sometimes I wish my filter worked *before* I spoke, not minutes later.

I probably shouldn't have mentioned the whole you-don't-look-like-them thing. Thankfully, he seemed to roll with it.

So much for a good first impression. He probably thinks I'm odd, which is unfortunate because I'm very normal most of the time. Note to self: take your meds on days you meet people for the first time.

Inhale. Hold. Release slowly. Oh well. Onward.

I throw on a pair of denim shorts, a t-shirt, and grab a zip-up hoodie. I decide showing less skin at the game will be a wise move. Nothing more vomit-inducing than drunk baseball fans salivating over a teenager.

I cringe at how I tried to test Shep's eyes when I leaned in front of him. I shouldn't have done that. For one because it wasn't cool—he is Carmen's cousin after all. But also, it didn't work. He didn't break eye contact. Did I mention the earthy scent that I picked up off his body? Like trees and chopped wood and charcoal barbecue.

So on the cliché scoreboard, I'm losing big time.

As I step out of my room, Carmen yells, "What. An. Ass! You're the only freeloader I know!"

For a second I think she's yelling at Shep, but then I see Carlo back out of Shep's room then book out of there. Haven't seen the kid move that fast since he had the stomach flu.

I sprint to Shep's room.

"I'm so sorry," Carmen says as I reach his room.

"Don't be. It's fine."

"What happened?" I ask.

"Nothing," he says. "Let's not make a big deal out of it."

"Already keeping secrets from me?" I ask, as I hop onto his desk.

"Watch out—" he says, reaching out to something behind me.

My butt hits whatever it is. I spin to grab it, but I'm too slow. The box hits the floor, followed by a crunching noise that can only mean one thing. I broke something fragile.

"Oh crap," I whisper then glance at Shep.

He is motionless, staring at the lifeless box. I am frozen, mortified.

Carmen slides next to me and looks over my shoulder. "Sam, what did you do?"

I wish she wouldn't ask these types of questions. It's fairly obvious what I did. I wish she would take one for the team and pretend she did it instead. My face feels warm and numb.

We all stare at the box and the face down picture frame that has mostly slid out. The shards of glass confirm what we all heard.

"I'll get a hand vac," Carmen says and runs out.

I stare at him. "I'm so sorry," I say.

His eyes are stuck on the scene of destruction. "It's okay," he says. His tone is honest, but his face tells me this frame was important. Probably his Mom's. This is going from bad to horrible.

"Was it an antique? I'll buy you a new frame right now. Any style you want."

But he doesn't say anything for a few moments. "Don't worry

about it," he finally says and lowers himself to the floor. "The picture is what I care about."

I lower myself also. He gingerly slides the frame out of the box, but appears unsure as to how to flip the frame. We're studying the remains. "I don't want the picture to get scratched up. It's the only copy I have," he says.

"I think I can use my nails to grasp the edges of the backing board and just lift it up," I say.

He nods. "Okay. Good idea. Just be careful," Shep whispers.

Time to redeem yourself, I think.

At that instant, Carmen returns and joins us on the floor. The three of us are huddled around the frame. I reach for it.

"Gently," Carmen says. "Don't screw up like you normally do."

I glare at her. "There is plenty of pressure on me already. No need to mention that I'm a clinical klutz."

He stares at me with his hazel puppy eyes. Something happens to my heart and my lungs.

"Clinical?" he asks.

I nod. "I have ACDC."

He chuckles. "You have a what?"

"She means ADHD," Carmen corrects.

"What she said," I say and try to produce my own puppy eyes.

For a moment I think he may say something poetic, release me of my guilt. "Let's focus," he says instead.

"When we were younger," I say as I gently turn the clips on the back of the picture frame, "like a month or two ago, Carmen and I played a marathon session of operation. You know that game?"

"Is that the one that you have to use a tweezer to pull out plastic pieces from small openings without touching the edges?"

"That's the one," Carmen says.

"Yeah, I know it," he says. "I played it when I was five."

I eye him after I remove the rear plate of the frame. He's grinning. "So you're good at it?" he asks. "Is that why you volunteered to do this?"

"Nah, I was horrible. I didn't even win once. But I think I've learned from my failures."

He mumbles something, but I tune out his negativity. I can do this.

I slip the tips of my finger nails into the edges and pull out the heavy backing board and hand it to him. I nudge the picture a hair from one of the edges and pull it out.

Success!

No scratches, no damage. I am a rockstar. It's a picture of Shep with a woman who must be his mom because she has a slamming resemblance to Carmen. She has her arm around his shoulder and he has tipped his head on hers. They were a beautiful family.

"There," I say, offering him the picture. But he's not looking at it. Both Carmen and Shep are focused on the backing board instead.

"What is that?" Carmen asks, but I can't see what they're looking at.

"I have no idea," he says, his voice low and distant.

When he rises, we all follow and cluster around him, peering over his shoulders. A large yellow envelope has been taped to the backing board.

At that instant, José shows up. "What did Sam break now?" he asks, but stops dead when he sees the object of our fascination. José moves me aside and places his hand on Shep's shoulder. "I was going to give you a few days before we spoke about this, but I guess fate has stepped in."

I shrink away, knowing full well that it was me, not fate.

"You knew about this?" Shep asks. The poor kid's eyes are bloodshot.

He nods. "Olivia left us a specific request."

FIVE

SHEP

AT THE KITCHEN TABLE, Carmen and Sam flank me, while my aunt continues to look over her shoulder, waiting for José to return. I stare at the oversized envelope in front of me. On it, written in my mom's frail handwriting are clear instructions: *For Shepard - speak to José before opening.*

Clearly, she predicted the chance that I might stumble onto this before my uncle had spoken to me. Whatever is inside the envelope must be important. My uncle joins us, in his hand a legal file box. From it, he removes one letter-sized envelope and another stack of letters bound by a rubber band.

"Go ahead and open the envelope she left you," he tells me.

Carmen squeezes my arm. I glance at her. Her eyes glow with empathy.

I grab the envelope and slide my finger under the sealed flap.

What is this, Mom?

I tear through it and a sense of fear and excitement sits on my chest. I pull out the tri-folded, yellow construction paper. As I open the flaps, the paper's brittle texture confirms this is an old document.

In bold red, the ornate title stares at me: *15 Days of Surfing.*

Beneath the title it says, *Summer of 2000!* On first glance, the document looks like it's a marked up map, but it's more than that.

The use of color markers, highlighters, and even the handwriting is definitely all Mom. This is exactly how Mom had marked up our various travel maps. The main drawing is California's southern coast. Written over the drawing is a list of numbered locations. I recognize some of these places: Encinitas; San Onofre; Venice; and a bunch more. She has also drawn a surfing banner which says, *Sleep Less Surf More.* On the lower left corner, is a list of activities: Sleep under the stars; moonlit surfing; and a handful more.

I turn to my aunt and uncle. "I don't understand."

"Do you..." Carmen starts. "Do you mind if we look?"

I hand it to her while I wait. Sam walks around and joins Carmen to pore over the lists.

My uncle rubs his chin. "The summer of 2000 was your mom's last summer here before she went to the University of Texas. This was her last surf trip. This trip pitted me and your mom against Papi, your grandpa, who did not want her to do anything of the sort."

Papi, the grandfather who I've never really met or spoken to. He apparently showed up at her funeral, but he avoided me then disappeared. He is the reason, according to her, she went to Texas in the first place.

"I fought for my little sister. We won. She went. Months later we found out she had gotten pregnant during the trip."

I absorb the details. Golden nuggets of information that she had never shared with me. This trip is when I happened. I knew she was young when she had me, but these details are all new to me.

"But... what am I supposed to do with this list?"

My uncle hands an envelope from his box to me. He then pulls out a Styrofoam container that holds what looks like a dozen or so blue vials.

"These are her ashes," he says as he runs his palm over the bottles. "Olivia wanted her ashes to be released at those same specific beaches you see on your list."

I sink into the chair. I don't get it. Why would she make this part of her will? Or put on all this fanfare? She could've just asked me directly and it would've been done.

"She wants her ashes returned to the water, while riding a wave, on a surfboard. This is her wish."

Say what? My heart hammers away at my ribs. I'm trying to process this. All of it. She wants her ashes spread at a bunch of beaches... while surfing? I don't surf. I don't even go in the water. He may not know that, but Mom clearly did.

He turns to Carmen. "She hoped that you'd do this for her."

Wait, what? Why would Mom want anyone else involved? This should be mine to do. Alone. I study Carmen. Her eyes are red and she's nodding vigorously.

Would I do anything for her? Of course. But I can't do this. Warmth breaks out at the nape of my neck.

And there it is. This is what happened the last time I went to the beach with my friends. I was on dry sand—far from the break. But this isn't just fear, there's something else. I can't put my finger on it, other than to say that my time with Mom should be private time.

I find the words that won't make me sound petulant.

"But why like this?" I ask, my voice small and nearly lost. I need to understand her reason for doing it in *this* way.

"I expect her reasons will be explained in the letter I handed you."

I stare at the sealed letter.

"Carmen, there's one more thing," José says. "On July twenty-ninth is the annual memorial benefit at Pismo Beach for surfers who've passed away. She wanted you to ride in her name. You're already registered."

"Absolutely," Carmen says, with no hesitation whatsoever.

He gives her a thumbs up. "On her list, Pismo Beach was the last location she visited. We can talk logistics later, but my guess is three to five sites per day then move on. We just have to hit Pismo Beach on the twenty-ninth."

Is he envisioning a family road trip? I'm touched that they would do this for her. And I feel fortunate that my cousin happens to be a surfer. But... I have to think this through.

I take the map from the girls and scan down the list. Day thirteen was *Pismo Beach*. The two days following were supposed to be *Santa Barbara* and *County Line*, but both are crossed out. Did she stay in Pismo for the last three days, or did she cut the trip short? Maybe something happened when she got there? I pause. Is that when it happened? Is that where she met the guy who would impregnate her?

I need to speak up, say something, but right now I'm struggling with basic words.

"Read her letter," José says, practically reading my mind. "Then take it from there."

"Okay," I say as I rise and grab the unopened envelope and her list. Without another word I head upstairs to my room.

They say nothing, but I can hear their thoughts.

SIX

SHEP

I LOCK the door then drop on my bed. I take a deep breath, then tear open the envelope and slide out the letter.

My dear boy... My handsome young man,

I messed up. I let you down. I let me down.

I promised you so much, had planned for so much more. It was supposed to be you and me. We were going to do everything together. Travel the world. But there I went and got sick.

I'm sorry, Shep.

There are things I need to tell you. Stories I owe you. I tried to explain why I worried about you and the choices you were making, but you couldn't listen, because you didn't have context. Maybe you'll hear me now. The truth is that the truth is not very easy to discern. Only by living it can you really understand.

My request—my dying wish, I suppose—is for you to go on

26

this fifteen-day trip like I did back in 2000. Relive my surf trip. That's when it happened.

Fifteen days to know me, the other me.

Fifteen days to get answers.

Fifteen days to reacquaint yourself with the surf if the waves call you.

I'm not proud of my past. I'm afraid you won't like the other me. But I'm asking you to give me your hand and trust me. I suspect after fifteen days with the old me, you'll learn the truth. Because that was the summer I got pregnant. The summer God was preparing both you and me. You'll learn something new about me. And in the process, you'll finally get what you've asked about for years—details about your father.

I love you. I will always be there with you. And if you listen—really listen—I promise to whisper to you once in a while.

Mom

P.S. You asked me if I believed you. Of course. My question all along was, do you believe you?

I squeeze the bridge of my nose and force back the tears. So much for being 'all right.' Man, I miss her. A lot. I rise off the bed and walk to the bathroom, studying my face. A face unlike anyone else in my family.

My father. Is it possible?

When I was younger, I thought about him a lot, hoping that one day he'd walk back into our lives. But he didn't and all my thoughts of him, whoever he was, eventually turned to anger.

What could I possibly learn about him during a fifteen-day trip? Did she leave clues? I suddenly remember all those other envelopes José had. Is that what she has in mind? A scavenger hunt?

I scan the letter one more time, but this time, my eyes freeze on her final question to me: *Do you believe you?*

Thankfully, it doesn't matter now. I don't have to be involved.

I FIND my way around the house to Uncle José's study. It's a large office with bookshelves, an office desk, and an oversized drafting table. He's hunched over drawings, studying details. I don't want to bother him now. I step backward just when he notices me.

"Shep, come in, come in."

"I don't want to disturb."

"Nah, come over here and check this out. It's a new project in Hidden Hills."

I approach him and study the drawing. I'm not trained in reading drawings, but the circular home looks like a docked flying saucer. It's large with what look like two tennis courts. I glance at the name on the corner of the sheet. "Nicos Architects LLP." The project's name is *Ace*.

"It's huge," I say.

"A tennis star. I guess she's also a celebrity. We get a lot of those around here." He pulls away from the table and points to one of the two chairs that face his desk.

"What's on your mind?" he asks as we sit.

I take a deep breath. "She never told me she surfed."

He shrugs. "I can't explain that. It was her love," he says, and his eyes turn glassy. "She was phenomenal. Each time I saw her, she had gotten better. I may sound like a proud big brother, but it wasn't just me." He leans forward in his chair. "Pros, sponsors, they were all interested. They knew she had something special. A gift. But she seldom competed. Probably because she didn't want Papi to drop the hammer."

Sponsors? She was more than just a casual surfer. I nearly smile.

My athletic gifts came from her. "But this is awesome. Why wouldn't she tell me something so cool?"

"My guess is that if she ever mentioned that she had been on the cusp of a competitive career with a legitimate chance as a pro surfer, you would've interpreted that to mean that she gave up her career for you."

"Well, she did," I say.

"Careers come and go. Raising a child is a one-shot deal."

A few moments pass by. "She was an awesome mom."

"I know."

"I wish I had told her that."

"She knew."

I can only hope he's right. I told her I loved her here and there. But never told her that she was enough. That she was perfect, or how much I respected her. Countless opportunities wasted.

"What's on your mind, Shep? You look worried about something."

"I don't know if I can do this trip," I say.

He flinches. "Why? You get to travel to amazing spots, while honoring your—"

"I have a fear of the ocean."

His mouth goes slack. "Seriously?"

I put aside my pride and tell him about the drowning incident and the shark attack.

After a few moments, he places his hand on my shoulder. "Olivia knew this would be difficult for you. Even so, she asked. Maybe she knows something about you that you haven't picked up on yet."

I let the moments drift. "You had another stack of envelopes earlier. What are those?"

"Pages from her personal journal. Her diary from when she went on that trip. Each one to be read after you've reached the destination."

I was right. That's how she's going to reveal the past to me. "Have you read them?"

29

"Absolutely not." He pauses. "And—I'm sorry for saying this, but it is an explicit instruction—you won't read them either unless you go on the road trip. Otherwise, I am to hold onto to the letters until after you graduate from college."

Oh yes, College. That constant reminder of why I kept my distance when the accusations began to fly and why I need to join my new school's football team. I need that scholarship. That ticket to freedom.

That's for later. Right now, I have to deal with this. Why in the water? Why with so much attention? That's when it dawns on me. What's really weighing on me is fear. I'm afraid of what I'll find.

She said she wasn't proud of herself. If she felt that way, then it will be rough. I love and respect her. To me she was perfection. She could do no wrong. Almost annoying how good she was. I don't want to lose that. I don't want her to transform into something else. And I don't want my uncle's family to find out either. This is private.

On the flip side, I also can't deny something else... I want more time with her. I wish he would just give me the letters, the vials, and let me do this my way.

"Sleep on it," he says, snapping me out of my thoughts. "Worse comes to worst, we'll take all thirteen jars to Pismo Beach on the twenty-ninth. That is the epicenter."

"What do you mean?"

"It's clear that something happened there. She stayed at Pismo for the last three days."

I nod then rise. He joins me.

"Do you have more pictures of her from when she surfed?"

He reaches over and grabs a frame that's on his desk facing away from us. He hands it to me.

A color picture of her in action, wearing a wetsuit on what appears to be a yellow and black striped surfboard. It looks like she's streaking up the wave, as if she's about to fly out of the water. The nose of the board is pointing north, but her upper-body and face have completely coiled in the opposite direction. I assume it's the moment before she swivels the board back down the wave.

It's an awesome picture of her. I snort. If only my buddies had seen these pictures. Poor Billy, who always got tongue-tied when she spoke to him, would never consider another girl in school again.

I shake my head. "Amazing," I say, my voice distant. "That's my mom, doing something unrecognizable. As if her face has been photoshopped on someone else's body."

"Nothing fake here. That's your mom. She was a ripper, cutting 'em up like nobody's business, intimidating the crap out of anyone who wanted to keep up with her."

I don't know what a ripper means and what she was cutting, but I try to picture the mom I know with the one he's describing. She worshipped in church with her arms held up high. The only thing intimidating about her was her unshakable faith.

"My Carmen has Olivia's attitude on the surf. When she first told me she wanted to compete, I nearly tried to talk her out of it. Then I recalled how much it killed Olivia when Papi stopped her from pursuing it. Who knows—if she had started when she wanted to, she could've gone pro at sixteen. I guess we'll never know."

My phone chimes with a text message from Billy, my buddy from back home.

Billy: *Dude, things aren't looking good here.*

My face goes numb.

"You okay?" José asks.

I find a smile, force it on, then look up at him. "All's good."

SEVEN

SHEP

THE BASEBALL GAME is a nice distraction. The rowdy crowd is buzzing because the Dodgers have a two-run lead. The seats... well, like everything else here, they're the type of seats I could only dream of. They're fantastic. To my right is Carlo. His face stuck on his phone. He hasn't apologized for what he said earlier. I suspect I won't get one anytime soon. Next to him is José, who has been telling Carlo to, "Get off that thing already." To my left are Carmen and Sam, chitchatting, sharing popcorn, barely aware of the game.

No one has mentioned the list, or surfing, or anything about my mother. I think I appreciate the space they're giving me. But maybe I need someone to tell me to grow a pair and deal with whatever I find out. If Mom had been here she'd give me tough love and point out that at least I'll know the truth. I'd been asking her for details, but now that I may actually find out, I'm not sure I'm ready to deal with what comes with that avalanche.

As for Billy's text, I haven't replied to him yet. I don't want to know what's happening back home. I don't want to care. But the problem is that I do care. Maybe he's exaggerating, or has heard false rumors. I'll call him tomorrow. I need time to just settle.

"I gotta pee," Carmen says in between innings.

"Thanks for the announcement," Sam says. "And please don't even ask me to go with. I just can't in that disgusting excuse for a bathroom."

Insight of the day: apparently even women's public bathrooms are nasty.

"More wall sits will strengthen your thighs," Carmen says. "That's the only way you'll learn how to levitate above the can."

"Just hurry up," Sam says. "The inning's about to start. The batter's at the plate."

Carmen shoots her a look. "Yes, I better be fast because baseball is such a fast-paced sport. I may miss something epic."

I laugh, but the guys behind us are not amused by her wit. When Carmen scoots through, Sam shifts over and sits next to me.

"Still wearing the hat, I see," she says.

I glance at her. "You want to wear it?" I ask.

Her smile is immediate. "Okay, fine."

Just as I reach for it, the batter makes contact. The crack of the broken bat echoes through the stadium and the ball goes foul. Directly toward us.

I see it in slow motion. Just like when I'm on the field, every micro-move, decision, and action has to be perfectly executed. The ball's coming at us. It may just miss, but hit someone else.

Eyes wide open, I follow the ball's trajectory. I use my left arm like a barricade across Sam's chest and push her backward. Her eyes go wide and her hair flails as she recoils toward her seat.

In that same moment, I stretch my right hand to intercept. The ball slams into my palm. My palm doesn't budge. The ball is a foot from Carlo's face. Trace powder from the impact slowly dissipates in front of him.

For a moment, the world is on pause as I stare at the snatched ball in my hand, then at Carlo who now sees my fist in front of his face, baseball in my hand.

Sam is the first to react. "Un-freakin'-believable!" she yells and the crowd around us erupts too. She jumps to her feet, yelling something to the crowd, pumping her arms, encouraging everyone to stand and yell. People behind me are slapping me on the shoulder, congratulating me, yelling one thing or another.

"Are you okay?" I ask Carlo.

The phone is still in his hands, but he's not looking at it anymore. He blinks then stares at me. "Yeah."

"Look at the screen," José says. "You're on the screen!"

I scan around and see the replay in slow motion. Over and over again. They captured the whole thing. One arm pushing Sam back, the other bare-handing the foul ball. That's when the stabbing pain of my old injury sears through my right shoulder. The pain radiates, but the crowd's cheers are like medicine. Just like when I played.

"Stand up," Sam says. She's on her feet, trying to get me to stand next to her. "Get up!"

I rise and the cheers transform into a roar. I take off my hat, salute the crowd and take a bow. And in a moment of I don't know what, I place my hat on Sam's head.

Her face turns red and her smile widens even more.

So she takes a bow, too.

DURING THE DRIVE BACK, Carmen is seething silently. José is unsuccessfully trying to make small talk. Carlo is in the front seat focused on the road ahead, no phone in sight. I'm in the middle of the back row. No, it doesn't make sense for the tallest of the bunch to be sitting in the back and in the middle, to boot. But Carmen made me sit there.

"You've got the largest hands I've ever seen," Sam says and grabs my now famous hand. My palm is still red from the full-speed impact.

She's turning it around, opening my fingers, closing them, studying the shape. She zeroes in on my pinky.

"Dude! Your pinky is almost as long as your middle finger. Now that I've seen it I can't unsee it."

I decide to not mention the nickname kids used to call me before I got bigger, stronger, and faster than most of them.

"Hmpf," Carmen spits.

Sam pops her head forward and stares past me to Carmen. "Get over it already," Sam says. "It's not like we timed it to happen when you weren't there."

Carmen leans forward and throws Sam a look. "Get over it? Just like that?"

"Look, if you had better bladder control, it would've been you instead of me."

"Oh that's great. Just great! You and Shep are all over social media. You'll be on freakin' *Sports Center*. And where am I? Doing the Spider-Man in a public restroom, unsuccessfully peeing all over the place."

Sam snorts but quickly covers her mouth. "Sorry. Sorry. Not funny."

Carmen mumbles something then leans back again.

Sam is still holding my right hand in hers.

We're all silent for a while.

"It was pretty badass," Carmen finally says.

"And hot," Sam whispers so silently that I don't quite know if that was what she breathed or if she even meant for me to hear it.

I don't react. I pretend I heard nothing, but I become very aware of the fact that her bare thigh is making contact with mine, her powerful hand is holding mine, and her shoulder is squeezed into mine—the same one that was injured but right now is feeling a rush of heat. Then I notice José's eyes in the rear-view mirror, watching me intently.

Sam nudges my shoulder with hers. "How's the shoulder?"

We are unnaturally close to each other. If I turn, I'll be right in her face. If I don't, I'll miss out. So I turn.

"Feelin' better already."

EIGHT

SAMANTHA

HE'S all over the internet. So am I, clearly. But I'm a bit surprised at how viral this thing has gotten. I mean, yeah, it's an awesome one-hander and all, but it's not like he survived a thirty-footer at the hands of Jaws in Maui. The popularity may have something to do with his looks. Some people are so vain. Just because he's a tall, square-jawed, hazel-eyed, unassuming gunslinger, doesn't mean people should ogle over him. Sad.

My phone rings. Nomi wants to FaceTime. It dawns on me that it's nearly 2:00 a.m. in Georgia. Why is she still awake? Are they filming into the wee hours?

"What's up, Sis?" I say as I accept the call.

Her beautiful face fills the screen.

"You're all over Instagram and Facebook and ESPN!"

"You're not the only big star in this family."

She leans closer. Her green eyes, peaceful and serene, remind me of the moment I fell in love—the day they brought her home. "I am hardly a star," she says. "Maybe a light bulb. So tell me, who is he?"

"Who, Shep? He's Carmen's cousin."

"Are you... dating him or something?"

I snort. "Not!"

"Seriously? Based on what I saw you two looked very cozy." Her eyes peer into mine. She's smelling blood.

"Not even close."

She pouts. "Let me guess: he's not a surfer, so it's a non-starter."

"You preach the truth, Sister. What happened with the scene that creeped you out? Is it all settled?"

She breaks eye contact while nodding. "Yeah, it's all good now. Mr. Carlson shared some good news. They're considering a spin-off for my role. Too early to tell, but he likes what he's seeing."

She's not telling me the truth. I hate that industry. Nomi wasn't the first to give it a go. I started when I was ten. Even at that age I could see how they stared at me. Cringy, the whole lot. Wanting me to dress a certain way, move my hips with a specific pop, toss my hair. I couldn't quite figure it out back then, but I knew I wanted out. So when I crawled my way out, Mom immediately convinced Nomi to start. Her small role on a Disney Channel show got her noticed by the "right" people.

Now she's on the fast track. Which means there'll be more predators after her. I'll take the sharks in the ocean any day of the week over some of those in the Industry.

"Just be careful," I tell her. "Listen to your gut and to your older sister. I'm really very smart."

She grins, kisses her fingertips then smashes them onto the camera. "I better get some sleep," she says. "Be good."

"Always."

I hop over to Facebook and as expected the video is trending. I jump to the comments.

Whoever he is, I want him to know I'm available.

I always liked cowboys.

That face. Those guns. Who's that bimbo next to him?!

"Bimbo?" I yell at my monitor.

"You say something?"

I spin to the door as Carmen strolls in and glances at my monitor.

"Seriously?" she asks.

"What?"

"Are you seriously watching my cousin's video over and over again?"

I feel my cheeks flush. "No," I say with a squeak and a hint of incredulity. "I'm watching myself."

"Yeah. Okay." She plops on my bed sideways. I hop off my chair and plop right next to her.

"Do you think he'll do the trip?" I ask after a few moments of silence.

"Don't know. Something about a beach phobia. And let's face it, you and I sound like insane people to him."

"Not me. I'm perfectly rational."

More silence.

"Kevin's been calling me," Carmen whispers.

"Block his number. Don't give him an opening." I'm getting irritated. I don't want to get angry. I just want her to be smart.

"He was drunk," Carmen says.

"And that justifies what he tried to do?" My voice rises unintentionally.

Her eyes go wide. "Keep it down. And he didn't do anything."

"Because you were able to fight him off. Because you're strong. Anyone else—" I can't finish the thought. I can't imagine my best friend damaged.

She sits up. "I'm not taking him back. I'm not stupid."

"But you don't want to report him either."

"People make mistakes."

I cover my face with both hands. There are things I should say, but the words don't come out because it'll only make things worse. Instead I stare into her eyes. "What if he tries it again? With someone else? And this time she's not as lucky as you? What then?"

NINE

SHEP

THROUGH THE LARGE WINDOW, I watch how the light breeze causes the trees to tremble and how the accent lighting shimmers throughout the yard. The sun is probably another hour or so away from rising. I've been in a trance, watching and doing nothing productive. My thoughts are hijacked with potential revelations in Mom's letters: she belonged to a cult; she was abducted by aliens; my father is billionaire Elon Musk.

Frankly, those are the best case scenarios. What if she was assaulted? What if I'm the result of something horrible? I would never want anyone to find out about that. Who am I kidding? I don't want to know about that either.

That's when I see them. Carmen and Sam, heading out for a morning run. They're talking to each other while they stretch. These two are serious athletes. Like I was. I used to be driven, focused on standing out. Since the scandal at school, I've just been hiding out.

They take off and I feel a hint of jealousy. I want to have that again. Up to a couple of months ago, I was focused on my future, because every college was recruiting me. I had the pick of the litter.

Even now, there are websites that have ranked me nationally, tracking the colleges I'm considering.

What the sites don't show is that I'm on shaky ground. Yes, my championship junior season elevated my value. I was enjoying— maybe even abusing—the privilege of being a star athlete.

Then I went to that party with my teammates. Another wild party, like the others. Unlike the others, in one night, our world imploded. Accusations flew, lives were turned upside down, and just because trouble always comes in threes, Mom was told she had months to live.

Nothing else mattered after that.

I glance at my mom's picture.

She never stopped calling me her Silver Surfer. "You're like liquid metal," Mom said when I first started playing football. "Strong, fast, and malleable. You are on another realm of skill. Don't waste it."

Even as a kid, I knew she was right. But after what I learned yesterday, I see how wasting my talent would've been a particular slap in her face. She left it all behind for me so that I'd have a future, a shot.

My team back home is in shambles right now because of the trial that's about to start. Unlike the rest of them, I have a chance here. A fresh start, away from that mess. Officially, I have to try out, but the coach has told Uncle José that my spot is practically guaranteed.

Will my new teammates ask about what happened? Maybe. Will they wonder if I was involved? I can't even imagine the consequences if the story follows me here. My uncle knows that there was trouble on campus, but like mom, he doesn't know what I know. I hope no one here ever finds out.

Billy's text from yesterday sits in my text in-box, unanswered. I still don't know what he meant, but I have an uncomfortable feeling that things are going to get worse before they get better.

I stare at Mom's picture, deep into her eyes. What would she tell me to do if she was here?

Best way to start, is to start. I smile. She had so many cheesy one-liners.

I get on my feet. Cheesy or not, I suspect my uncle has a home gym.

I'LL BET three dozen eggs this home gym was Carmen's idea. The entire room is wall-to-wall mirrors, a sound system connected to a tablet with a killer selection of music, perfect lighting, and top-notch equipment. What else could I ask for? Will they let me live here forever?

I've been at it for just under an hour and it feels awesome. Even my shoulder has stopped complaining. When I exercise, the voices in my head calm down and sometimes I find answers. This time, I'm not searching for that though, because I may not like the answers. Instead I enjoy the peace.

I'm working on seated lat pull-downs when I hear the door to the gym open from behind me.

"Good morning, hero," Sam says.

"I see you found the most important room in the house," Carmen says. "What do you think?"

I release the bar, grab my towel and rise to meet them. I know I'm a sweaty mess, but athletes understand each other. That's not just sweat. That's evidence of hard work.

"I think your dad dropped some serious cash on this gym."

She raises her hand and I give her the high five she's looking for. I glance at Sam. No matter what condition I find her in, she's a sight. Yes, she hums to her own tune. Different, for sure, but not in a weird way.

"Check out his pecs," she says, then actually pokes my chest.

Okay that was weird.

"Did you see those?" she asks Carmen.

"Yes, Sam." Carmen's eyes are closed, a look of hopeless exasperation.

"They're like plates."

"Um. Thanks? I guess."

She fidgets. "Look, they're impressive and all, but it's too much. Those muscles will weigh you down on a surfboard—if you were a surfer. Which you're not. Clearly. But if you ever decide to try a real sport, you'll need to trim down."

My mouth drops open. "Real sport?"

"Sam, is this necessary? At seven in the morning?"

She faces Carmen. "Okay, fine. Football players have some athleticism, sure. But they primarily beef up so that they can hit each other harder and say, 'My guns are bigger than your guns.' 'Yeah, bro!' 'Kick ass, bro.' And please don't pretend I'm wrong."

Her caricature version of my tribe is insulting at best. "You're wrong."

"Well of course you'd say that, Shep. You're one of them." She smiles at me like I'm so innocent that she can't get upset at me for my silliness. "You can't think outside of that mindset. You need that rush. You live for when you're on the grass, the lights are on you, the cheerleaders are adoring you, and the crowd is cheering your name."

She definitely understands some aspects of the game. How? It clicks. "You dated a football player, didn't you? That's why you're so bitter"

She crosses her arms and grins. "Nope."

I don't believe her.

"My ex is," Carmen says. I see sadness in her eyes and my heart drops.

Countless thoughts run through my head but the most important is why. Why is he her ex? What happened? Did he hurt her?

"Forget him. It doesn't matter anymore. Sam, I was gonna show him the quiver. You want to come with?"

"Sure."

"What's a quiver?" I ask.

"Our boards."

WE ENTER what appears to be the garage, or an extension of the garage. But this is like no garage I've ever seen. The floors are textured with a checkerboard pattern. Storage systems line one of the walls. Another wall has chrome workbenches and toolboxes.

I follow Sam and Carmen to an alcove. A wall of surfboards, neatly organized. Different sizes, patterns, and colors.

"These are mine," Carmen says, pointing to what looks like half a dozen. "I use shortboards for the most part."

"Why are they different lengths?" I ask.

"Shortboards, like the ones I use, are for ripping. I love to shred the waves."

There's that alien language again.

"These are Sam's."

Sam has a few also, but these are a bit longer. One is really long.

"That's huge."

"Yeah Dad's a longboarder, too," Carmen says, as she points to two longboards next to each other. I didn't realize José also surfs.

"This is the one I wanted to show you," she says and walks over to the last board.

It's a black and yellow striped board, like a honey bee. Carmen pulls it out and flips it so I can see the surface. There is a yin and yang symbol at the tip of the board.

"This was your mom's," Carmen says and my world goes silent.

She's still saying something, but I'm not paying attention. I hold the board and run my hands over the smooth surface. My mom rode on this. When she was my age, this was hers. Her sport. How awesome is this?

I remember the first time I stood on the board and rode the wave. I remember the smile on her face. The utter joy.

A sensation brings me back to here and now. I feel reverberation from the board, like it's in motion, like it's alive and talking to me, trying to tell me something.

And if you listen—really listen—I promise to whisper to you once in a while.

As if drawn in by a magnetic force, I lock my eyes onto the board.

"Are you okay?" Sam asks and places a hand on my back.

The tether breaks and I pull away. "I'm fine," I say and hand the board to Carmen, who carefully places it back.

"This one's your mom's too," Sam points to one of the longboards next to José's.

"That's where you guys are," my uncle says as he walks into the garage. "Checking out the boards?"

My uncle walks up to Mom's board and runs his hand over it. "When she left, I promised I'd take care of her boards. Did you tell him?" he asks Carmen.

"Was about to."

He turns to me. "Well, Olivia wanted to make sure I kept them in primo condition for you."

I try to maintain my composure. I'm a bit derailed. I glance at the board. It's just an object. A thing. Yet, for some reason I feel like she's here with me.

"When I surf for your mom at the Pismo Beach memorial," Carmen says, "can I ride your mom's board?"

I step backward.

"You okay, son?" José asks.

I nod but can't produce words. So I force them out. "Yeah, just remembered I need to do something."

I turn and walk out of the garage, head up the stairs, and walk directly into the shower. I need silence, shut off all other sounds. I turn the knob until I can't stand the heat. Until the entire bathroom is so thick with steam that I can barely see anything. I allow myself to get lost. The sound of the rushing water, now muted by the thickening steam, engulfs me. I recall Mom's words.

I suspect after fifteen days with the old me, you'll learn the truth.

All those envelopes hold details written by her. She wants me to know something.

TEN

SHEP

I HEAD toward the kitchen and hear their voices.

"We pushed him," José says.

"It's my fault," Carmen says. "I should've waited, but something was happening when he held the board, so I took the opening."

She's right about that.

"Ugh. I'm so mad at myself," is what I think she says, but her voice is muffled.

"He's strong," José says. "like Olivia."

"Maybe you guys should let me do the convincing," Sam says. That's almost hilarious.

"Now what do we do?" Carmen asks. She sounds distraught. I can't let her feel like this.

"Good morning," I say as I round the corner into the kitchen.

They all spin and straighten.

"I've been thinking." I place the list on the counter. "If we're going to do this, we'd have to start in two days. Otherwise, we won't land in Pismo on time."

"Do what, exactly?" Carmen asks. Her eyes are expectant.

"This road trip thing. I'd like to recreate it. Mom did this trip over

45

fifteen-days. If we start soon, we can retrace her voyage. But I'm not surfing. I'll need your help for that."

"Hells yes!" Carmen blurts out. She's straining to hide her wide, all-tooth smile.

I don't know what I'll discover about Mom. What I do know is that she kept this story from everyone, even her brother. So I need to protect her secrets. I'll go with them, but the details, the discovery will be mine to keep.

Sam and Carmen exchange excited glances then turn to José.

He looks concerned, one eyebrow up. "Fifteen days? I don't know. That's a very long time."

I had hoped that maybe Mom had told him in advance. He clearly doesn't know. Even though he's a busy guy, I have to try. "That's what she requested of me in her letter," I say.

His concern softens.

"It's PCH, Dad," Carmen says. "Except for Pismo, none of the other spots are more than a couple of hours away from home."

I can tell he's struggling. Agreeing to his sister's request means committing to a long-term trip. He finally nods. "Fine. Go for it."

"Awesome!" Carmen says and pumps her fist.

Mom had a reason why she wanted me to do this. In some crazy way, this will be our last trip together. Separated by eighteen years, but together nonetheless.

I'm scared, no doubt, but at the same time, excited because I want to see what Mom saw, experience what she experienced. I can't have her back, but I can experience her life when she was a teenager. I can't think of a better way to be with her one last time. I had hoped that one day I'd complete all our planned trips. The first one is not quite like I had planned, but I'll make the best of it.

Also, can't deny that the possibility of finding my father is on my mind, too. There. I said it. I know it's not smart. I know it's not healthy, but he is my father. After Mom passed away, I spent weeks finding comfort in the idea of the lone wolf. But what if I still have a pack I could join? Maybe I'll be disappointed or pissed or relieved when I do finally meet him. Either way, finding him will put an end to a question that has never had an answer.

"So how do we do this?" I ask. "I mean, what's the best way to go to all these places and do everything she did?"

"Follow me," José says.

ON THE WEST side of the house is an oversized gate. He punches a code and the gate opens.

"Our RV. It's not high tech, but it's easy to maneuver and has all the necessities. Even a secure rack for surfboards."

It's beautiful, but it doesn't seem large enough. "How many people does it fit?" I ask.

"It has two beds. A queen in the back and the kitchen bench converts into a twin," my uncle explains.

The math doesn't add up. "How will we all fit?"

"It's only you and Carmen. How many were you expecting?"

I hesitate. I thought it would be a family thing. This may not be as bad as I originally thought. No matter what happens there, my uncle will not need to find out.

"What about me?" Sam asks.

José is stunned by her question. So am I.

"I don't think that'll be appropriate," he says.

Sam spins to Carmen. "You'd go without me? Fifteen days of surfing across the Pacific Coast Highway without me? Your surf buddy? Your sister?"

Carmen's been nodding with each word. She eyes her dad. "Why can't she come with us? There's safety in numbers."

José runs his hand over his face. "Look, I'm uncomfortable with..." He looks at me then at Sam.

I think I understand. He has unstated concerns about me. Maybe he also suspects something about me and the situation back home. "I can sleep inside a tent, if you have one. The girls can be inside, I'll be outside."

José's eyes dart around, considering this option.

"I'm a bit slow this morning," Sam says. "My coffee hasn't kicked in, so let's please back up the rusted truck for a sec and clarify why he has to be outside?" Sam asks. "Shep's not going to do anything ungentleman-like."

He glares at her. "It's not Shep I'm worried about."

We're all silent for a moment.

"Well then. I think *I'm* mildly offended," Sam mumbles.

When Carmen laughs, Sam gives Carmen the evil eye and then she glances at me, practically challenging me. I'm staying out of that.

"So what do you say, Dad? Sam and I have taken this bad girl out before on smaller trips. We know our way around it."

"When you two are together, your IQ drops by a factor of two."

"That's a slight exaggeration," Sam argues.

His right brow arches. "Really? Who was it that crashed into a mail box in broad daylight on a wide residential street?"

"We thought we saw a deer. We got freaked out," Sam says.

"You said it was a dog," he says.

"Right. That's what I just said. A dear dog."

She can't be for real. But she seems very proud of herself and truthfully, I'm in awe of how she just rolls with whatever is thrown her way.

Even so, the less, the better. This is shaping into a high school road trip, which is not what I wanted. I thought this would be a—I pause. This's exactly what Mom did. I am recreating what she did eighteen years ago.

My uncle is rubbing his goatee. "I suppose it'll be fine," he finally says. He turns to me. "Are you okay driving this?"

"Yes, sir. I can ride anything."

"Can you ride waves?" Sam asks.

My phone buzzes just as I'm about get into it with her.

"Let me walk you through the RV," José says.

I glance at the message. It's a text from Billy.

"Give me one sec," I say. "I'll be right there."

I take a few steps away from them and check the messages. Billy has sent me a link to an article from the local paper. I read the headline once but the words don't compute. I lean against the wall and read it again.

'*A Victim or a Predator? Details about accuser surface days before first day of trial.*'

Just then, he sends another text.

Billy: *Has anyone contacted you?*

PART TWO

"Waves are not measured in feet and inches,
they are measured in increments of fear."
~Buzzy Trent

ELEVEN

SHEP

THE TEXT CONVERSATION is still lingering in my mind. I relive the exchange once again.

Billy: *Has anyone contacted you?*

Me: *No, why would anyone want to speak to me?*

Billy: *You know...*

Dot, dot, dot. They mean nothing, or everything.

I can't help but wonder if Mom suspected this would happen. Is that why she wanted me to go on this trip? To keep my mind on something else while things shook out.

Whatever her motivation, I am grateful and lose myself in the details of the trip. We've gone through the RV, studying the various compartments, capabilities, and features. I'm focused on water, electrical, and septic systems. These are the things that really matter because if at the moment of truth we can't flush, everything goes out the window. Thankfully, Carmen is an expert and very detail-oriented. We definitely share the same blood. Sam, on the other hand, is lounging on the bed and texting away.

"Have you told your dad yet?" Carmen asks Sam.

"He doesn't care. And after this battle with Mom, she won't

either."

I glance at Carmen. She shakes her head.

"Is Nomi okay?" Carmen asks. I don't recognize the name.

"She better be or I'm taking the next flight down to Georgia to rescue her." She hops off the bed then slides her phone in her back pocket. "There. That felt good." She smiles. Not a forced smile, per se, but one that declares whatever happens, happens.

"You still need to let your dad know about the trip."

"I'll text him."

"Is he away?" I ask, hoping to get a bit more insight into this girl.

"Nah. He's probably with his executive assistant."

I pause, hoping there's a punch line, but none comes. Uncomfortable pieces of the puzzle are coming together.

She saunters past us. "Gonna get some clothes from the house. I'll mention it to him if he's there."

Carmen and I remain silent until the door closes.

"What was that all about?"

She sighs. "Absentee parents is the right term, I think. Yeah, it's a tough one."

"Is that why she stays with you guys?"

She nods. "They live across the street. We'd see the pizza delivery guy bring food twice a day. One night we asked her to join us for dinner. Then breakfast and then... we asked her parents if it would be okay for her to stay when they were out. They didn't even blink. They thought it was a great idea. 'Like a slumber party,' her mom said. It's been nearly a year now."

"That's a lot of slumbering."

"I'm not complaining. I love her, even though sometimes she's out there."

I cough.

"Okay, maybe a bit more than sometimes," she says with a smile. "But she's a rock. Even when logically she should be the one asking for support, she's on the front lines giving it. I can count on her for anything."

TOMORROW, we hit the road. Today, we've been studying the list and planning for what's ahead. Gotta admit, I'm nervous and exited and a bunch of things in between. Which in an inexplicable way reminds me of standardized tests. I have always hated the multiple choice questions that give way too many options. You know what I mean?

For example:

a) You're excited to start a new adventure

b) You're nervous because ocean and sharks and death

c) You're thrilled because you'll get to learn something new about your mom

d) You're scared because you'll get to learn something new about your mom.

But the question doesn't end there, because that would be too easy. They go on to really mess with you, because the real choices are: always a) but sometimes b); never a) always d); often b), but you can't forget c); and so on.

Here's the thing. The real answer is Yes and No to all of the above. These are all the emotions and calculations I'm processing approximately sixty times per second. I go from wanting to jump in the flipping camper right now, to jumping in my truck and heading to Alaska.

All the math leads to one distinct answer: the trip will happen. Closure will be found. Even if I find no answers, that is, in fact, the answer.

So we're huddled around the kitchen table, the list and a map of the left coast in front of us. Carmen has a notepad with a detailed timeline. Rosie's been a machine, calling campgrounds and beaches to reserve spots for us based on Carmen's schedule.

The list is split into two columns: the left is the "Surf Destination" and the right is the "I Can Do This" list of activities or challenges.

I scan through the locations:

Day 1 — ENCINITAS
Day 2 — BLACK'S BEACH + OCEANSIDE
Day 3 — SAN ONOFRE "COTTONS"
Day 4 — DOHENY BEACH
Day 5 — BROOKS STREET
Day 6 — THE WEDGE
Day 7 — SURF CITY HUNTINGTON
Day 8 — EL PORTO
Day 9 — VENICE
Day 10 — SURFRIDER
Day 11 — ZUMA + LEO CARILLO
Day 12 — RINCON
Day 13 — PISMO
Day 14 — SANTA BARBARA
Day 15 — COUNTY LINE

Cross referencing the list against the highlighted, marked-up map, it looks like eighteen years ago they drove south to San Diego on day one, then inched northbound, passing Malibu, up to Pismo then back south to Malibu which was home.

But the plan of the return trip changed. She stayed in Pismo Beach.

"Here's the list of all the locations that I've booked camp spots along with confirmation numbers," Rosie says and hands it to Carmen. "These ones, no luck, so you'll just have to get creative once there."

"We'll find a nice neighborhood and park on the street if we have to," Sam says.

"I'm off to the market to buy you guys the meats and eggs and whatever else you asked for." Rosie leaves and we focus back on the list.

"Gotta tell you," Sam says, "some of these spots are for advanced surfers. The waves are intimidating and the talent there is top notch."

Carmen grins. "Olivia must've been a badass."

Pride rushes through me. Mom mixed it up with the big boys. Why did she go on this trip, I wonder? Was it really to get one more big trip in because she knew once college started she wouldn't be able to surf regularly?

"What about the 'I Can Do This' list?" Carmen asks.

"No," I jump in quickly. "Mom didn't say anything about those in her letter."

Sam shakes her head. "So what? Do it anyway. Make this trip as much yours as it was hers."

"They are doable," Carmen says. "Like look at this one: Dance from when the sun sets to when the sun rises."

"I'll dance with you," Sam says.

"I don't dance," I mumble.

"Sure you do," she says. "Anyone can twerk."

I almost laugh, but knowing her as little as I do, this list would be an invitation to even more 'out there ideas.' "Like I said, let's stay focused."

They both pout, but don't push it.

"So..." Carmen starts. "What are you? Six-two, one-hundred-ninety pounds?"

I eye her. "Just under two-hundred. Why do you ask?"

She shakes her head. "No reason." She glances at Sam. "Thirty-four inch waist?"

"Close enough."

"What are you two talking about?"

"Never mind," she says, and without another word they both leave me alone in the kitchen.

Too much time under the sun, clearly. I scan the list again and wonder how big of a role this other list had in whatever it is that she experienced. I run through it one more time.

1. Be awake for 24 hours
2. Dance from when the sun sets to when the sun rises
3. Shave my hair
4. Surf naked

5. Change someone else's life forever

6. Survive a shark attack

7. Moonlit surfing

8. Be kissed by a stranger

9. Sleep under the stars

10. Do something unexpected

11. Go to a nude beach

12. Work out on Muscle Beach

13. Find a ghost

14. Hear God's whisper

15. Fall in love

Unlike the locations list where she has put a large checkmark next to each and crossed out Santa Barbara and County Line, there's no way to know which ones were completed or even attempted.

This list may be an omen for what I may be in for. If I had come across this list on the internet for some random person, I would've thought of them as cool and adventurous. But this is Mom we're talking about. How could she have considered surfing in the nude and going to a nude beach? She was so conservative and spiritual that they seem in complete contrast to the woman I knew. Maybe her friends put her up to it and she skillfully avoided them? That would be classic Mom.

Then again, one of the challenges tells me this is all Mom. When I was younger, she insisted on teaching me how to dance. She called it a critical skill because as she said, *"One day, you'll find that girl who'll replace me. On that day, I want you to dance until the sun excuses the moon, and the day starts anew."* That's exactly what challenge number two says.

I study the last two and breathe shakily: Fall in love; hear God's whisper. Did she fall in love? Was it with my father? And what does she mean by God's whisper?

I don't know, but I hope to find out.

TWELVE
SHEP

IT'S BEEN a long day of planning. It's late. We should be in bed. Instead, we're lounging around the fire pit in the backyard. The night breeze is cool, a bit damp. The crickets are participating in the largest open-door concert in the western hemisphere, and the moon is about ten days away from showing its full glory.

"We should go to sleep," Carmen says, but she's already more asleep than awake.

"Carmen! The whole point of a road trip is to live it up. Not be on a tight schedule. We're not preparing for the Olympics."

"I should be," Carmen mumbles then stumbles out of her chair. "That's it. I'm off to bed."

"Night," Sam says, but stays put.

When Carmen closes the sliding door, I glance at Sam. She's staring at me.

"What was she like?" she asks.

"Mom?" I shift in my seat. "Perfect. Tough. All heart." I pause. "She was generous even with those things we desperately needed for ourselves. A good, decent person."

"That's because she was a surfer."

I grin.

"So she never told you she was one of us?"

"No, never. And I would've never guessed it either. She was the furthest thing from a surfer girl."

"Hey. What's that supposed to mean?"

I put up my hands. "Look, she was the school librarian. Not a cool, aloof, skateboarder-on-land and surfer-at-sea woman. She was the church volunteer. The person who'd latch on to the soul-saving-cause-of-the-month. Don't get me wrong, she totally believed in her causes, she just had too many."

"And what causes did you have?"

"Causes?" I chuckle. "Three of them. Me, me, and me. I was on the football team with a future that millions pray for, but only a few hundred will ever taste. I worked at it daily, because I wanted that shot. Even the work I did on the ranch was for personal benefit. Four o'clock every morning, running chores to help the family that had taken us in because I didn't want us to lose our only shelter."

"A legit cowboy." Under this lighting, her grin radiates. "And now you're about to be transformed into a beach bum. Did you guys ever talk about moving back here?"

"Never even discussed it. Even if we put aside the fact that we couldn't afford a box under a freeway in L.A., our hometown was everything. She loved serving, helping, being part of the community."

It was because of how much the community loved her that everyone gave me a pass after she got ill. They didn't bother me or question me. But that may change now.

"Wish I had met her," Sam says, pulling me out of the memory.

"What are your parents like?" I toss out.

"Exactly like your mom. Just completely different." She runs her hands through her hair, quickly separating long strands which are then brought together into braids. The fire's reflection gives her hair a glow. She glances up at me. "I basically have no parents."

"But you do."

"They exist, yes. But do they know what I've been up to? Did they congratulate me when I won gold for my school's swim team? Do they care that when I'm on a board, riding a wave, I forget their names and faces?" Her eyes glisten, but she's not crying. Not yet. "What am I gonna do? Cry over ghost parents? Or that for now, one child means more to them than the other? Am I going to resent them?" A tear streaks down. "Absolutely not." She hasn't even registered her tear. "So I go on with life."

I cross my arms. "I didn't take you for a philosopher."

She rises, towering over me. "Nah, that's just real speak. People who surf don't load up others with bull. We call things as they are and find the joy in life. Because we know something no one else does." She extends her hand. I take it and she hoists me.

"And what's that?"

"That when we're walking on water, we are that much closer to God."

WHEN WE REACH MY ROOM, Sam keeps walking toward hers. I open my door and watch her stride on, her head down, but her shoulders wide and proud. She opens the door then glances at me.

"Tomorrow. The start of epic."

"Tomorrow."

She winks then enters her room. When I hear the click of her door I cross into my room and take off my t-shirt. I glance at the time on my phone. Nearly eleven o'clock and we plan to be up at 4:00 a.m. Carmen was right. We should've slept earlier. That's okay. I'm sure I'll be able to doze out in seconds flat. It's not like I have anything on my mind. It's not like I'm about to relive my mom's fifteen-day journey when she was my age.

Knock, knock.

I take a wide step toward the door and open it. It's Sam.

"Hey, what's up?" I ask.

Her eyes glide down my exposed top then dart back up. "Just wanted to thank you."

"For?"

"Not pushing me out. You could've. You could've said you wanted this to be a family thing, but you didn't and I feel... well, thankful. And stuff."

"You're welcome. And stuff. Just remember this conversation when I get mad at you over the next couple of weeks."

"Why would you get mad at me? I'm an angel. Practically."

"Yeah. I can see that. Practically."

She gives me a sly smile. "I even have wings. How else do you think I glide on water?"

I'm about to say something when she steps forward and lands a soft kiss on my cheek. A million-billion-trillion beads break out all over my body. I know my chest and shoulder and arms are covered with them. *Please don't look. Please don't look.* But she does. Then smiles.

Crap! Crap! Crap!

"You do realize what just happened, right?" she says.

I shrug, incapable of saying something coherent when I feel like such a tool.

"You, my friend, just took care of challenge number eight: Be kissed by a stranger."

I clear my throat. "I don't know if you qualify as a stranger."

"You're wrong about that. I'm very strange. Good night," she says then shuts the door behind her.

That was... interesting, I think as I drop on my bed. *No, that was unexpected.*

On my dresser, someone has left the stack of Mom's letters. I grab them and yank the rubber band off. The sticky note is a gentle reminder from my uncle.

Only open the one for the specific day.

The honor system. I flip through them. There are fifteen of them, each numbered and sealed. I am tempted to read them. All of them, right now.

Instead I grab my travel bag and shove them in. Next to my bag is the four by four foam carrier that houses thirteen blue jars, each with a portion of my mom's ashes inside. Lucky number thirteen is labeled Pismo. The last stop where she stayed for three days.

I pull one out and nearly shiver. She's here with me. In my hand.

And for the next fifteen days, she'll be with me at each stop.

I'm trusting you, Mom.

THIRTEEN

DAY 1 - SHEP

I'M ALREADY awake and ready when my alarm goes off. I step out of my room and gingerly walk through the hallway, my rucksack over my shoulder and the case of vials in my hands. As I take the steps down, I hear murmuring voices.

"Mornin'," I say. "Ready to load up the RV?"

"Look, it's sunshine," Sam says.

I eye her. "Sunshine?"

"Just like sunshine, you show up after all the rain."

I frown. "Is that surfer talk? Because I don't get it."

"What she's trying to say in her colorful way is that we're almost done," José says. "Grab a cup of coffee and let's load up the last of it."

Turns out none of them could sleep, so they did most of the work. We only have to rack up the boards. They are taking way too many, in my humble opinion, but I roll with it. José and I latch the surfboards to the back of the RV. We then place three longboards on top of the roof and strap them in place. One is Mom's. I double check all the hooks and locks.

"Paranoid much?" Sam coughs as she walks past me.

José pulls me aside. "Carmen has a couple of credit cards. She also has cash. She has a AAA card in case the RV breaks down, also—"

The horn blares. We both turn to the RV and see Sam's bright face sticking out of the window.

"Come on already. Kiss or hug or whatever and let's go!"

"Listen," José whispers, "don't let her drive."

"No doubt." I decide to ask the question. "Does Carmen know about the letters?"

He shakes her head. "She knows there's more, because she saw them, but does not know what they are. I figured if you want to tell them, you will."

I nod in gratitude. Just then, Rosie runs out, her nightgown haphazardly wrapped around her. "Have fun. Be safe."

With that I run up the RV's steps, slide into the driver seat, and crank the engine.

"Road trip!" both Sam and Carmen yell as we march forward.

I swing the RV out of the looping driveway, tip my hat to Mom's truck, then hit the road. *All right, Mom. Let's see what you planned for us.*

IT WILL BE 5:00 a.m. soon. No traffic and no issues, but we still have a couple of hours to go before we reach our first destination.

"We're making good time," Carmen says.

Sam is sitting next to me and Carmen is hanging out in between us on the floor.

"We'll get there by seven, maybe seven-thirty if this holds up." She rises. "I'm gonna lay out on the bed for a bit. Catch a few."

"Slacker," Sam says.

"Hater," Carmen mumbles then plops down on the bed.

I glance at her in the mirror. "Hey, is that legal?" I ask.

"Sure," she says. "Unless we're caught. In which case, I'm not sure."

That does not give me confidence.

"This is going to be awesome," Sam says then slides on a pair of aviator sunglasses. "Alone without anyone to tell us what to do and when to do it. We make the rules. And we rock it. Just like *Lord of the Flies.*"

I remember that novel. Things didn't go so well in that story.

Sam then rolls up her blue turquoise hoodie, framing her face. Loose strands of hair poke out from the edges of her hoodie. She is objectively pretty. She leans her head back and from the slits on the side of her lenses, I can see that her eyes are closed. She begins to hum a song I can't place.

She pulls her feet out of her sandals and plants them on the dashboard. She has long tanned toes, the nails painted neon green. Wrapped around her ankle are bracelets adorned with charms and shells. My eyes travel the length of her legs, studying the deep cuts on her calves, over her knee, and under her pronounced hamstring.

I peel my eyes away from her calm, yet powerful physique and concentrate on the road. It's best I focus on the task at hand. I won't get annoyed just because she's taking a nap. I won't dwell on how I wish she would just talk to me about whatever. I won't get irked at the fact that her way of being relaxes me. Nope, I'm good. I'll just speak to myself for the next few hours. I'm good.

In a couple of hours, I will read the first letter. No worries. I got this.

FOURTEEN
DAY 1 - SAMANTHA

MY EYES POP open and my feet slam down as I jerk forward, but something pulls me back. A stretch of highway lays in front of me.

"Whoa, you okay?" someone asks.

I spin to the voice and the world comes back into focus. I'm in the RV. I must've dozed off. I straighten up and rub the spot where the seatbelt dug into my chest when I snapped up.

"Well that sucked," I say and bring my feet up to the chair and hug my legs. My voice is a bit hoarse.

"Bad dream?"

I shrug. "I dunno. I don't remember my dreams." I shiver from the AC's cool air. "It's like an icebox in here."

He glances over. "Dang, Sam. You have goosebumps all over your legs."

I eye him. "I think your eyes should be on the road and not on my legs."

The RV swerves. "I wasn't... when you said—I just—you know, noticed," he nearly whines.

"Hey," Carmen moans from behind.

"Sorry," he says. His pale neck turns red. He adjusts his hat, shoving it down.

"Settle down up there," Carmen says.

"Eyes on the prize, Shepard," I whisper.

Shep's jaw muscles pulsate.

"Fifteen miles to go," he yells out.

I lean back, satisfied. He's so cute when he squirms. This is going to be a fun trip.

WE'RE ONLY a handful of miles from Encinitas. Just as traffic on the *5 freeway* begins to slow, we exit and take the *101 highway*, the southern extension of *Pacific Coast Highway*. On our left, hundreds of houses litter the roads that hug the hills. To the right is my friend, the Pacific. A beat-up guardrail is the only thing that separates me from being with the ocean again.

"Next right," Carmen says. "San Elijo Campground."

Shep takes the turn carefully and inches up to the entry booth. I step out of the RV while Carmen and Shep work out the reservation with the lady from the park.

"Be careful," Shep calls out. He's so protective.

"Always," I say.

I breathe deep, taking in the smell of the ocean and sand. I pick up another scent. Bacon. I walk toward the aroma. About fifty feet in, I find the camper and the men who are cooking breakfast on their grill. Three older men. Their eyes are swollen, evidence that they're more asleep than awake. Probably spent the night drinking.

One of them notices me. "Good morning," he says.

"Hey," I reply then keep on waking.

"We have plenty if you're hungry."

I just smile and keep walking. Yeah, I'd just accept your invitation and have bacon and eggs with you, because hey, we're all trustworthy. His leering eyes tell me exactly who he is and what he's about. I can practically feel their eyes on me, tracking me.

From behind, the tap of the horn pulls my attention. "Down to nineteen," Carmen says as they slowly pass me. "We got oceanside *with* hookup!"

"Score."

By the time I reach them, the RV is parked and Carmen is already out looking over the bluff. Shep's unloading the small grill.

"I'm gonna prepare breakfast," he says as I walk by him to join Carmen.

"Overcast," she says. "Small, textured surf."

"Two footers, at best." I track the direction of the winds. "Surfers in the water. Waiting."

"Let's get our boards," she says and we immediately turn back to the RV.

"We're going to hit the water," Carmen tells Shep.

He freezes. "What about breakfast?"

"Priorities, Shep. Priorities," she says then punches his shoulder.

I walk by and punch his shoulder, too. "You heard the woman." I step inside, close the door, then pop it open again. "Don't come in, we're changing."

His little ears turn red, but he still manages to tip his hat.

We quickly change. Like me, Carmen is wearing her bikini under her clothes. No point in wasting time. She's wearing a hot green cross-back top. Very functional. Nothing worse that discovering a boob has popped out. We don't bother with wetsuits. Down here, the water is outright warm.

"Ready?" she asks.

"You know it."

We hop out and go to the rear of the RV. The board rack has been unlocked. Shep is leaning against the RV.

"Need help taking them down?" he asks.

"Do you need help milking a cow?" I reply.

He scoffs then says, "I'm gonna lock her up and join y'all on the beach."

"Why don't all y'all you change into your board shorts?"

He shrugs. "We'll see."

He disappears after we grab the shortboards which are ideal for the conditions. With them tucked under our arms, we march toward the walkway.

Carmen picks up her pace. Not me. The process is sometimes as wonderful as the surf. I love everything about getting ready, from studying the waves to breathing in the scents of the ocean. Each beach has its own unique fingerprint. Also, I prefer to study the surfers that are already there and see what skill level I'm going up against. Not Carmen. The water could be bobbing with twenty pros and she'll get right into the mix, without hesitation.

"The overcast is burning away," she says. "The troops are sensing the shift."

A handful of surfers, not too far from us, run into the water. "We better join them before we lose the next set of waves."

We place our boards down. "Time for salad dressing," she says.

Methodically we apply sunscreen. This is not suntan lotion. We're not trying to get sexy. This is protection so we can do this for as long as we can stand upright.

"You look like a geisha."

We both glare at Shep who saunters in. "You'd be wise to protect that pasty white skin of yours," I say.

His face contorts and he looks down at his exposed arms. "Pasty?" he whispers.

"Yes, pasty," I repeat.

He sets his beach chair down and drops his rucksack. "Go on then. Pass it over so I can apply some."

Carmen throws it at him and he snatches it. The way his muscles ripple when he grabs the errant toss reminds me of the baseball game.

I toss a wax bar to Carmen and we kneel in front of our sea chariots. I rip it open and the sweet scent completes the sensory experience.

The sound of crashing waves pulls my focus toward the water. The ocean is awakening.

FIFTEEN

DAY 1 - SHEP

I PEEL off my t-shirt and apply the lotion on my arms, neck, and shoulders. Then take some more and apply it to my face.

"Get your nose," Carmen says. "First thing to burn."

As I apply lotion to my nose, I glance over the bluffs toward the campground. I hope mom's board is safe. Although they're covered and locked down, I can't imagine losing them. I almost wish we hadn't brought them.

I drop on my beach chair, cover my head with my hat, and pull out a water bottle. As I take a drag I watch the girls. Kneeling on the sand, both are rubbing something on the board. Almost like they're sanding it down.

"What are you doing?" I ask.

"Wax," Carmen responds without breaking stride.

Sam leans over and my eyes freeze on the sand. The sand that's stuck to her butt and thighs. As she waxes with the right hand, with her left hand she swats down some of the sand.

I snap my eyes away from her before either one of them catches me in the act and jumps to conclusions. I scan around, to see if anyone's checking out the girls. No one obvious. It dawns on me that plenty of guys will be interested in them. One more thing I have to worry about when I should be focused on Mom's request.

The roar of the ocean pulls my thoughts to the deep. The good news is that I'm not hyperventilating. Looking back at when I went to the beach with friends, I think I was freaking out because I knew they would pressure me to jump in and the last thing I wanted was for them to think that I was a coward... which for the record, I was. Maybe that's why fear kicked in. Here, on this beach, I know the girls won't pressure me.

"Check it out," Carmen says. "The swells are coming."

I scan around, to see what she's talking about. I don't see anything out of the ordinary. "What's a swell?" I ask. "Like 'swell people are coming?'"

Sam laughs.

"No dweeb," Carmen says, her smile friendly and awesome. "It means a group of waves."

I squint into the distance. I don't see anything. "How do you know?" I ask.

"You have to study the waves. Look at the patterns," Sam explains. "You have to take your time."

"Surfing is not for the impatient," Carmen adds. "Often you're just hanging for twenty, thirty minutes waiting for a batch of waves to come."

Although it was close to a decade ago, that one time I surfed I don't recall waiting. Then again, a lot of that day has been erased from memory. What's left is a very dramatic story that always got me a whole bunch of sympathy. Somehow, I doubt these girls will give a rip. They've probably seen and experienced worse.

I study the people who are already in the water, bobbing up and down like black dots in the ocean. "With all those people competing for the same waves, how do you get a turn?"

"Sometimes, you get screwed. Sometimes, you screw," Sam says. "Enough chit chat," she says and rises.

Gotta admit, they look really cool. Yes, they look hot, but more than that, they look powerful and in tune with their bodies and the environment. I remember my mom's pictures and notice they're not wearing wetsuits. "Aren't you going to get cold in the water?"

"We're going to skin it," Sam says and along with Carmen they tuck their boards underneath their arms and jog-walk to the water.

Skin it? I need to learn this lingo somehow. I pull out my phone and search for it. Boom. A bunch of sites with a glossary of 'Surfer Lingo.' It seems I'm not the only one who needs to decode their language.

I'm about to scroll through the list, but decide to watch the girls in action first. They step in and once they're shin deep, they glide their boards in front and lay on them. With their heads up, they dog paddle. They're smooth and effortless in their movement. I could probably do that. Seems easy.

Time to test my newfound strength on the beach. I adjust my hat and walk toward the shore. This is the closest I've been to the ocean in over a decade. The waves break in front of me, inches away, and leave their foam before they pull back to the ocean. There, not too bad.

I scan the water and find the girls. Sam does this sexy thing as she paddles. Her legs are up, her feet crossed, and her perfectly formed hamstrings shine like newly-polished stone. I probably shouldn't be staring at her like that. Carmen may think I have the hots for her or something. Which, for the record, I don't. I've been going on the record a lot today. As an athlete, I appreciate that her body is a perfect demonstration of athletic dedication.

Yeah, that sounds about right.

A wave, not too large, grows in front of them. Sam, who is slightly ahead, goes over it while Carmen pushes the tip of her board down, diving into the wave. For a couple of moments I don't see her. I take a step forward, but as the wave ebbs, she reappears right next to Sam.

They join the black dots.

Three guys in full-body wetsuits run past me into the water.

"I'm telling you, that's the same chick that passed by our camp," one says.

"Let's say hi," another one says and they run in, throwing water and sand in their wake.

I cross my arms. They must be talking about Sam and Carmen. There's three of them and one of me. Not great odds, but something tells me that Carmen and Sam aren't daffodils. They'll mix it up with the best of them.

Looks like they're the only women in the water among at least a dozen guys. Most of the guys have wetsuits, but the girls are braving the waters like warriors. Yeah, there's no doubt—these two are badasses.

The herd of surfers are continually in motion, positioning and repositioning. Just then, the surface swells and a guy with a red board makes a move for it. So does a second surfer on a white board, less than a second behind. A third one breaks in the opposite direction. The wave appears to be splitting to both the left and right.

Red paddles, fast, keeping up with the wave as it rises. White overtakes the red but as he takes the wave, he nosedives. Red catches the wave and streaks down. It's a small wave, maybe three feet? Hard to judge from here, but he accelerates down the wave's face going toward his left, his center of gravity low. He glances at the wave over his right shoulder. Just then a smaller wave sideswipes him, forcing him to dive into the water.

"Ouch," I call out.

But just as quickly, he's back on his board, paddling back toward the rest of the surfers.

Another wave puffs up. Sam and Carmen must be in the right position because although a couple of guys try to react, they just as quickly pull back. Sam and Carmen paddle out with the wave that's forming.

They're like synchronized swimmers, paddling in unison, keeping up with the wave. I grin like a hyena because they're paddling so fast and hard that I don't think the other dudes before could've kept up with them. No wonder Carmen and Sam's shoulders are so well-developed.

In an instant they're both on their feet. A smooth and elegant movement. Now they're streaking down the face. They're too close. They'll slam into each other.

But they don't. Unlike the earlier wave that created a left-bound wave, this one seems to be going straight down, with a slight left pull. It's a small wave. Nevertheless, they're making the most of it.

Their boards must be at most two feet apart from each other. Are they talking to each other? Sure looks like it. They begin pumping their legs, like pistons. Are they trying to accelerate the shortboards? It doesn't matter because the wave has lost its strength.

The girls straighten up and glance each other, laughing about something. Sam closes the gap, then steps on Carmen's board. Sam leans on Carmen, Carmen tries to compensate, but it's no use, equilibrium is lost. They both dive in.

They re-emerge and quickly mount their boards and paddle again toward the group of surfers.

One of the older guys catches a nice wave and streaks across. In one swift move, he hops on the board, balances himself then pumps up and down, just like the girls did earlier. He's speeding up. My assumption was right, that motion generates velocity. He then takes a wide movement back toward the wave and someone near me yells, "Beautiful turn."

I consider looking up the term "turn." But decide against it since it probably just means "to turn" like in normal human English.

He's back on the wave's path, building up more speed. He directs his board up the wave's face then aggressively moves the board back, leaving a spray of water.

"Insane carve," the person next to me says.

I'll probably look that one up later.

Irrespective of what the guy next to me thinks, I'm not impressed. He was one of the dudes that's old enough to be Sam's dad. I pray that he eats it. When he tries that 'insane carve' again, the wave doesn't play along with him. He and his board fly.

Prayer answered.

"Wipeout!" the surfer next to me declares.

That's a term I don't have to look up. I know what that means by example and it'll be committed to memory.

For some reason, everybody cheers. Including the girls. I don't get it. He just ate wet sand. Why would they celebrate that?

A few minutes later, after others ride more waves, the waves (or is it swells?) disappear, but the surfers remain in the water. In no time at all, the girls are surrounded by the guys, chitchatting.

Okay, I admit, what they did looked like fun, but I remind myself that any minute now, one of them will be shark breakfast.

I go back to my chair and do what I came here for. I pull out the first envelope.

SIXTEEN

DAY 1 - SHEP

I'VE BEEN STUDYING the envelope for a couple of minutes. It should be so simple. I break the seal and read her notes. Words that she wrote eighteen years ago. I get to experience her world, from her eyes when she was my age. Maybe even get the name that goes with the title of "father."

Whoever he is, she never found someone else to replace him. When I was young, there was a guy that came over briefly. They must've been dating, but one night I heard them arguing and that was it, he was gone. Within a couple of weeks, we started going to church. After that, I never saw another man in her life.

I stare at the envelope and tear the seal. I pull out a small sheet, folded in half. The left edge has been carefully torn out of the diary. The paper has a soft but thick texture. I take a deep breath and unfold it.

My mom's handwriting stares back at me. I scan the paper. On the top left is the date, July 10, 2000. Beside the date it says, "Day 1." The day's accounts are split up in sections. Each section separated by something she's drawn. It looks like the serrated edge of a knife, but with only three teeth. Or is it three shark fins? Then it clicks: three stylized waves.

Everything seemed to evolve around the ocean for her. I glance at the sea. *Eighteen years ago, Mom was here, at this beach.*

I lower my eyes to the paper and read.

July 10, 2000 — Day 1

I write this with my butt firmly planted in the warm sands of Encinitas.

Still seems unreal that I'm actually here—on a road trip with my best friends, visiting the best surfing locations from San Diego to Pismo.

I am living the dream. Literally.

The entire drive down I expected something would go wrong and we'd be forced back home. It wasn't until we parked the van and I stepped onto this precious sand that I knew this is really real. Sharon and Tracey were arguing about something (probably over the fact that Tracey decided to bring her smelly boyfriend with her). But I didn't pay attention to any of that. I focused on the swells that waved at me like an old friend, inviting me to be one with them.

I cried for no reason. Something washed through me and the only thing I could think of was the sense of gratitude I felt for my big bro. He fought for me. And I won. I needed this. After the last couple of months at school, after Tom, I needed to break away and live it up.

I am stoked, beyond words. I can't help but think that this trip will forever stay with me.

Enough words. The ocean needs me.

The surf was amazing. We were killin' it out there. And what's even more amazing is the water. It's actually warm. I'm glad I listened to Sharon and skipped the wetsuit. I've never been able to surf this long without a suit. The water in Malibu is downright painful after a while. But here... oh man... is it weird to say that the way the water glided against my bare skin was tantalizing? And when I caught a little barrel, the way it wrapped itself around me and misted all over my body... man, I was totally feelin' it. I felt alive. All woman.

Speaking of which, Tracey must be regretting that she brought her loser boyfriend. The surfer boys here are hot and they are hot for us. We're the only ladies surfing. Good odds.

Some idiot gave me crap, so I clipped him then dropped in on him a bit later. We exchanged words and I gave him a piece of my mind (and one of my fingers). I don't really remember what I told him, but over fine Jamaican joints, Sharon retold the story. Apparently, I told him he should consider consuming bull testicles. We laughed until we cried.

We surfed in the afternoon into the early evening. The waves were rough—thick and nasty, like they were angry at us. One of the guys got messed up bad at Sea Side Reef. Apparently the floor is rocky. The wave hammered him into it and when he came out, he was all bloody and goofy. Felt bad for him.

I had a talk with the ocean though. I asked for her to give me one and she did. I caught a beauty and pulled off a soul arch. All the guys gave me mad respect after that.

Remember that idiot who gave me lip during the morning? He and I made out around the campfire. Yeah, not my finest moment. He's still an idiot. But at least he's a good kisser. One challenge down!

Laters,
O

I don't think I blinked for the duration of the letter. I am frozen, unable to make sense of this entry. Did she just admit to smoking weed and making out with some random guy and taking about hot guys? And who is Tom?

Forget that: Why would she want me to see this stuff about her?

Did she do more than just make out with him? Was this guy my father? This is depressing and confusing.

This is the same woman who spoke to city council about cracking down on vape use at schools. She's the same person who nearly had a heart attack when she caught me and my buddies sharing a joint in the barn.

And what's with making out with some loser? She spoke to me about purity all the time. Not that I listened, but, come on.

Just as I'm about to really get on my soap box, I recall the request from her letter: *I'm not proud of my past,* she wrote, *but I'm asking you to give me your hand and trust me.*

I take a deep breath. *Sorry, Mom.*

I put the sheet back into the envelope and slip it into my bag. I'm not loving this. And I particularly don't like how I'm reacting to it. I need to get a grip. I grab the water bottle, take a sip and find I'm slowly regretting this trip.

That is until I catch Sam in action.

She's on a solid wave, going left-bound. She's low on the board, her arms expertly counter-balancing the ride. She then pops the board and takes a fast turn, rides up the face of the wave then snaps her board back down the wave. She repeats the maneuver and this time when she snaps it back, she sprays a deluge of white foam. She does it one more time and when she goes back down the face, the wave loses its energy.

She lowers herself on the board and paddles back toward the crowd of surfers. Her legs are up and her feet are crisscrossed. She shines like her body was dipped in liquid gold.

Just then, she turns her face in my direction. She's deep in the water, so I can't tell if she's looking at me. But I raise my fist and pump it.

She repeats my gesture and smiles. Bright white teeth shine back at me.

SEVENTEEN
DAY 1 - SAMANTHA

CARMEN and I snatch one more wave and ride it to the sand.

"I'm spent," Carmen says as we grab our boards and splatter our way toward Shep, who has been lounging, watching us the whole time.

"Hope you enjoyed the show," I say as we reach him, nearly hovering over him, dripping salt water all over him.

"Stop that," he says and rolls away from us.

Almost in unison, we both whip our hair toward him, sending a spray of water bullets.

"What's the matter with you two?"

"We're hungry," Carmen says. "And all you're doing is taking a nap while you could've been making us breakfast, or lunch, or whatever."

He adjusts his hat then grabs his chair and bag. "I feel used," he murmurs.

"Welcome to day one," I say.

He eyes me then heads toward the wooden steps that will lead us back to the campground.

I catch up to him. "What did you think?"

"What? Of the surfing?"

"No, of the seagulls."

"It's whatever," he says.

I bump him. I grab his hat and place it on my head. Serves him right.

"It's a fine sport, but a bit slow for my taste."

"Slow?" Carmen and I yell at the same time.

"What are you even talking about? We were smokin' out there," Carmen says.

"Once you were on the wave, sure. But until then... man, it took forever."

"He's a football player," I explain to Carmen.

"Oh, I see," she says.

He pauses and looks at both of us. "And what's that supposed to mean?"

"It's not your fault."

His jaw opens more. "Are you calling me dumb?"

"No, no. Just ignorant."

"What the—?"

"Ignorant about what makes surfing the most addictive sport known to mankind."

He relaxes his shoulders. "Let's hear it."

As we stroll to the camper, I momentarily visualize the board under my feet and allow the words to come naturally. "Surfing is a relationship, a connection with the water. It's about floating on a board, bobbing with the motion of the ocean. It's about being one of the few, while the many on the coast stare at us, clueless. They don't know that we're reading the wind and the water. We're feeling the adrenaline of the waves and how the formation of the sea floor causes the water to behave differently. We're experiencing the flow of energy rolling through the water.

"Then there's the relationship with the wave. An innocent swell transforms into a tower. We have an understanding—the wave will challenge us to feel her, to adjust with her. And if we respect her, if we hear what she's trying to tell us, then maybe she'll let us stay for a while longer.

"But we never forget who's in charge. This is a glorious, miraculous sport with a dark side. She can take you down and hold you down and split your board and your back. She won't even shed a tear. She'll move on and forget you were ever even there."

We have reached our RV. He's just staring at me.

"Football is a fine sport. You have to be an exceptional athlete to play it, I'm sure." I slide my board on the rack then turn to him. "But to surf is divine. It's reserved for the extraordinary."

I WOULD CONSIDER LICKING THE FREAKIN' plate, but anything else will cause a bulge to appear on my exposed belly.

"That, cuz, was an epic omelette," Carmen says.

"You're welcome," he says as he places his last forkful in his mouth. His hazel eyes sparkle with excess green in this sunlight. His eyes land on mine, like he's studying me. He then shifts his eyes to Carmen.

"Why are you guys smiling like that?" he asks. "You look like you're high."

"We are," Carmen says. "Just not on drugs. This is what we call stoked."

"It's all about the feels," I say.

"I see," he says.

I gaze at Shep. "Ready to give it a shot?"

He glances at me. "What? Surfing? No way. When I look at the ocean all I see are shark fins."

"It's more likely that you'll get attacked by a shark on land than in the ocean," I say.

They both stare at me. "Okay, maybe not more likely but just as likely."

They continue to stare at me. "Never mind." I cross my arms and sink into my chair. I shouldn't try to sound intelligent when I'm tired and flying high at the same time.

"I'm not gonna push you, Shep," Carmen says. "But you should consider it. You should focus on why you should surf. Not why you shouldn't. And you should think about Tía Olivia's objective. She wanted you to go through with this so that you'd experience what she experienced. So that you'd get to know something about her."

He's holding on to each word. For the first time, I think he may actually try it.

"Like I said, I won't push, but I will encourage. Sam will push."

He grins and when he does, my chest constricts and something too large to be in my gut twists. It causes me to breathe shakily. I know that sensation. It's a messy one.

Carmen rises. "I need a nap, but in the afternoon, I'll take the first vial," she says.

"Do me a favor," he says, his voice low, almost hoarse. "Go out there with Mom's board. I think it's appropriate."

She engulfs him in a hug. *Give them space. Leave them alone.* I drop my eyes and focus on my toes. *Oh who am I kidding?* I jump in and collect them both into my embrace. I love group hugs.

EIGHTEEN

DAY 1 - SHEP

THE THREE OF us are on the sand, studying the waves.

"Over there," Sam says, pointing to something deep in the ocean that I obviously can't see or interpret.

"Okay," Carmen says then turns to me. Her palm is open.

I take a deep breath, then put the vial in her hand. Her fingers wrap around it. I glance into her eyes and see determination. Like a soldier, ready to take the hill. I wish I could do this for Mom. But at least I have Carmen.

Carmen grabs my mom's smaller board and heads into the water. Sam stands by me, her own board on the sand next to us.

The sun is probably two hours away from setting, but it's already casting a warm glow on the silvery water. I watch my cousin as she steps into the water and after a few wide steps, slides onto the board and paddles.

The waves are a little bigger now with more frequency, but she easily glides over the few that come her way. She reaches the area that Sam had pointed out.

"Now we wait," Sam says.

I don't reply. Instead when Sam walks closer to the waterline, I follow her. I stop when she stops. The cold water should be sending shivers up my spine, but what I'm experiencing at this moment overshadows any other feeling I may have.

I know it's my imagination, or wishful mind, but I feel like Mom's here with us, watching us.

Carmen is bobbing in there, turning, paddling, resetting. A couple of decent looking waves nudge her, but she doesn't take them.

After a few minutes, she paddles to her right.

"Right there," Sam says and points to something that I just don't see. I don't know what these girls pick up on, but I have a feeling that it's more instinct than science.

Just then I see how the ocean wobbles and a wave forms, as if a puppet master is pulling it off the surface with invisible strings.

I can't see Carmen's face, but I can feel her determination to catch it.

"Faster," Sam breathes.

Carmen's powerful shoulders come through for her, she gets there just in time to turn the tip of the board into the wave's direction.

She takes one, two, three deep pulls and grinds it out.

"She's got it," Sam says.

I hope she's right, because today I've seen plenty of surfers not catch more obvious waves. But within two seconds, she and my mom's board are sliding down the wave. The wave doesn't have height, but it looks massive—thick.

In a blink, Carmen hops on the board and keeps her body low. She maneuvers the board, staying close to the wave.

"Will she catch a tunnel?" I ask.

She glances at me, smiling. "You mean a barrel? No, not with this type of wave."

As she says that, Carmen straightens a bit. Her focus shifts back and forth between the wave she's riding and what I assume is the bottle in her hand. I can't actually see it happening. She's still too far away, but when she points to the sky, I know I'm right.

She lowers her body and pumps the board, gaining speed. She

stretches her hand out and as the white foam of the wave covers the board, she tips her hand, releasing my mom's remains behind her.

Sam wraps her arm around my back, then rests her head on my shoulder.

Between watching a portion of my mom's ashes join the beach that she loved and Sam's physical proximity, I realize how much I appreciate her standing next to me. Carmen was right. Sam is like a rock.

In awe, I watch my cousin finish her duty with grace. She drops into the water, then grabs the board and walks toward us.

Sam releases my shoulder and meets Carmen in the water. "You nailed it," she says and takes the empty blue jar then helps her with her board.

"Thanks for doing this," I say.

She hugs me for a few moments. And although she's wet and cold, I couldn't care less.

She pulls away then places one hand on my shoulder and the other on Sam's. "You guys'll think I'm off my rocker, but, man I felt her."

"No way," Sam says.

"Totally. Like she was there, on the board, with me."

I should be laughing at the silliness. Instead, I feel jealousy because on some level I believe.

AFTER DINNER, although they tried to convince me to sleep inside the RV, I stuck to my promise and set up the tent. To my surprise, the sounds of the ocean quickly tenderized me into a dreamless sleep.

Until a sound worthy of the depths of hell pulls me right back out. I hesitate, wondering if it's real or a sound from my dream world.

There it is again.

Like a chain being pulled through a tin can. I sit up and turn on the lantern.

Again.

This is not a dream. It's really happening. Is that a bear? Or a mountain lion, smelling our food?

Once again, but this time, it stops momentarily, then continues.

It can't be. I stand up, unzip the tent then walk up to the RV, step in, and—

No, it's not the engine or the heater. It's one of the girls, snoring.

I walk gingerly into the camper and find both girls sleeping on the queen bed. Carmen has a pillow over her head.

Sam is on her back, in pajama bottoms and a white tank top undershirt. Her legs and arms are spread wide, her mouth open and her hair is all over the place. Mystery solved. Evidence that no one is perfect. This is an inhuman sound.

The chainsaw massacre continues. I'll never be able to sleep. If I close the window most of the sound would be trapped in here. How can Carmen sleep through this mess? I glance at the nightstand next to Carmen and notice a stash of small bags. I reach over and grab one.

Earplugs!

I tear it open, shove them in, and feel grateful for science.

NINETEEN

DAY 2 - SHEP

"WAKE UP," someone says, but the voice is muffled.

I pop my head from under the sleeping bag and rub my eyes, trying to focus on the source of the voice. Sam. She's speaking, but her voice is low. I squint, trying to figure why she sounds like she's under water. Then I remember. I yank out the earplugs.

"—running on the beach?" Sam finishes, but I only catch the end of her question.

"Sorry, what was that?" I ask.

Her eyes go wide. "Why are you wearing earplugs?"

"No way, he wore earplugs?" I hear Carmen ask but I can't see her.

"Why?" Her eyes are hard, focused on mine. "Why. Are you. Wearing earplugs?"

Think quick. Evasive action. "Um. You know, the sound of the ocean... and, um..."

Carmen breaks into a belly laugh. "Dude, he totally couldn't sleep because you were snoring like a hog."

Sam gives me a dirty look. "Is this true? Was it because of me?"

I can barely maintain eye contact. "Maybe."

"Liars! Both of you. There is no evidence that I snore."

"I have recordings," Carmen says. "Many of them."

"Fabricated. Fake news." I can see the smile that's trying to break out, while she trains her glare on me.

I sit up. "So... What was that about running?"

WE TAKE a five-mile route along the shoreline. The coastal air takes some getting used to. My lungs are not used to the thicker, wet air. But with time, I'll acclimate...or die. What I may never adapt to is the heavy sand. My feet bury on impact so it takes more effort to pull them out. I'm leaving an explosion of sand bombs behind me. The girls on the other hand don't break stride. It's like they were born to run in this environment.

Here's the deal, each mile on sand feels like two miles on land. I am tempted many times to stop running, to rest, but I have to get myself back to competitive shape. I haven't even scrimmaged with my new team. I've been out of the training cycle for months. My ticket to college and then the next level is with a football scholarship. My future died in Texas, because our program got hammered. I can't afford to lose my shot here.

I doubt anyone here would be aware of the scandal. If they look me up, all they'll see is that I'm a five-star student-athlete. That may be good enough. On the other hand, it only takes one curious person to open a can of worms. What I don't know is the football culture at this school. I know they had a solid team last year and barely lost in the semi-finals. What can I expect, I wonder? Carmen's ex is or was on the football team. I wonder why they broke up. She's running ahead of us, earbuds in. I speed up a bit and catch up to Sam.

"You okay?" Sam asks.

"Curious about Carmen's ex." We reduce our speed and walk up the stairs. "What happened with what's-his-face?"

"What's-his-face's name is Kevin. Two things happened within a span of a couple of weeks. For one, there was the incident with the cheerleader."

I'm generally not a violent guy, but people like him push me into rampage mode. You hurt someone while at the same time screw around with someone else because you think you deserve it. If he's still on the team, this may prove to be problematic. I moderate my breathing as we approach our camper. "And by incident do you mean he cheated on her?"

I turn on the instant-boil water kettle.

"To be fair, we don't know if he actually cheated on her. But the intent, at a bare minimum, was there. Here's how it went down: we got intel that Kevin was at a party and he was all over Sheila-I-know-the-Kardashians."

A scene I'm all too familiar with. When you're a standout athlete, you have a future, prospects. Everyone's attracted to you. Even if you're with someone, there's always someone waiting in the wings, ready to come in and make the move. Some are willing to do anything.

"Personally I thought that was great news. She needs to be dating a surfer, not some low-life football player." She hesitates. "No offense."

"Plenty of offense taken. We'll deal with that later. Back to Carmen and friend-of-the-Kardashians. What did Carmen do?"

The kettle bubbles violently. I pour a cup for Sam.

"What any self-respecting person would do. Carmen and I snuck out of the house and went to the party to confront him."

I pour a cup for me too, just as Carmen joins us. For a moment I'm sure Sam will change the topic, but she goes on.

"So I find him on the couch with Sheila right next to him, her bare legs draped over his." She turns to Carmen. "Was she even wearing shorts? I mean, all I remember is seeing a whole lot of skin."

"I'm sure she had something on," Carmen says, looking a bit uneasy.

Sam shrugs. "Anyway, so Carmen shows up in front of him and says a few things—"

"What? What did you say?" I ask Carmen.

"He was a bit slow to the take, because of the beers and his state of sexual intoxication, but once he realized it was me, he threw her legs off and tried to stand. But Sam was behind him, so she pushed him back down."

"I yelled, 'Sit your ass down, son,'" Sam says.

Both Carmen and I turn to her.

"Okay, I didn't say that, but I really wanted to say something cool and dramatic. You know, the type of stuff that generations will talk about."

"So what did you actually say?" I ask.

She shrugs. "Nothing. Just pushed him down."

"Fascinating," I say then turn to Carmen. "Then what happened?" I ask.

Sam interrupts. "Carmen crosses her arms and says, 'No need to stand on my account.' She then points to his pants and says, 'Your Chapstick's showing.'"

My mouth drops open. "You didn't."

Sam is cracking up at this point and Carmen appears very proud of herself. "I did," she says. "It really was a Chapstick, but the others there didn't know that."

My cousin is a warrior-and-a-half. I laugh but then it dawns on me that this was incident number one. Sam said there were two incidents. "Even after this, you stayed with him. Why?"

Her face darkens. "He seemed genuinely apologetic and things were going good again."

She doesn't offer anything more. I look at Sam who is drinking her coffee while she's eyeing Carmen.

"And then...?" I finally ask.

Carmen turns her attention to the ocean, takes a deep breath then back to me. "At another party, he tried to force himself on me."

My vision goes blurry and my throat constricts. "Tried?" I choke out.

"Nothing happened," Carmen says.

"But it could have," Sam says. Carmen turns to her. They're staring at each other. "Carmen happens to be strong and she wasn't drunk. So it ended there. Here's the kicker: a year earlier, someone had claimed she had been nearly assaulted by him. Problem was that she didn't have the best reputation and Kevin, well he—"

"And he," I interrupt, "was untouchable because he was the star athlete. He got a free pass."

Different cities, same culture. In some schools it's about sexual hazing rituals. In others, it's letting the boys be boys. They argue that the girls were there for a reason, after all. An argument I know too well.

I'm feeling ill. They're staring at me. "I'm sorry this happened to you," I say.

She smiles. "Nothing happened. I'm fine."

Although she's right, the thought that's slamming around in my head is, *What about the others?*

TWENTY
DAY 2 - SHEP

AFTER BREAKFAST, we leave Encinitas and go to Black's Beach, the next destination on Mom's list. We drive south and in less than an hour we reach the Torrey Pines hang-glider port turnoff.

"Park in the dirt," Carmen says.

"We'll walk down the hill," Sam says.

I shut off the engine, get my bag and Mom's ashes. "How high up are we?" I ask as I join them at the rear of the RV.

"Three," Carmen says.

"Three what?"

"Three hundred feet."

"Down a steep pathway," Sam adds.

My eyes dry up, possibly because they are as wide open as I can get them. "We're going to take boards down a steep three-hundred-foot trail?"

"Also, sometimes the gusts of wind can get pushy so you have to be careful as you navigate down the path. But the views down there are to die for," Carmen says. "Not literally, but you know, they're beautiful."

If they can do it, so can I. I wait... nope, that feeble pep-talk didn't work. I'm still worried. I secure my bag then grab my mom's surf-board. Carmen and Sam grab their shortboards. Here we go.

"Best of all, it's a clothing optional beach," Sam says, just as they march off.

For a few seconds, I forget about the anxiety. Instead, I think of Mom's list and wonder if she went for it here. Before I can stop the thought, other images enter my mind. Most of them include Sam. Does she plan to *participate*?

I shake it off, then speed up to catch up to them at the edge of the bluff. I'm not afraid of heights. I don't suffer from vertigo. But for just a moment, I lose my footing.

"Whoa there," Sam says. "You okay?"

I shake it off. "Man, this is scary and beautiful all in the same instant."

"Wait till you see the naked hotties," Sam says and begins the trek down.

I'm way too focused on the placement of my feet to play one-liner tennis right now or to properly enjoy the view. But each time I glance up, I think of what Mom would've seen and thought of in this place. This is unreal.

Eventually we reach the base. I'm out of breath and this was the easy part of the journey. I can't imagine what going back will feel like. We need to find a donkey for the trek back up.

We find a spot close to the water for the girls to prep their boards.

"Black's Beach is truly a jewel," Carmen says. "I don't think there's another place in San Diego that is as consistent with as many good waves and surfers as this place."

"The water looks perfect," Sam says.

I step up to the water, but not too close. The water is crystal clear and the waves have a shape to them that I didn't see at Encinitas. Only a few surfers are in the water. We have chosen a good day, it seems.

I turn to face the girls and see Sam applying sunscreen.

"Are you going to skin it?" I ask.

She grins. "Look at you. Using big words already."

I'm proud of myself. I've been studying the surfer lingo site.

"Yeah, I prefer feeling the water on my skin," she says. "It's just a different experience. Here in La Jolla, the water is warm."

She throws her hair forward and applies lotion to her shoulders, her neck, arms and down to her tight abs. When she applies the sunscreen to her sides, for the first time, I notice the hidden ink. A small tattoo of a stylized wave—like the one mom has drawn in her journals—etched on her skin, gracing her upper ribs, dangerously close to the side of her breast, where there is a distinct skin tone difference—the tanned and untanned skin.

Yup, it's official. One ounce of ink has suddenly propelled her into the next tier of hotness. I can't help but wonder if she's dating anyone. I haven't seen any evidence, so it leads me to a couple of possible conclusions: she's very picky (only surfers must apply) or she's a mass murderer. I'll hold off judgment for now, but seriously, I wonder why she's not with anyone. She's bright, very attractive... a bit insane. That must be it.

I plop my chair into the soft sand, drop my butt in the seat, and watch the ocean.

My train of thought is broken because of the display of nature in front of me. The waves look ominous. Driving down here I had a brief internal debate about possibly entering the water. Not surf or anything stupid like that, but to step in the water. Get my knees wet and prove that the shallow ends are not dangerous. But given these waves, no way.

"Beautiful set," Carmen says. "Nothing reckless, okay? These waves can grab and hold you for a long while."

Yes, sir. That's enough for me to confirm that my ass will stay firmly planted in this chair right here.

"Got it," Sam says and with that they both run into the water.

I look around, but don't see any nude hotties.

I sink deeper into the chair and instantly I'm hit with exhaustion. Surprisingly, the ocean's persistent roar calms me. Maybe some of

Mom's love for the beach has genetically entered my soul, too. I adjust my hat to cover my face and decide to take a few.

I WAKE up from the sound of distant voices.

I sit up and look around. A cute blonde, maybe my age, is at the water's edge holding a thin, small board. She appears to be studying the waves that break on the beach.

Just then she runs parallel to the water's edge, the small board in both hands at the ready. She throws the board on the wet sand in front of her. The board skids as fast as her. She hops onto the board and like a skateboarder, controls the thin board into the wave, carving —practically slicing in a curving pattern—across the face of the breaking wave. She literally rides the face of the one-foot wave and completes a turn, spraying a bit of water. When she reaches the sand again, she hops off the board.

She grabs her board then returns to where she started—near me— preparing for another wave. Her long wet hair shines as it swings from left to right.

That was sort of cool. Like combining skateboarding and surfing, but staying close to the shore. I bet I could do that.

I turn my attention to the water. There are at least a dozen or two surfers clustered now. I squint, focusing on who's out there. It's all men, again. I bet it's the same guys from the campground. But they are so deep in the ocean that I can't tell if they're talking to each other. If I only had binoculars. I lean over and grab Carmen's backpack. She won't mind. I open the bag and see a GoPro camera. No zoom lens. She also has another small video camera. This one does.

I power it up and through the viewfinder I focus in on the black blobs then zoom in. The girls are sitting on their boards, the tips of the boards sticking up. As suspected, some of the same guys are there, stalking them. I study Sam's face as best as I can. Yup, she's laughing, flirting.

I turn off the camera and put it back in the bag.

"Wow," the blonde says.

I look up and catch sight of what has stunned her—a beast of a wave. I had not seen anything like that in Encinitas. When the wave crashes, it looks like a monster, devouring whatever is in its path.

I walk over to the edge of the water. Nope, no panic attack. But just in case, I survey the water and verify that there are no sharks near me. I return my attention to the girls.

They're all repositioning, trying to prepare for the batch of waves that are coming.

One of the guys takes a wave. A second one attempts to also, but he crashes down hard the moment the wave opens up, while a third surfer pulls back. The first surfer skids down the face of the wave, but the wave is catching up from his right.

I witness a barrel for the first time. That's right, I know words. Mom used it in yesterday's diary, and I happen to know that the hollow, covered portion of the wave that sort of looks like a tunnel is in fact called a barrel. The surfer's just outside the cave the wave's creating. He's pumping his legs, pulling ahead of the wave by a head. Then he somehow slows himself down. It's hard to see what he's doing but it's clear he wants to stay inside the abyss.

Without warning, the wave collapses on him and he disappears in the white foam. A lot of white foam. I stand on my tiptoes, trying to find him.

"Where is he?" the blonde says, who has somehow ended up right next to me.

"Not sure," I say.

The next three seconds are long. Stretched out. Maybe a shark ate him. Once the foam dissipates, a head pops out and a board reappears.

"That was scary," she says.

I don't respond, because just then Carmen takes a wave. My heart leaps into my throat. She's on her feet streaking over the wave before I've even had a chance to worry. Thankfully, this wave isn't as ugly as the last one. She carves out then points her board back up the face of the wave. She snaps the board just as she summits the lip of the wave. A huge spray of water is left in her trail. Back down the face of the wave and just as quickly she rips another one.

Her movement is dynamic, powerful, and beautiful all at the same time. She rides low to the board, her arms continually changing balance and direction of the board.

I'm in awe of my cousin.

"Fierce! She's bitchin'!" the blonde says.

"She's my cousin," I say, the pride unmistakable. Not sure if this makes me cool by association, but I think it should count for something.

"She's rad."

Yeah, she is.

"Another one," the girl says.

Now Sam is on the move.

Air doesn't enter my lungs momentarily.

The wave is a beast. It rises higher and higher, a roar of an aquatic lion. But Sam takes it without hesitation. She skims the face of the wave, then drops down a good five feet without making contact with water. I'm sure she'll lose her footing when she hits the water again, but somehow, she's able to control her center of gravity and master the board. She's under the ominous shadow of the wave. I'm having an anxiety attack just watching her.

She's moving fast. She has to or risk getting crushed by the huge mass that follows her. She pumps her legs, up and down, up and down, gaining speed.

"Go, go, go!" Blonde yells.

I grin, more pride, more euphoria. Wow, she's amazing.

The batch of surfers begin yelling so loud that even from this distance I can hear them.

Sam is just outside of the barrel. Then she's inside it. Then we can't see her. She's either still inside it, or being demolished by it.

"Oh crap," the blonde says.

Before I can even think, I sprint along the shore in the direction she'd been riding. I throw off my hat ready to jump in.

One step in, then a second, I'm about to commit to the water when cheers break though. I stop and scan for the source of celebration.

Then I see her, way ahead of the wave that's now imploding. Sam's standing tall, her hands pumping up and down, asking for the crowd to get louder, just like she had when I barehanded the baseball at the Dodgers game.

I feel stupid.

Then terrified.

I quickly turn to run back on the sand. Just as I get my feet under me, a wave grabs and trips me. I crawl my way back to safety.

"You okay?" The blonde offers a hand.

I take it and smile. "Other than my ego, I'm great."

She produces a pretty smile. "Are you a lifeguard or something?"

Oh she's funny. "Not."

She grins. "I'm Brit."

"Shep."

We walk back toward my stuff.

"Do you surf, too?" she asks.

"No, I watch them do their thing."

"Your cousin and... girlfriend?" she asks.

California girls are forward. I can respect that. "No, just a friend."

She nods. "Do you want to try skim boarding?"

"Is that what you were doing?"

"Yeah, it's fun and you don't have to sit out there like shark bait."

She totally gets me.

So she proceeds to show me the basic idea. Run, toss in wet sand in the same direction of your motion, hop on board and ride like lightning.

"Easy enough," I say, hoping I don't make a complete ass of myself. A partial-ass is okay, and almost respectable.

"Let me show you," she says and waits for what she calls the whitewash of the wave—that's the foamy stuff of a broken wave. A couple come and go, but she waits. "Like this one," she yells and runs.

She hops, directs the board closer to the water line, then lowers herself like a legitimate surfer. She snaps the board, producing a decent splash.

She grabs the board then runs back to me.

"Easy," she says.

I take the board from her and get the distinct impression that she's totally expecting me to be good at this. I suspect Brit has been skateboarding all her life. She has mastered the movement.

"Don't do any tricks the first time. Just get on the board and go straight with the water line."

Tricks? I don't know what she means, but I just hope I can stand on the board long enough.

She takes my hat and wears it. Another one who seems to think it's okay to wear a stranger's hat.

"So I just need to wait for the right wave to—"

"Now! Go! Go! Go!"

I hop into action and run as fast as possible. Like she showed me, I toss the board, run a few steps then I leap toward the board, praying upon prayer that the laws of physics apply to me just as much as the next person.

I make contact and for a micro-second, I'm certain I'll fly off, but I don't. I lower my body, just like Brit, feet shoulder-width apart, and I glide the distance.

"Awesome!" she yells.

Once the board slows down, I jump off. I am sincerely happy. That was awesome. And easy. Sort of.

From the distance I hear something. I scan the ocean and see Sam and Carmen waving at me. They saw my brilliant move. That's right, football players can do this stuff, too. I walk up to Brit.

"Go again," she says. "Do the same thing."

"Okay," I say. But since Sam is watching me, it's high time I show her what a real athlete can do with this beach stuff.

I watch the waves. This one looks good.

"Go, go, go!" Brit yells in confirmation. I'm amazing myself. I'm even building an instinct for this stuff. Easy peasy.

I sprint. I have speed. Acceleration. Even on the beach, I can outrun anyone in a forty-yard dash.

I toss the board and quickly hop on it. I've got good speed. From the corner of my eye I see a small wave coming at me. Time to show I can rip, too.

In my mind's eye, I see how Carmen and Sam cut up the wave, so I carve the floor toward the wave and just when I should be completing the turn, I feel the board separate from the sand. Time to snap the board and spray some.

I snap the board. Then I fly in one direction. The board in another.

"No!" is what I think I hear Brit yell.

I am aware of two things: (1) I am a good ten feet up in the air, and (2) my arms are thrashing around, but thankfully I don't yell. Mainly because I've lost my voice from the sheer terror.

I hit the sand. Hard. The wind gets knocked out of me.

I roll around then end up on my back.

When I open my eyes, I see the green-eyed blonde looking down at me. She seems disappointed. "I did say no tricks."

Yes, I've made a complete ass of myself.

TWENTY-ONE
DAY 2 - SHEP

I'M BACK on my beach chair, pretending that my shoulder isn't ravaged and my ego isn't thrashed. Brit didn't stick around after that mess. Just when I think things can't get worse, a couple in their fifties walk past me. Naked. Sam's sense of humor is grinding on me. She's lucky that I'm in awe of her.

She's so calm, so collected. And when she's negotiating with those nasty waves, she doesn't change at all. Still the same person. Consistent.

But that's not why I'm here. *All right, Mom. Let's see what you have in store for me today.* I pull out the second envelope from my bag and tear it open. This one's thicker, more pages.

July 11, 2000 — Day 2

Okay, that walk... long! But the view... wow! Just amazing. No picture, no painting could capture that breathtaking setting. I feel so connected to the immenseness of nature.

Once I got over being so naturey, I turned my attention to the details. Specifically of the ocean. From where I stood, the rippling water was like begging me to surf her. I practically ran down the path (and almost tripped and died... but clearly didn't).

I haven't jumped in yet. This is delayed gratification. I have a feeling once I'm in, I may not want to come out. The water is crystal clear. I mean holy crap. I love this.

Okay, time to wax the board and get to the real business at hand. We're here early enough that we have the water to ourselves. Sharon had a great idea. Let's see if we go through with it and then I may or may not write about it!

Sharon got banged up. This place doesn't mess around. You have to respect the wave. I told her. She stole a wave and as is always the case, wave-karma caught up with her. I feel bad. She has a nasty cut on her shoulder blade, but beyond patching it up, what can we do?

I, on the other hand, did well, thank you very much for asking. Got a bunch of people huddled around me in the lineup and again later on the beach. Clearly, it's for my skills. Or it could be because I am one of very few women in the water and all the guys hope my itsy-bitsy pieces of swimware will fall off me and they can sneak a peek.

Why would they think such thoughts, you ask? Well... Sharon (before she left traces of her DNA in the ocean) reminded us that this was a nude beach. So yeah, once in the water, we each took a turn at surfing naked. Might as well knock a challenge off our list, right? For the record: an amazing rush! So much freedom and at the same time scary as hell, because the whole time you're thinking, someone will see us, someone will see us, someone will see us. And you really don't want some under-sexed horny pot-head to be the one who sees you. I was the last and as luck would have it, just as I completed my run and was paddling back to the girls to get my bikini back on, an army of guys arrived. There may have been catcalls. Or that could have been the ringing in my ears from the rushing blood. I don't know if they saw my exposed ass when I paddled back, but the way they were hanging around me afterward... well, like I said, I hope it was for my mad skillz.

Back to the water!

He's here! Quick is here! I need courage now. Like, an Everest-sized load of courage.

I knew there was a chance we'd cross paths. But when I saw him, I totally chickened out and hid.

I know. I know. After what I went through with Tom, the last thing I'd want is a relationship, but this is Quick... He's actually here.

My friends don't know about him, about our past together. Even when his fame grew, I never mentioned that Quick Silver and I had been together a couple of summers ago. So when Sharon said he's in the water, all I could do was just stare at him. When that boy's surfing, he seriously shines.

Every surfer recognizes him now. I, on the other hand, know that he's not only gifted on the board, but he's an amazing guy. The person I should've been with.

Why am I writing this, instead of going up to him? Why am I not asking him to pick up where we left off two summers ago? Scared, I guess. That he'll fall short of who he was a couple of years ago.

That summer at surf camp, I fell for him immediately. At first he tried to be the responsible instructor by keeping his distance. But that only lasted three days. He spent more and more time with me. Helping me, guiding me, encouraging me. I remember the smiles, his hand on my back, our first kiss. I was about to turn sixteen, he was about to turn eighteen.

We made the most of it that summer because we knew time was against us. He was on the verge of starting his professional tour and between us he didn't want to go to jail. We both understood that once he was eighteen, we'd be playing with fire until I turned eighteen, too. Not that we had been intimate or anything, but still. If he had asked, I would've said yes. And on that last day before he left, I made sure he asked.

We made a promise back then: we would meet again when the time was right.

We went our separate ways after that. It was hard, but it was the right thing, we both said so, so I did my best to believe it. When I started eleventh grade, I tried to track his career, but it wasn't easy. We wrote a few letters, but he was never home so his replies would come months later. Eventually, life happened and we stopped writing.

So when I heard that he was going to be doing a few small events this summer at local hotspots, I started planning. And here he is, less than 100 feet away from me. And I'm here, hiding, writing, instead of acting.

Will he still remember me? Why would he, when all the surfer girls around the world are after him?

Then again, it's destiny, right? I mean, yeah, I sort of stalked him, but even so, it was a long shot. Why else are we on the same beach, at the same time, during a trip that was not supposed to happen? Given all this, clearly I'd have the wind at my back. I would walk right up to him and remind him, right?

Not so much. I'm still the same coward. I hope he'll come right up to me. Otherwise, I may have to find the courage. Wish me luck!

It didn't happen. I even said a little prayer for him to come to me, to seek me. But it didn't happen.

When we packed and went up the trail I kept hoping that he'd come after me. A scene out of a movie where the hero realizes who the girl is and sweeps her off her feet.

The only thing that was swept off my feet was the sand.

We drove off and he was nowhere in sight.

When we arrived at Oceanside, I was all quiet and out of it. So we smoked weed, but this time it didn't make me loose and happy. I wasn't even willing to surf. All I did was float in the water. Took my longboard and literally rested on it in the water. Good thing I wasn't attacked by a shark.

It was relaxing, but didn't change my mood. The others wanted to get drinks and get high, I wasn't interested. All I thought of was how I wish I had made the first move.

I've decided I won't sleep tonight. I can't because he's on my mind. I planned, then I dropped the ball. I should cut out that piece of my past and move on, because clearly I'm not going to do anything about it. But what can I say. I feel what I feel. I'll give myself twenty-four hours (maybe forty-eight) to sulk, then I'll get back on track.

On the brighter side, if I hold off on sleep, I'll cross off one more off my challenge list.

Until tomorrow.
O.

I quietly put the letter away. *Is it him? Is this my father?*
"Wow," I breathe.

It must be. Am I seriously this close to finding him? Quick Silver isn't a name, but I bet at one point she mentions his real name. This has to be her plan for me. I thought I'd get to spend a trip with my mom, but it looks like she'll hand him to me, in a letter written nearly two decades ago.

A pro surfer... then why did he just abandon us? I want to run up the trail, tear open the rest of the letters, and get to the answers.

Then again, maybe this is just the start of the rollercoaster she rode that summer. This could be a pattern of her flailing heart. In two days, she's talked about two different guys. And then there's Tom, someone who I guess she was with just before this trip. A horrible thought enters my head. What if she reveals even more guys?

I read through the letter again. *She surfed naked.* And smoked weed again...

Honestly, this is not how I want to think of my mom.

"Hey, Shep."

I look up, it's Carmen and Sam, dripping all over the place. I quickly shove the letter into my bag, but I know they saw it.

"It's time," Carmen says. "The ashes, please."

I reach into the bag and pull out the vial. She takes it and grabs my mom's unused, but pre-waxed board.

I get off my chair and walk up to the water line. Sam joins me.

We watch Carmen jump into the water and paddle over and under the waves.

"Did you get hurt?" Sam asks. She's not looking at me.

For a moment I think she's talking about the letter, but then I remember the flight of the wannabe surfer with Brit.

"No... Maybe. Just a bit."

"Shoulder?"

"Maybe."

She's silent for a while. Just when I think she's going to let it drop, she says, "Was she worth it?"

I turn to her. She eyes me.

"No," I say as I adjust my hat.

She casually takes my hat, places it on her head then winks at me. "Let's not share our hat with others, shall we?"

Ours? I don't argue with the California beach goddess. She returns her attention to Carmen.

The other surfers allow her to take the next wave. Do they know? It doesn't matter, because she catches the wave.

"A clean three-footer," Sam says.

Carmen effortlessly hops on the board and rides the wave. It's docile. It seems to understand and respect what Carmen's up to. She's fairly close to us now so I can see her in detail. She opens the bottle, then carves the wave, and as she rips through, she releases the ashes.

I love you, Mom.

I miss you.

But you're worrying me.

SHORTLY AFTER, we leave Black's Beach. The trek uphill confirms that a) I'm not in as good a shape as I thought, and b) I was right when I predicted the climb up would be worse. Where is that donkey I asked about? My quads are burning, my calves are numb, and my shoulder is a complete mess. Balancing my mom's board on my head up that steep cliff is just what I needed to completely snap any remaining tendons. All we need is a nice wind gust so that we all fall to our death. The end.

Somehow we make it to the camper. Silently, we load the RV then hit PCH toward Oceanside. No one is talking because we're all tired.

By early afternoon, we have already set up camp, showered, and have eaten the sandwiches Carmen prepared. We all look drained, our eyes more closed than open.

"Nap?" Sam declares.

"Nap," Carmen confirms.

They traipse inside while I connect the hammock because a nap sounds just about perfect. But when I try to lean down, a shooting pain in my shoulder causes me to grunt.

"What's wrong?"

Sam is by the RV's door. I roll off the hammock and squeeze my shoulder. "I need pain meds and ice."

"Got it," she says and goes inside. A few moments later she hands me two blue pills and a water bottle.

I swallow it down with greed.

"Sit over here and let's take a look at your shoulder," she says as she walks me to the picnic bench.

I try rolling up the t-shirt's sleeve, to expose my shoulder, but Sam stops me. "Just take the shirt off."

After a brief hesitation, I do. She studies my shoulder, as if she can see through the skin and muscle and tissue.

"I'll be right back." She runs off then returns with a bottle. "Baby oil," she announces.

She squirts some on my shoulder. It's cold but pleasant. She pours some into her palm and hands me the bottle.

She grinds her hands together, then gently begins working my shoulder. She rides her knuckles over tight muscles, squeezes toxins out of the muscle tissues, and manhandles my shoulder, tricep, and bicep. This feels good, great, in fact. I realize my eyes are closed. I also realize that I may fall asleep if she keeps this up.

Then her fingers glide up to my neck. With both hands, she rubs the sides of my neck then squeezes the middle with her thumbs.

This hurts. But a good hurt.

She's causing me to feel.

To learn to rely.

I'm not ready.

And with that thought, I go out.

The next thing I know, I'm waking up, Sam asleep by me on the bench, and her fingers are resting inside my hair.

TWENTY-TWO

DAY 2 - SHEP

THE PIER at Oceanside is rather boring, if I'm being honest. It's just a pier with a restaurant. That's it. Then again, maybe boring is just what I need. Reading Mom's journal feels like an out of body experience. I know the main actor of the story, but the role she's playing is completely foreign to me. It's still awesome, if I'm being honest. It's my mom. Things I never knew about her. Experiencing her joys at a time she was carefree. For that I am grateful. But it's only day two and there's plenty that gives me concern.

I lean against the railing and stare into the vastness of the ocean. An unexpected calm joins me. I should be scared, because any minute now an earthquake will hit and the pier will buckle, sending me into the awaiting jaws of a shark. Instead, I'm at peace.

I drag my eyes away from the horizon and find the girls in the water to the north of the pier. The best part is that I can actually see them better because I am as deep as they are, with a bird's eye view. What's annoying is that yet again, they are surrounded by guys.

I must admit, it's cool how they're all just floating in the water, all straddling their boards like I used to mount the horses we had on the ranch. Like the horses, the waves continually move the surfers.

They're resting. Connecting. The community of surfers.

Any minute now, they'll all feel it. That motion in the ocean that tells them a set of waves is coming.

I pull away from the rail and walk back down the pier. Seagulls are yelling at me, at each other. A stout lady, probably in her sixties, is fishing off the pier, her worn-out oversized hat evidence of her decades of experience. The bucket next to her proves that she's got game. A dozen or more fishing rods adorn both sides of the pier. Most just leaning against the railings.

As I reach the sand, I glance back toward the mass of humanity in the water. Although, the ocean is vast, the surfers seem to congregate where the others are. I don't get it. Go somewhere else and you don't have to fight over the waves. I recall what Sam and Carmen said. *You have to study the waves.* Can they actually tell where the swells will form?

I hear the moaning, followed by the thunder generated by the ocean. I spin around. The set has come and it's a nasty one. I train my eyes on the girls.

Within seconds, chaos ensues.

At least four or five surfers per curl and a handful of waves all at the same time, crossing each other. The influx are vicious, ridiculous.

The surfers are getting pounded. Some are having a hard time just keeping their head above water. One after another they're getting beat up.

Sam and Carmen aren't doing much better. They dive into the water, continually, just trying to find a point where the waves will give them a chance to reset. Just watching them being manhandled is exhausting and scary. I can't imagine what they're feeling.

It reminds me of a cartoon I saw when I was a kid. The wave turns into the shape of a hand, grabs the surfboard, then slams the surfer away like a baseball.

The situation would be funny if I wasn't worried. The surfers are constantly thrown off their boards, but none are escaping. None are making a run for it. Instead, they're withstanding the storm by dropping backward or diving in when they realize the wave is about to win.

Then I see Carmen streaking by. She's gained so much speed that I'm sure a sonic boom is about to follow her. She maneuvers her board, going up the wave's face at a wide angle. Like a voice inside my skull, I hear *Run.* So I sprint along the coast, keeping her in my sight.

I expect her to turn the board back toward the base, but no. She's going up, and going, not slowing down or changing directions.

Then I see why. Her path has turned into a vortex of imploding waves, colliding and exploding into each other.

"Turn!" I yell, knowing full well that she can't hear me.

Then it happens.

She flies.

Like a rocket, she's a projectile, torpedoed into space.

She brings her hands together like an Olympic diver, the string to her surfboard tightens, and the board follows her until the tether snaps.

Like a spear, she disappears into the water.

I pick up my pace and scan the surfers. I can't see her. Where is she?

I see Sam. She's pulling something from the water, but the oscillating waves make it hard for me to see what. The path clears. Sam has fished out Carmen's board and is now helping her up onto it.

Sam is paddling and pulling toward the beach. They bypass where the waves are breaking to find a less violent path to the beach. Why isn't Carmen doing anything? Did she get knocked out? Did she swallow water?

Screw it!

I attack the water and by the time I'm waist high, I dive in, swimming toward them.

"Here," Sam yells out.

I reach them and help pull Carmen toward the shore. She's breathing, but not moving.

"Is she hurt?" I yell.

"Don't know," Sam says.

Once I'm close enough to shore, I lift Carmen and walk her to the sand and lay her down. She's plastered on the ground, not saying anything. Sam drags both boards and drops them nearby.

"Concussion?" I ask Sam.

Water speeds down her body. Goosebumps have overtaken her frame.

"Don't think so. That was a controlled dive."

"That was controlled? Nothing about that was controlled!"

"She's the one who initiated the dive. That's controlled. When the wave catches you off guard is when bad things happen."

I lean down next to Carmen.

Sam's knees hit the sand on the other side of her.

"Can you hear me?" I ask.

"Are you okay?" Sam asks.

Nothing for a few moments. She's breathing and there's eye movement behind her closed lids.

"Carmen, for the love of God, are you okay?"

She pops open her eyes. Her face has specks of sand and the strands of hair are held together by the grains. But she smiles.

"I..." she starts.

"You what?" I ask. "Are hurt? Did you break something?"

She shakes her head slightly.

"I"—a pause—"can fly."

My shoulders sag and my lungs accept air again.

"Yeah, you did!" Sam says. "Superman called and asked for his cape."

They both laugh uncontrollably.

I drop my ass on the sand, then fall backward, my arms splayed wide open.

These two will be the end of me.

I ADD another log to the campfire. Carmen is fine, physically. I do question her mental state though. All those two have been talking about during dinner is how she flew.

"You were up twenty feet!" has now evolved into, "Maybe forty or fifty feet!"

I have no clue how high she was. She was too high for my taste. My uncle trusted me with these two nut cases. I should lay down the law, but truth be told... it was amazing. If not for the fact that I was sure my cousin was knocked out cold and therefore drowning and therefore shark food, I would have been celebrating with them.

"Did you notice that your cousin dove into the water?" Sam asks. She's not just busting my chops. There's a bit of admiration in her eyes.

Carmen nods. "Maybe you're over your phobia?"

The same thought crossed my mind. I was so focused on saving them that my fear nearly disappeared. Second time in two days. "It's not phobia. It's a certainty that the last thing I'll see will be the inner cavity of a great white."

"Not down here," Sam says. "Maybe a baby white."

I glare at her.

"Well, whatever propelled you to do it, I am proud of you," Carmen says.

"Whatever propelled me? Oh I can tell you very specifically: the thought that you were dead."

She chuckles. "I don't plan to go out that easily."

The fire is burning low, so I grab a few more logs and add them to the pit.

"Shep, what's in those envelopes you're reading?"

I can't maintain eye contact with Carmen.

"Well? What's the story?" Sam asks.

I lift my chin and smile. I hate what I have to do. "It's nothing."

"Clearly, he's not ready to share," Sam says. "Because something's going on. It's either the letters or something else."

117

Carmen's face tells me she's feeling the same as Sam, but not voicing it.

"It's nothing. Really," I say.

"Your problem is that your face is too honest. So when you lie, it's obvious. You are transparent," Sam says.

My transparent face is exactly why I avoided the district attorney, but I can't tell them that.

Carmen leans forward. "You know you can tell us anything, right?"

I nod, but don't say anything. I dealt with the scandal on my own. I dealt with grieving Mom's death also. I'll see my way through these letters. I don't need to embarrass myself in front of the only family I have left.

"Whenever you're ready," she says.

"I'm gonna make s'mores," Sam says and runs inside the RV.

Carmen's studying me. I hope she'll leave it alone. The silence stretches uncomfortably and like a lifeline, the door slams open and Sam stumbles out with a box of Graham crackers, a bag of marshmallows, a jar of Nutella, and kabob skewers. She pierces three marshmallows and hands us each a skewer.

"Nutella instead of chocolate?" I ask.

She gives me a dirty look. "If you actually have to ask, you and I have very little to discuss from this point forward."

"What I mean is, I'm happy to see that you also recognized the flaw of the original recipe used by millions. Clearly, Nutella is the superior choice."

"Coward," Carmen coughs.

I place the charred marshmallow on one cracker. Sam hands me another cracker smeared with Nutella, which I quickly squeeze on top of the marshmallow. I shove the whole thing into my mouth before it falls apart.

I chew. Taste. Chew some more. Taste. Then stop.

"Oh man," I say with a full mouth.

"You're welcome," Sam says. "Next time, accept my ideas like you accept the laws of physics."

"Yes, ma'am."

"So," Sam starts, "do you have any indication in those secret letters of yours if any of the challenges were completed at this point?"

I debate how much to share and decide I can share that information without much risk. Also, let's face it, I need to get some of this off my chest.

"It seems that at this stage in the trip she had knocked off two challenges."

"Which ones?" Carmen asks.

"Well..." I start and immediately realize the first challenge she completed is not the type of thing I want anyone to know about.

"What? Spit it out," Sam says.

"I need to know that I can share in confidence."

"Of course," Carmen says.

I take a deep breath. "At Black's she surfed naked."

Silence.

"Wow," whispers Carmen. "My aunt is even cooler than I thought."

"I so want to try that," Sam says.

Immediately, the idea of her surfing naked etches a vivid image in my mind's eye. I am grateful, fortunate in fact, that it's dark out, because I have no doubt that my ears are lava red.

"Not me," Carmen says.

"Why?" Sam asks.

"Because my cousin is here. What's the matter with you?"

"Okay, let's change the topic," I say.

"What if we were all naked?" Sam shoves in. "Then it won't be weird."

We both turn to her, unable to even grasp at her logic.

"You know, when in Rome and all."

"That saying does not apply. At all," Carmen says.

Sam shrugs. "Whatever."

Carmen shakes involuntarily then turns to me. "What was the other challenge she finished?"

I decide to hide 'kissing the stranger' challenge from the girls. "Here, at Oceanside, she didn't sleep for twenty-four hours."

"Awesome!" Sam says. "We should definitely do that one."

I study her. "We?"

"Come on, when in Rome..."

"It still doesn't apply," Carmen says.

"One big happy family. Let's do it. We can each try to see how many of the challenges we'll accomplish."

Carmen eyes me. "Up to you, Shep."

"I was gonna do it, so if you want to join in, fine." As soon as I speak those words, I pause, in shock. Where did that come from? I was not planning on doing any of them.

"Seriously?" Carmen asks and a smile washes over her entire face.

"Now we're talking," Sam says and gives Carmen a high five then turns to me.

I study her outstretched hand. *Well crap.* I reciprocate.

"Let's make some coffee," Sam says. "I love Rome!"

———

IT'S 1:00 A.M.

We played board games, until we got bored.

We tried to play Pictionary until it became clear you can't with three players.

We've been playing poker, Texas Hold'em, of course. I've massacred them. My bowl of Cheerios is nearly overflowing.

"Since we're staying awake," Carmen says, her eyes bloodshot, "we should leave here at five or earlier. This way we can take full day advantage of San Onofre."

"Sounds good," I say as I sip the hot chocolate.

"I'm glad we're doing this outdoors," Sam says, her voice low without any inflections. "The cool air will keep us awake." One eye continues to drape close while the other eye seems to be focusing on nothing in particular.

They surfed all day. They should get rest. It's silly of them to try this.

Sam lays her forehead on the table.

"You're cheating," Carmen says.

"No, no. I'm thinking. Just thinking. Thinking..."

In less than thirty seconds the snoring begins.

"She's so weak," Carmen says.

I pop my loot into my mouth. "She's not strong like you," I say.

"Nope."

We stare at each other.

"I gotta pee," she says, and is barely able to stand up.

"Okay, I'll be here. Waiting."

"Just give me a minute." She stumbles to the door, pulls herself up, then closes it behind her.

A few seconds later, the camper shakes a bit. I'd bet my winnings she's on the bed.

I go around the bench and lay my hand on Sam's back. Even in rest, her body is tight, strong, and warm. "Wake up," I whisper into her ear. I pick up the scent of her hair... smells like fruit. This is the best shampoo ever created.

I try again.

"Sam, go to bed," I say.

Her snoring stops. "I'm just thinking," she mumbles.

"Don't you need to use the restroom?" I ask.

She pulls her head up, her forehead marked red. "Yeah. I need to pee," she says.

I help her up, open the door, and she wobbles inside. I wait for it and within seconds the RV shakes again. Two down. Me to go.

PART THREE

"My passion for surfing was more than my fear of sharks."
~Bethany Hamilton

TWENTY-THREE
DAY 3 - SHEP

AT 4:00 A.M., I slowly pull the RV out of the campground. Maybe it's not safe to drive while they sleep, but at this time of day and if I drive slowly, the twenty-mile drive should be uneventful.

The sun has yet to make an appearance, which makes this whole experience of not sleeping all that more surreal. I silently admit to myself that I'm glad I crossed off one of the challenges. And yes it's a bit selfish, but I'm also glad I was on my own. It allowed me to have something of my own with Mom.

Being awake gave me the chance to think about a bunch of things like why I don't want them to know about the letters and about he-who-I'm-not-ready-to-discuss: my father. If I find him, will I want to punch him, or hug him? The girls don't know any of this. If they did, they would totally judge me and tell me that I'm setting myself up for disappointment. Frankly, that's just silly. I can't get much more disappointed—he's been absent for seventeen years. But now that Mom's gone and she has sent me off on this trip, she clearly wants me to find my dad.

The word gets caught in my mouth. Dad—a term I've never used before. I sure could've used a dad many times over the last few years.

But I never mentioned anything like that to Mom. I didn't want to hurt her. I didn't want her to think she wasn't enough, because she was.

But she's no longer here.

It would be nice if—

"Hey, cuz," a tired voice from the rear calls out. "What time is it?"

"Early."

I hear her feet hit the floor. "Awesome," she says. "We can surf as the sun rises."

This girl is insane.

"Wake up," she says. "We're on the move."

A groan travels down the camper. "Does this mean we failed the challenge?"

"You two did," I say. "I rocked it."

"I was so close," Sam says. No. She wasn't.

THE CAMPGROUND'S not open yet, so we find a good spot nearby and park the camper. Carmen goes into the narrow bathroom to change.

"Was that a nuclear facility we just passed?" I ask.

"What, the two boobs?" Sam asks. "Yeah, it was."

"Doesn't that mean the water is radioactive?"

"You're way too paranoid," Sam says. She grabs her bikini top and bottom and jumps on her bed and goes under the sheets.

"What are you doing?" I ask, a bit taken aback.

"I'm changing. If you won't get out, I have no choice but to get creative."

"Fine, fine, I'll get out."

As I open the door, Carmen bumps her way out of the bathroom. "Hurry up," she starts to say to Sam, but stops and stares at her friend. "Seriously?"

"Leave me be. I'll be done in a sec."

Carmen and I go to the boards and take them down.

"Shep, there is a lot of beach here. That means a lot of walking. We're going to surf at different spots on this patch of beach. Old Man's, San O, Trestles, Lowers, all of it."

I'm staring at her in disbelief. "You guys'll be exhausted by the time the day is done."

"This place is worth it." She runs her hand through her hair. "Also, a lot of these spots are for beginners. I mean, you know. In case... you know."

I study her. "Thanks for the heads up," I say, but don't give her room to continue.

Sam jumps out in a hot bikini.

"That looks so good," Carmen says.

To which Sam raises her arms above her head and slowly turns. I catch sight of the wave tattoo on her side again. Then I get an eyeful of the bikini bottom.

Not a g-string, but high up. I feel Carmen's eyes on me. I quickly dig my face into my bag, hoping my ears don't light up. But I can feel them. My stupid ears are burning hot.

"Do you like it?" Sam asks.

Please don't be talking to me. Please.

"Shep, I'm talking to you."

Of course she is. I gather myself and look up, focus directly on her eyes.

"What do you think?" she asks.

I swallow. "Perfect," I say.

She beams. "I haven't tried this brand before. I just hope it doesn't slide off when I'm surfing."

She saunters over, grabs her bag and board, and heads toward the trail.

I glance at Carmen. She's studying me. She asks me questions, interrogating me better than any CIA officer could. She corners me, shames me into confessions, and nearly makes me cry. All with just one look.

"Let's go," she says.

I nod, not daring to use words.

I SHOULD'VE SLEPT.

This is the most walking I've done in forever. We started at the southern edge of this strip of beach called Old Man's. It was right next to the nuclear plant which was bad enough, but the shirtless old men with beer bellies gave the place a more "deep south" feel instead of "mecca of surfing" feel.

Because of our early start, only the diehards were sharing the waves, like Carmen and Sam. But as early morning surrenders to mid-morning, the beaches are now invaded by surfers and beachgoers of all types.

I've had my mom's longboard this time, because Cottons is what Mom had handwritten on her list. Turns out Cottons is a decent longboard stop. Not sure what that means and why one board is used in some beaches over others. But I trust that they know what they're talking about.

"Longboards are the best way for a beginner to start," Carmen throws out. These two seriously make me wonder if they can read minds. I pretend I didn't hear her. My focus right now is to find a spot where I can rest and read the third letter.

"A lot of marines here," Carmen says as they prepare to go into the water of what she's been calling the Lowers.

"Sci-fi," Sam says.

"That's Semper Fi," Carmen corrects. "You knew that, , right?"

"Exactly what I said," Sam says.

I don't know if I want to strangle her or hug her. She's a beautiful disaster. How can she be so carefree, yet sure-footed, when her family life is so unstable? What does she know that I don't?

"What a shame," Carmen says as she stares into the ocean.

She takes the words out of my mouth. The water here is over-crowded. "This is ridiculous," I say.

Just then a fight breaks out in the water.

"What happened?" Carmen asks, but none of us were paying attention.

Some guy with long blond dreadlocks standing by us imparts his wisdom. "The typical," he says. "Longboarders against the short-boarders. Or the locals who don't take to tourists who drop in on them."

I turn to Carmen, hoping she can explain.

"Dropping in is when one surfer steals someone else's wave. There's a whole thing about who has the wave. Newbies mess that up all the time."

On some level I get it, but seriously, do they have to get into a fight? We watch as the combatants get out of the water and continue the fight on sand.

"Do we have to stay here?" I ask.

Carmen pays me no attention. Instead, she grabs her board, eyes Sam, and they both run into the water. They get into the mix with the dozens of surfers.

The number of surfers are only outmatched by the staggering number of beautiful women on the beach. In fact, everyone looks great. This is like a movie set where they've cast extras at their peak physical condition.

You name the age, it's here. Some look piss-poor while others look like they just stepped out of their oceanside homes. I wonder if pro surfers are here, too? Not that I'd recognize any. I think of Quick Silver, whoever he really is, and my mom at these same beaches.

An idea dawns on me. I search the internet for 'surfer quick silver.' Although I get a billion hits, none of them are about a specific surfer. It's about a brand.

I drop on the sand and decide it's time. I take out Mom's next letter.

July 12, 2000 — Day 3

What an amazing day! Churches, Middles, Lowers... I could stay here forever. I wanted to stay at Cottons even longer, but the rest were too tired. I don't know what it was about that spot, but something called me to stay there as long as I could.

I tried to convince the girls to stay another day, but Sharon is being a stickler for the schedule. I love that I'm here with them (would've been better without the loser boyfriend), but if I had been here alone, I would've stayed another day.

Confession: When the day started, I was looking for him. Yeah, Quick. But no luck. I've been thinking about him which is really annoying because I want to be thinking about the waves and the sand. But whenever I get quiet time, he shows up and I become a mess again.

On the brighter side of things, I didn't sleep last night. Yay me, one more off the list!

I felt odd writing about this earlier, so I didn't. Confession two: I know why I wanted to stay at Cottons. And if I can't write down the truth here, where can I?

I heard the voice. After months of silence, I heard it again. And it was beautiful. It made me stronger, more in tune. I feel like I am a better surfer tonight than I was this morning.

Feeling grateful.

Good night,
O.

─── 〜 ─── 〜 ─── 〜 ───

I put the letter away and stand up. *What voice? Is this a surfer thing?*

Nothing about my father, which now makes me wonder if Quick really is my father. This voice business is something I'll have to ask the girls about. Get deeper into what surfers experience when they're in the water.

I don't get it. She loved surfing. Why didn't she surf when we were in Texas? Was it just because I was being a petulant ass about it? And that time I surfed, why didn't she jump on the board? Why wouldn't she relive her passion? Why didn't she teach me? How can you talk about this with so much love and then stop it, cold turkey?

I hesitate. When it all went to crap back home, didn't I consider quitting football?

I stroll to the shoreline and scan for the girls, but no luck. Way too many people.

It dawns on me that I could get a quick shuteye here. I pull the towel out of my bag, lay it on my mom's longboard, then lay on it. I use my bag as the pillow and my hat to keep my face in the shade. Just rest for a bit.

I feel my body release the tension. My eyelids want to close shop, but I fight them for now. There is an orchestration at play on the beach. The sound of the waves crashing back into the ocean, as the seagulls cry, and the cacophony of the beach dwellers' voices, slamming into each other, producing a sustained echo, a roar unlike any other.

It's a beautiful, soothing sound.

I drift and in the moments before I'm out, I see a man on a surfboard. Bald. The reflection of the sun off the water makes him illuminate. He's fast and controlled. Ripping one wave after another, doing aerial tricks, like skateboarders and snowboarders.

He is amazing.

Is he...?

TWENTY-FOUR
DAY 3 - SHEP

THE GIRLS WAKE me out of my power nap and we walk over to Middles. "Nice and decent waves without the crowds," Carmen says. "This is perfect."

With that, they both run into the water and do their thing. I drop onto the sand, my mom's board next to me, and I watch them. They look so good doing their magic. I have a feeling that any guy who watches a girl surf will immediately fall in love. They show such amazing control and grace.

Although it is an individual sport, they are not in it alone. They count on the wave. Both as a teammate and an adversary.

I wanted to be a running back from the first time I started watching football. What I loved about that position was that although I was officially part of the team, I also realized that I could be an individual contributor. I wanted that ball in my hands because I knew that I could manufacture yards and touchdowns by just studying what was in front of me and predicting what would open up based on the dozens of plays unfolding on the field. Time would slow down. I could see it all happening and all I had to do was be faster to the open spots before the defenders. Yes, I needed the offensive line, but I created the yards based on what was in front of me in that instant.

I miss football. I miss being in charge. When this is all done, I'll need to hit the field hard and fast. I need to get back to top form.

A college-age girl is studying the waves. The way she stands and the way the wind flows through her hair reminds me of Mom's picture on José's wall. A teenager who was powerful and sure-footed. All that changed after this same surf trip eighteen years ago.

A wave roars, causing me to glance at Mom's board. The curve at the tip of the board smiles at me.

Screw it.

I grab the board and march toward the water.

Between the crashing of the surf and the thumping of my heart in my throat, I can't hear anything else. Every movement on the water's surface is a potential shark. Each scraping of seaweed against my legs is a bite.

I have a remote sensation that the girls are watching me, maybe even cheering. I also have a stinging awareness that the water is considerably colder than I expected. But I can't turn back now. I am committed.

In fact, I should be committed to an asylum. What type of stupidity is this? Why can't I just stop my feet?

I am in waist-high water, the longboard floating at my side, like a well-behaved pit bull who at the slightest provocation will launch itself at my jugular.

I run my palm across the smooth surface of the board.

Please be nice, I think.

A couple of steps and I angle the board slightly. It's time to get on it. Holding it from both edges, I slide my body on it.

And slide right off.

That was embarrassing.

I need to better balance myself I guess. I don't remember this part being hard, but then again that was nearly ten years ago.

Once more, I grab it and push myself on. The board teeters left and right. Holding on to the sides for dear life, I flex my core and command it to achieve balance.

It does.

Next step: paddle.

I'm not sure if I'm positioned properly on the board. Should I be closer to the tip or to the rear. I guess it doesn't matter too much. I imitate what I've seen Carmen and Sam do. I reach out with one hand, sink into the water, and pull back. The board and I move up slightly. Or at least I think we do. I repeat with my other hand. Back and forth and soon, I pick up speed.

Awesome. This is working.

I decide to put a bit more into it. I accelerate my motion. The board tips a bit too much to one side and before I can react, I slide right off.

What the hell, man!

I attempt to stand on the sand, but can't reach. I realize I'm above six feet deep now. Sharks love this depth.

My heartbeat accelerates.

Don't waste time. Get up already.

I hold onto the board and slide myself up, shimmying here and there. The board is uninterested in my needs and wants, but I fight until my upper body is well-positioned. Just as I throw a leg over and squeak my way onto the board, I see a wave coming at me. Not a big wave, but a wave nonetheless.

I scroll through what I've seen the girls do. Go over it, go into it, and then sometimes they roll into the water.

I decide to go into it.

I look at the wave, grab my board and push the nose in. But nothing happens. I do it again. The wave is coming at me. Only a few feet away.

I push down.

Nothing.

Only two feet.

I push down hard. Still nothing.

I snap up and the wave hits me and bumps me off the board.

I grab the board, then slap the water. This is ridiculous. I can't even stay on the board. How are they standing on this freakin' thing?

I glance at the surfers some thirty yards away. Crap. The girls are watching me intently. The guys on the other hand are snickering and chatting while covering their mouths, eyeing me, like I'm a moron (which for the record, I am).

I can do this.

I tip the board and slither my way back on top again. I glance over and paddling toward me are Sam and Carmen. I want to get this done without their help. I can do this on my own. For the record, I should've done this on my own, so I don't need help. Also, if both my mom and dad were surfers, then this crap has to be in my genes.

I paddle. I get overly aggressive and nearly slide off again. I get deep enough and see another small wave coming at me. This is my chance, before the girls reach me, I'll catch the wave and show them. Mom called me her Silver Surfer. I must still have some of it. I turn the board around by thrusting my weight in the direction of the shore. I glance over my shoulder.

Here it comes.

I'll nail this one.

As the wave approaches, I feel the nearness of the girls.

"Paddle, paddle!" Sam says.

I don't need help, thank you very much, but I follow her advice anyway. My timing is nearly perfect because I am just ahead of the wave. This feels right. The wave begins to overtake me, so I paddle more.

"Hop!" I think I hear.

I place my hands to the side of the board, gripping it tight, I focus on the sand and with a swift athletic move, I pop my feet from the rear to just beneath me.

Perfect.

Until it's not.

The board tips one way. I adjust. Then the other way. I try to adjust again, and then my feet slip out from under me and momentarily I'm airborne. Until I'm not and I drop onto the board then plop into the water.

The wave carries my board and me with it. Like a dying fish caught by a master fisherman, I am dead-weight. I've been under for too long. My heartbeat accelerates.

Fight it off, I hear in my head. So I move around and with my toes I make contact with the sand and slow down the movement.

I surface, take a deep breath, submerge and swim toward the board. From beneath, I see the two approaching boards. *So freakin' embarrassing.* I quickly scan my surroundings, to make sure no sharks are nearby, because that's just what this adventure needs.

I push up and as my head pops out of the water, Sam and Carmen reach me.

"Are you okay?" Sam asks, concerned, while Carmen reaches for my errant board.

"I'm fine," I mumble. I glance over at the other surfers and some are still laughing.

"So, here's the deal," Carmen says. "Next time—"

"I know, I know, ask you guys to help me, give me pointers, teach me a few things before I jump in."

"Yeah, that would be good too," she says, then eyes me. "It would also be a good idea to wax the board."

I stare at her.

"That's what keeps us glued to the board."

Sam gives me a sympathetic smile.

"Wax," I say, my voice dry. "Freakin' wax."

"Give me your hand, cowboy," Sam says. "Let's see if we can get you and your pony here back to shore."

It's settled. I want to strangle her.

TWENTY-FIVE

DAY 3 - SHEP

WE'RE MARCHING TOWARD COTTONS. The girls are on either side of me, not saying much.

"You can go ahead and laugh," I finally say. I'm sure they want to make comments, throw jabs, and discuss my epic fail.

"Laugh?" Carmen asks. "You mean celebrate."

"Big time," Sam echoes.

I stop. "Come on. I made an ass of myself."

Carmen stares at me, deep into my eyes. "You showed courage and determination. Trying to do what you did, without any preparation or training or guidance takes bravery."

"And a bit of stupidity," adds Sam.

I spin to her.

"But more bravery," she says, grinning. "I'm kidding, dude. Seriously. When I saw you jumping in the water... man, I was so stoked. I mean, you were going for it."

"Well, thanks. That was my first and last attempt," I say.

"Now you're making an ass of yourself," Carmen says.

"You were so close to evolving and bam! Your knuckles started to drag on the sand again," Sam says.

I don't respond. No point.

We march until we get to Cottons. The waves are soft, gentle. Hardly anything that would be worthy of a surfer's time. But this is where Mom says she heard the "voice," whatever that means.

Carmen lowers her board on the sand then takes mine.

"Bottle please," she says.

I dig it out of my bag and hand it to her.

She looks at the bottle and whispers something as she tucks it away.

"What did you say?"

She turns to me, blushing. "I thanked her for trusting me." She turns then marches into the water.

I should be doing this for Mom. But what she needs is something her own son can't do. I won't admit it to them, but I want to learn. I wanted to do this on my own terms. But it seems that my terms are not going to work out as planned.

In the background, the sun makes its ascent. We've been here for ten hours straight, from one beach to another. This spot is the calmest by far, with the least amount of people in the water or on the shore.

I lower myself to the sand. Sam sits next to me, thigh to thigh. I look at my reddened toes and glance at her deeply-tanned ones. At that instant, she wiggles them.

"You need to spray your feet too, if you don't want them to turn lobster red."

"Thanks for the tip."

"My pleasure." She takes a deep breath and exhales. "It's been a good day," she says.

My immediate instinct is to argue that point, but truth is, it was a good day.

"I'm not typically petulant," I say. "Usually, I'm the one who's telling the team that we can do this. At half-time of the championship game, we were down by two touchdowns. Coach gave his speech, the quarterback yelled at everyone, and when they were done, I said what I really believed. I told them that we have the opposition team exactly where we wanted them. We all laughed until we cried. But something happened because we actually began to believe that this was our plan all along. We let them get an edge on us so that we could embarrass them in the second half."

Her face is inches away from mine, holding on to each word, like I'm the most fascinating person in the world. I have more to say, but she's so beautiful and has so much peace in her eyes that all I can think of is that this is possibly the best moment I have ever had in my sordid life.

"Go on," she whispers.

"That's what we did. We were unstoppable. Both offense and defense played like we were possessed. We won by three touchdowns. We scored five unanswered times. I say all this to impress you, clearly."

She chuckles. "Clearly."

"But also to say that I'm not a sad sap or mister grumpy pants. It's just that lately, I haven't had a lot of reasons to feel like I can be unstoppable again."

"We're not giving up on you, Shep. We made a commitment to your mom the day we got in the RV. We'll make it."

With simple words she calms my world. Okay, I'm glad she came with us. We return our attention to the water and Carmen, who's been bobbing around waiting for the right wave.

It dawns on me that I achieved something big today. Although sharks were on my mind, I survived. I am not a magnet for those beasts after all. And furthermore, when I was negotiating with the board and the waves, all those thoughts—including the trial—were gone. I'm not saying I'm not afraid of sharks. I'm just realizing that I could possibly take more chances in the water now.

Carmen repositions herself and instantly, the ocean gives her a nice one. She paddles with the surf, then slides on with grace and ease. I haven't seen her on a longboard before. I wonder if she'll change her style.

She straightens a bit, her arms hanging at her side, she's relaxed and loose, she maneuvers the board to stay in the white foam of the wave, then takes out the bottle and does the honor.

Sam lays her head on my shoulder.

Her wet hair sends a pleasant shiver up and down my spine.

No, I don't really want to strangle her. Instead I close my eyes and breathe her in.

WHEN WE REACH THE RV, the sun is already flirting with the horizon. We stow everything away, then drive to our reserved spot at the campground.

By the time we bathe and devour some burgers from Carl's Jr., we're nearly ready to turn in.

"Anything we can knock off the list while we're here?" Carmen asks.

I pull the list out of my bag and the girls huddle around me. Sam's hair hangs low, tickling the side of my face. I don't complain, because she smells nice.

"Number ten," Sam says. "That's done."

I look at it.

10. *Do something unexpected*

I think about it for a minute then grin. "Big time," Carmen says. "When you took the board to the waves, you killed that challenge. Numbers one and ten are done."

"And number eight," Sam says casually.

Carmen turns to me. "When did that happen? Who kissed you?"

"I kissed him," Sam says.

Carmen's eyes go wide.

"On his cheek, gutter-brain."

I decide to change the topic. "I guess I can do number nine tonight. *Sleep under the stars.* It's not too cold. So I can put my sleeping bag on the hammock."

Maybe doing these challenges isn't that hard after all.

"We're just nailing these left and right," Carmen says.

"You can knock off number eleven tomorrow if you want."

I scroll through the list and pause when I find it:

11. *Go to a nude beach*

"That's not happening," I say.

"There's a secluded one here in San O," Sam says. She's always so helpful.

"How do you know this stuff?" I ask.

She winks at me. "I know what I know."

"Well what I know is that I'm not doing that."

"You don't have to do jumping jacks or pushups. Just prance around."

"At least sixty seconds," Carmen adds.

"Maybe ninety."

"No, not doin' it," I say and put the list away.

"You should totally consider it. It is a big one to knock off the list."

I cross my arms and lean back.

I am not doing it. Nope.

"No way," I say and hop out of my chair.

They both stare at me. "We heard you the first fifteen times," Carmen says.

Sam smiles. "Oh, he's been thinkin' about it. Look at his ears and cheeks all red and bright."

Carmen stares at me. A smile spreads her lips apart. "Are you blushing?"

"Coffee? Sure, I'll make us some."

———

IT'S BEAUTIFUL OUT HERE. The only sound comes from the crashing waves. No speeding cars, no lights other than those created by the moon and the stars.

I can't even hear Sam snoring.

Sam. Yup, she's unique all right. And pleasant when she's not forcing me to do the things that I know I should be doing, but pretending like I don't want to do.

I adjust myself on the hammock and use the sleeping bag like a blanket. This is awesome. It's actually warm and I have an unobstructed view to the stars. This is a good way to go out.

The door of the RV opens.

I turn over. It's Sam, stepping out. She's wearing a large t-shirt with a kitten on it. Her sweatpants are rolled up just below the knees. Her hair has been put up into a bun. She's a wonderful mess.

She steps up to me, trying to see if I'm awake, I assume.

"Hi," I say.

She flinches. "Oh, hey. Sorry. Wasn't sure if you were up."

"Everything all right?"

"Yeah, yeah. Was having a hard time sleeping. It's warm in there. I figured maybe it's nicer out here."

"It's practically perfect."

She steps next to me and stares at the stars. "Wow, so pretty."

I stare at her profile. "Yes. Very."

She glances at me. "Make room for me," she says.

Before I've even had an opportunity to properly shift over, she's already getting in. Thankfully it's a large hammock, but even so, gravity has us stuck to each other.

I'm not complaining. My body may be humming though. I'm just very aware of her body next to mine.

"Now this is what it's all about," she says.

I swallow. "Yup," I whisper.

"We need to do more of this," she adds, then wiggles around until she's nestled into my side. She lays her head on my chest, throws one arm around me, and says, "Good night."

The vibration of her voice runs through my chest cavity.

"Good night," I whisper.

For the second night in a row, I don't sleep a wink.

TWENTY-SIX

DAY 4 - SHEP

BY THE TIME Carmen wakes up and steps out of the RV, I've already made bacon and coffee. I can finally prepare the eggs.

"Where's Sam?" she asks, her voice groggy.

I nod toward the hammock where Sam is blanketed by my sleeping bag.

Carmen's mouth opens then glances at me. "How long has she been here?"

"She slept here."

"Why?" She's suspicious, but is trying to keep a calm demeanor.

"Something about being too warm inside." I shrug. "It's fine, she didn't bother me."

She steps up to the hammock and pulls the sleeping bag off her. "Bacon!" she yells.

Sam practically catapults off the hammock. "Where?" she yells.

"Wake up already. Breakfast is ready."

I crack two eggs on the pan and grab two more. Sam plops back down, arms open wide, eyes sealed shut.

"Why are you here, anyway?" Carmen asks.

Sam pops one eye open, turns this way and that, probably trying to figure out where she is. "Oh yeah. That's right," she says. "I slept with Shep."

One egg explodes in my hand.

"Say what?" Carmen snaps. She glares at me then back to Sam.

"What?" Sam studies her as she rubs her eyes. Then it clicks. "Oh you thought slept. Like, slept. No I just slept with him, not *slept* with him." She throws her legs over. "Lately, your mind has gotten really comfy in the gutter."

She drags her feet to the camper, enters the camper and closes the door. The door swings open again and her head pops out. "Mornin' Shep."

"Mornin'," I say as she closes the door again. "Eggs are almost ready," I call out.

"Okay," she says, her voice now muted.

I can feel Carmen's eyes on me. But I don't look at her. There is nothing to be discussed. Nothing that I want to discuss, that is.

"SO ABOUT THE NUDE BEACH," Sam says in between bites, "I think we should go there right now, knock it off the list, then go to our next destination on Tía Olivia's list."

When did my mom become Sam's aunt?

"Great idea," Carmen says. "Let's do the nude thing, then go to Doheny and make a day of it. If we go early enough we can get a good camping spot."

"Okay, time out," I say. "Do I have any say in this?"

They both look at me, waiting for my decision.

"Ten seconds. That's it. Not a second more."

They glance at each other then back to me. "Sixty," Carmen says.

"Twenty, but I take my hat with me," I add.

Carmen breaks into a belly laugh. "It's your call, but that'll look really weird."

"I don't know," Sam says. "That may be a good look on him."

"You guys can't be there," I say. "That's just weird."

"Trust me," Carmen says, raising her hand. "I don't want to see anything that may scar me for life. But we do need to make sure you do it."

"Think of us like the officials from the *Guinness Book of World Records*. They have to be there to confirm."

I don't like the sound of this. "Fine. We go together, but you guys have to keep your distance."

"Absolutely," Carmen says. "We'll be close enough to confirm, but not so close to be able to see distinguishing marks on your butt."

"And no telling your parents about this," I add.

"What happens on the sand stays on the sand," Carmen says.

I stare at them. Sam is struggling with a smile. I don't like this. "And no cameras."

Sam raises her right hand. "Scout's honor."

If she's a scout then I'm a world-class surfer.

TWENTY-SEVEN
DAY 4 - SAMANTHA

THE THREE OF us walk through the campground parking lot. Shep is wearing board shorts and, as promised, his cowboy hat. Carmen and I are wearing boy shorts and bikini tops.

"Is it far?" Shep asks.

"Not too far," I say. I almost feel bad for him.

Carmen nearly laughs. I glare at her. She's going to blow it.

"You guys aren't going to do something really horrible to embarrass me, are you?" he asks.

I stop and stare up, deep into his eyes. "We will not embarrass you." I don't explain that he'll be fully responsible for embarrassing himself.

He's studying my eyes. He doesn't believe me. Not completely.

"Come on," Carmen says, "let's not waste time."

Near the end of the road we find the gate. A trailhead marker shows "Beach Trail Six."

"This is it," I say and march on.

We hike the trail, down toward the beach. The surf is not great, but we're here for another objective. We continue south on the beach away from the lifeguard tower. The area that is the clothing optional zone is up ahead.

"I guess we're here," Shep says.

Only a few people here, but their choice of attire makes it clear that we're in the right place. A middle-aged couple are tossing a Frisbee in their birthday suits. Some athletic endeavors should never be done when naked. Another man, in decent shape, is walking his dog. Both man and dog are buck naked. I glance further south and can almost make out the Camp Pendleton Marine Corps Base.

"Okay," I say, "You should probably... um... you know... get..."

Shep's Adams apple goes up and down as he scans the area. "I'll change there," he points to a large bush. "You guys need to create space from me. Away. Now."

"Absolutely," I say. "A good ten feet away."

He spins toward us. "Thirty. Minimum!"

"Look we need to make sure that you're not wearing flesh-colored briefs."

He doesn't say anything. He seems dejected. He stumbles his way there.

"This is going to be great!" I say.

Carmen eyes me. "First of all, it's weird. And second, I'm watching you."

"Hey, I'm watching you, too." I give her my best smile, the one that attempts to show that I have no agenda but a friendly laugh. It's not like I'm hoping for a quick peek, or see him with a full-body blush, or anything like that.

"What's the hold up?" I ask. This is taking way too long. It doesn't take much to pull off shorts.

"I'm coming," he says. "Go away."

Slowly I see his messy mound of hair pop out from behind the bush. He steps out. That ridiculous hat is completely covering everything.

Carmen's hands go to her face, cracking up and embarrassed at the same time. She spins around. "I've seen enough," she says. "Seriously. Stop."

At that he comes to a dead stop. "What gives?" He quickly backpedals behind the bush. "You two need to leave. Now!"

"Yes, sir, but before we do, we've got a simple question: why did *you* get naked?"

His face contorts. "The list." His eyes are searching ours.

"Cuz, the list specifically says '*Go to a Nude Beach.*'" Carmen lets the words sink. "Where did it say that *you* have to be naked?"

His right eye twitches. "You two set me up. Played games with words."

"We made recommendations," I say. "But you seemed very eager to get naked. Now if you really are into this birthday suit attire, there is the other challenge about surfing naked. Maybe—?"

He smiles as he calmly lifts his hat and places it back on his head. He was never naked. He's still wearing his board shorts. All he had done was roll them up.

"Cheater!" I yell.

"I'm so glad I won't have to live with a guilty conscious."

"You would've lied to us?" I ask. "You would've pretended like you did what we thought you were going to do just to cross it off the list?"

He grins. "Why yes. At the drop of a hat."

I nod in respect. "Well played, Shep. Well played," I say. "Can we talk about surfing naked now?"

TWENTY-EIGHT
DAY 4 - SAMANTHA

WE ARRIVE IN GOOD TIME. Doheny Beach in Dana Point is one of my favorites, probably because this is where I first got on a board when I was ten. The northern end is primo location for great surfing. From beginners to advanced surfers, they all congregate on this plot of sand. Less powerful waves, longboards, and some of the longest rides in Orange County.

By 8:30 a.m. we've made camp. Not just any spot, but right on the sand. This is by far the best spot we've had. Even better than Encinitas. Hard to believe that we were able to land right on the beach. You can surf, run back, change boards, then return to the water. This place would be an ideal beach for Shep to give surfing a legitimate shot.

I glance at him. How can I push him without it appearing like I'm pushing him? Maybe I can—

"This is perfect," Shep interrupts my thoughts. He's on the sand, barefoot. No shirt, no shoes, no problem. Not bad for the farm boy who didn't even want to go to the beach. His skin is changing tone, too. He's looking more and more like a California native.

He adjusts his hat, which sort of ruins my whole point about being a native, but hey, we're getting closer.

He glances at me and I realize I've been staring at him. I peel my eyes away and study the ocean with her gentle two foot west-north-west swells. Just at waist high. This will be ideal if he agrees. I just have to find a way to convince him. It may not be easy after his solo attempt, but—

"I want to learn," he says, his eyes fixated on the water. He turns to me. "Will you teach me?"

Seriously, I almost cry. But I need to be calm and collected. "Hells yeah!" I blurt out.

Carmen, who's been stretching at the water line, hears my explosion. "'Sup?" she yells back.

"He asked me, not you."

She frowns and walks toward us, kicking up a bit of sand as she picks up her speed. "Asked you what?"

"To teach him."

She glances at him. "Blood. That's what we share, Shep. Blood."

He grins at her. "You were going to let me expose my butt to the world."

She covers her face. "I know. I know. All that disgrace for nothing."

SHEP WALKS out of the camper wearing his first gift—the wetsuit Carmen bought him. The silver-colored suit with yellow trim gives him the form of an aquatic warrior. A Spartan of the oceans. I can practically see his abs pop out of the layers.

"Are you sure this is necessary?" he asks as he walks up to me. He's not comfortable in it. I don't blame him. A wetsuit takes getting used to. "The water wasn't that cold at San O."

"Your Texan bod may find this water a bit too cold."

He eyes me. "Us Texans can handle plenty."

"We're wasting time. Come here," I say and walk him over to the board I've placed on the sand.

"Carmen's surfing already?" he asks as he scans the water where a handful of people surf the calm swells.

"Yeah, she's always making the most of every wave."

He joins me on the sand as I kneel down next to the board.

"I want you to start with this one. It's a hybrid—not short, not long. It's a bit more buoyant than the short ones we typically use, but easier to learn on."

"Is this new?" he asks. "Looks unused."

I grin. That's his second gift. "Yeah, I bought it before we left."

"You didn't have enough boards?"

I glance at him. "I bought it for you. So I can teach you."

His eyes go wide. "Seriously?"

"Seriously," I say. "Are you ready to learn how to walk on water?"

"Ready."

I start with the basics. "We need to use a common language. There are terms you need to learn so when I call out something, you don't look at me like a sheep about to be eaten by a shark."

He shivers.

"Okay, bad example," I admit.

"Horrible example," he snaps. "Go on."

"The tip is the nose. The back is the tail. The sides are the rails. We don't wax the rails or the bottom. We want water to glide easily on the main contact points."

"Got it," he says.

I point at the chest line on the board and where the rearfoot typically lands. "We'll wax this region."

"Why not the entire top surface?"

"On longboards, we'd typically wax the whole thing because you'd probably want to nose ride."

"Explain."

I draw the outline of a longboard in the sand then step onto the fake board. "Longboarding is almost like dancing." I walk up and down the faux board, cross stepping and turning. "This dance connects me to the waves."

"You do that when surfing?" His eyes are sparkling.

"I try. Sometimes the ocean allows me. Most of the time, it doesn't. It takes a tremendous amount of presence, balance, and calm."

"Sounds amazing."

He has no idea how amazing, yet so frustrating it can be. Because no matter how much I try, I am incapable of being in the moment and letting go completely. I can do a lot on the longboard, but I have yet to hit a complete soul arch. I will though. One of these days, or years, I will. I glance at him. He's eager for more.

"Let's wax the board," I say.

I explain the difference between the base coat and wax. We mark his chest line with the base coat, then draw diagonal lines from the top. Once at the tail, we repeat with diagonals going the opposite direction toward the nose.

"Now we wax the board," I say and open the container then split the wax in half. "This is Sex Wax."

"I won't ask."

I eye him. "You are so junior high." I make him apply the wax in diagonals, verticals, horizontals and circulars. I don't have to make him do that, but watching him strain his muscles is a treat. Maybe I'm a bit junior high, too.

His hands are so large. He could cup my entire face in them, I bet. "Big hands," I mumble.

"What?" he asks.

"Can't get over the length of the pinky," I say.

He stops waxing and studies both hands. "Yeah, it used to be worse when I was younger. The pinkies were just as long as my middle finger. Back then, they called me Orangutan Boy."

"Orangutan. That could be your surfer nickname."

He glares at me.

"Or not," I quickly mumble.

Once he's done waxing, I rise. "Okay, grab your board. We're going to find flat water."

"How's that gonna make me a surfer?"

I step up to him. "Am I the teacher?"

"Yes."

"Then call me Sifu Sam from now on. And show me respect."

"Yes, sifu."

We stroll the beach until we find a good spot and walk into the water. At waist height we stop. "You need to be well-positioned on the board. Not too far up or back. Slide on."

He does. "Man, the board sticks to my wetsuit," he says.

"Wax is your friend." I tap his side. "Scoot over about two inches so that you're centered to the line. Then go back a bit so that your feet are near the tail, but not over."

We practice getting on and off a few times, to make sure he can always find his spot. I take advantage of the situation and tap his hips and shift his legs every chance I get. The things a surfing instructor can get away with are nearly criminal.

"Now we paddle," I say. "Hands cupped, big, long stokes. Your arms should go into the water just below elbows, chest up, feet together, strong core."

He eyes me. "Like this?" he asks, as he paddles.

For such a muscular body, he shows decent flexibility. More importantly, his form and movement are perfect. As if he has picked up the motion from watching us. I bet he's a visual and kinesthetic learner, like me. Either that or it's encoded in his DNA.

"Nearly perfect," I say and again use this opportunity to touch his chest and push down his back. I'm a horrible person, but my heart's in the right place.

After a few minutes of that, we move on to the duck dive.

"Is that because ducks dive like that?" he asks.

"It's because you have to duck before the wave slams your country ass off the board. The idea is to duck under the incoming wave while still moving forward. But once you duck, you want to go as deep as possible so that the energy of the wave doesn't push you backward."

We practice. Freakin' kid gets the hang of it quickly. We move on to the next skill.

"I kept on trying this move that one time and no matter what I did, the board didn't go in."

"Yeah, you can't do a duck dive with a longboard. You'll need to do a turtle roll."

I show him how to roll the board to the left or the right. "When you roll over, you stay underwater for a bit until the wave passes by, then you reverse the motion."

"I hate this one," he says.

"Why?"

"This is where I see the shark coming at me."

"That's the most ridiculous thing I've ever heard. You never see the shark coming. You feel it."

His color turns yellow.

"I was kidding you big oaf."

Not really.

THE SURF at Doheny couldn't be more perfect. Small, gentle breaking waves, waist deep means I don't have to worry about injuries.

"This is what we want," I say to Shep. "We want the white water. The foamy stuff of a broken wave."

"Seems weak."

"Seems weak, sifu!"

"Yes, sifu."

"You want to catch the wave on your belly, paddle hard until you feel the energy of the wave moving you. At that point grab and hold onto the tip."

"That's when I jump to my feet?"

"You will take belly rides a few times until you learn how to feel for the energy I'm talking about. Developing your sense for the wave will be a skill that will pay back forever."

He gets this easily. No issues. He's a natural.

"Time to learn how to transition from belly to feet."

"Now we're talkin'," he says.

We position ourselves. "Here's the process. Paddle your little heart out. Head up, watching the wave. Once you feel the wave pushing you, get your hands on the board's rails. Lift your chest up slightly, then spring up. The front foot will typically leap off, while the back foot will drag to position."

He is listening to me with such intensity that for a second I think he's going to kiss me. I hesitate.

"Then what?" he asks, instead of kissing me.

"Once on your feet, stay low, point straight ahead—face forward, feet diagonal to the board, shoulder-width apart. Clear?"

"Clear."

We wait for the right wave. "Like I said a bit ago, we initially want the white water. The broken waves. Eventually over the next few days we'll transition to the clean wave—the face of the wave. But we don't want to—"

He begins to paddle before I've even given him the go ahead. I study the wave and it may be okay. Probably not enough energy, but that's okay, he'll learn from the fall.

Instead, he catches the wave, moves his hands to the rails, and like a pro, jumps to his feet—his body low, his arms wide, his feet perfectly positioned.

I stare at him. Son of a surfer!

TWENTY-NINE
DAY 4 - SHEP

I GRIP the rail so tight that for a second I think I may grind my fingers into the board. My heart beats to the tune of thrash metal and my breathing becomes rapid. I hop to my feet and by pure luck I nail the spots.

I keep my body low, extend my arms, and then it happens.

I hear nothing but the rumbling beneath me.

I feel nothing but the wax that binds my feet to the board and the splashing wave that caresses my legs.

I'm standing. I'm skimming the surface of the water. I am surfing.

I'm doing this. Me!

And just for a moment, I am taken back to a decade ago, to the first time I did this. I remember this feeling. I remember my mom's divine smile.

The energy that's been carrying me drops a few notches. My knees wobble. More velocity is lost. The board loses some of its buoyancy. I try to compensate with my upper body, throwing my arms out more, then adjusting my core, trying to find a new point of balance, but it's useless. The wave is gone. I do as I've been instructed. I do a controlled drop into the water.

I'm at two feet of depth. So I snatch my board, swivel it and turn toward Sam.

Sam and Carmen are side by side, fists held high, celebrating.

I decide it's time I do this thing properly.

I turn away and head toward the shore.

WITH GREAT DIFFICULTY, I peel off the wetsuit and hang it inside the RV's shower. I want to feel everything. Just like Sam and Carmen. I want to skin it.

I run back into the water where Sam has been waiting for me. She's on her board, too. Carmen is waiting by her side.

"Give me a hug," Carmen says when I reach them.

She positions her board such that we're side-by-side, the nose of our boards pointing in opposite directions. We hug and stay like that for a few moments. When she pulls away, she caresses my face.

"So freakin' proud of you. You're playing all out."

I'm doing what Mom wanted me to do. Experiencing life from her eyes.

"I want a hug, too," Sam says.

She shows up on my other side and reaches over. We embrace and stay connected. The ocean's gentle movement sways us this way and that, but we're holding on so tight that we're now synchronized, both moving to the same rhythm.

"Break it up, you two," Carmen says. "There's more to learn."

We pull away. I avoid eye contact.

WE'RE BOTH DEEP, facing the sand, past where the waves break. She's still teaching, explaining.

"A wave will break to the right or left. Look at that one," she points to one to the left of us. "The face of the wave is moving to the left. You have to be aware of which direction you're going, otherwise you'll go right into the breaking wave. Full stop. Fail. You'll be an internet sensation all over again, for all the wrong reasons."

I study the waves for a bit. "What are we waiting for?"

She glares at me. "Above all, be aware of the other surfers in the water. It is better to get yelled at because you didn't take a wave that was yours than to drop in on someone else's wave."

"Okay, okay. I got it, what are we waiting for?"

"For one, I'm not done preparing you for this. Also, you need patience with this sport. Sometimes, this is what we do. We wait," she says. "When we're prepping the boards, we read the ocean, the current, and riptides. We're studying how the waves break. Are they heavy or soft? How deep is the break, or is it in the shallow area? If shallow, do we have to deal with rocks? When the water is full of others we have more to consider. A lot more."

I take this all in. She's right, I need to slow down and be more aware. "Back at San O the surfing was insane. I was anxious just watching you two."

"I love surfing for many reasons. But when people get aggressive in overcrowded beaches, it is not relaxing or enjoyable. It's the pits. It makes me wish less people wanted to surf."

The thought of battling with other people who are trying to get that high I just felt must feel personal. Like someone is trespassing on your home.

"Back to your lesson," she says. "We want to catch the wave just ahead of the white water, like that." She points at a wave in the distance. "When a wave is formed," she says and brings her hands together in the form of an "A," her fingertips touching each other, "the force of the wave is concentrated in the center peak. That's what we want. We want to take the shoulder because that's how we take off.

"For bigger waves, you will have to paddle harder and faster than what you've done so far. Otherwise, it'll pass right by you. When you've caught the wave, you snap to your feet—clean and fast. If you take too long, the wave is gone. On your feet, smoothly so that you can ride the wave. For today, just get on the board with the full wave's impact. Don't worry about turning or guiding the board."

"I think I got it."

"Okay, let's practice."

I mistime a handful of waves. I miss them because they're faster than I expected, or I left too early, which capsized me immediately. With practice, I eventually get the timing. Sort of. But then rit to eat it immediately after.

"Wipeouts are a rite of passage," Sam says.

"What's the opposite of stoked?"

She laughs. I love that full, honest laugh.

Just then the next wave shows up and I go for it. I paddle hard and consistently, using good form.

"Hop it," she yells.

I grab the rails then jump to my feet. I nail it. The energy of the wave and my full concentrated weight on the board accelerate me. For a micro second I am tempted to turn and snap and whatever it is they do, but I stick to the lesson.

"Lower your body!" she yells out. "Be aware!" is what I think she says, but she's too far away now.

I tuck in a bit more and the wave approves. For a few moments, as the gracious wave takes me on the ride of my life, I become aware of everything around me. My senses are even more pronounced now. Almost like I've awoken muscles that are capable of feeling a new sensation.

The texture of the wax, the spray of mist from the wave behind me, the wave's unpredictable movements beneath, the wetness and mass of the water, the taste of salt, the scent of the ocean, and nature's energy. Time slows. My heart beats with ease. The air I breathe flows gracefully.

I recognize this moment.

I've felt it before.

I'm in the zone.

A chill runs over my body. I'm feeling something else. Not sure what it is, but I don't want it to end.

But the energy dissipates and my board begins to sink slightly under my weight. *No, no. Not yet!*

I hop off the board backward and my feet hit sand. I grab my board and turn back to where I started.

Sam has both arms up in the air. I can't hear her, but I know she's celebrating my first real wave. I mount the board and paddle fast and hard toward her.

When I reach her all I want is to hug her. For teaching me how to do this. For exposing me to this feeling that I can't quite explain. But she raises her hand instead, ready for a high five. So I go with the flow.

"How was it?" she asks. Her eyes huge, radiating.

"Amazing."

In that moment I realize, Sam is doing what Mom should've done all those years back. It should've been Mom teaching me how to get to my feet, how to feel the wave, how to surf. But it's Sam who has filled that role. And I think I'm okay with that. Somehow, I think Mom is, too.

THE THREE OF us are huddled on a blanket on the sand. We are under the shade of our camper, devouring sandwiches Carmen prepared. I didn't want to stop when we were in the water, but now that I'm out, I feel the exhaustion.

"I've been thinking," Carmen says.

"Always dangerous," Sam mumbles.

Carmen throws a piece of tomato at Sam. Sam grabs it and eats it. "Yum," she says.

I marvel at the quality of their friendship.

"Anyway," Carmen says, "I think it's time to hand off the torch. What do you think, Shep?"

I come to. "Sorry, what? What torch?"

She holds onto my eyes. "Olivia's ashes. I think you should take over. Same with the memorial at Pismo."

I straighten. The thought hadn't crossed my mind, but maybe she's right. If I dedicated enough time, I may be able to ride for my mom at Pismo beach.

"You are more than capable," Sam says.

"But what about the other beaches that aren't easy and calm like this one?"

They look at each other and nod. "Yeah, fair point," Carmen says. "But even in the heavier beaches, you don't have to go into the mix of serious surfers. You can go off to an area of smaller waves that doesn't interest them."

"I suppose," I say, but wonder if that's what Mom wanted. Did she want us to just clock it in, or do it properly?

"Let's take it a day at a time," Sam says. "Can you handle it here? Yes. Should you do it here? Absolutely."

"Okay," I say. "Let's go do it."

"Slow down tiger," she says. "Need to rest the body. Give time to recover and your next session will be that much more badass."

"Agreed," Carmen says. "Enjoy the external calm. And re-live the feels you had when you were on the board."

"I was in the zone," I say. "Just like when I play football. That indescribable moment where you can do no wrong. I didn't think I could ever recreate that state of mind and body doing anything else. It was amazing."

"You see," Carmen says to Sam. "It's happening."

"We are witnessing evolution from ape man to surfer," Sam says.

They both laugh. I give them their victory lap. I lean back and take a long sip from my water bottle. I feel a level of calm and joy that I can't say I've felt before. The sun is caressing my skin and the sounds of the breaking waves and hoarse seagull cries ease me into a state of untroubled mind.

"I can see it on your face," Carmen says.

I glance at her. "What?"

"You, lil' cuz, are stoked."

"Big time," Sam says.

I grin and close my eyes.

***

BY MID-AFTERNOON, we're ready to hit the waves again. Sam and Carmen want to show me how to do basic maneuvers in the water before I leave my mom's ashes in the water.

I decide to read Mom's fourth letter before I go in. So I ask them to go in and catch some while I do my thing.

I rip the letter open.

July 13, 2000 — Day 4

When we parked the van, I knew today would be a different type of fun. For one, we parked on the ocean side. The best spot possible.

The surf is gentle, so it's time for the longboard. I'm feelin' it.

Before I go in, on the tales of the awkward front, Sharon and her stupid (and smelly boyfriend) were up to something in their sleeping bag. While I was still in the van! I felt like throwing up. I used to think I'd miss my friends when I move to Texas. Truth is, I'll miss the waves. I wish I had gotten accepted by San Diego or Santa Barbara. I wish I had tried harder.

A lot of newbies at Doheny, but it was still fun. They saw me doing things with the longboard they haven't seen girls do. I felt the vibe. At times I was walking up and down my board like I was dancing to a tune orchestrated by the ocean.

Check this out: I pulled an epic soul arch. Twice!
A bunch of young boys hovered around me wanting auto-graphs. From me! They think I'm a pro. I felt a different type of high today, and for the first time wondered what it would feel like if I went down a pro career. Why not?

Because Papi, that's why!

The early evening surf was awesome. The lights from the campers were my guide. I took the shortboard and cut it up. It was pretty cool to show off.

And yet... and yet I feel incomplete. I wanted to hear the voice again, but the waves weren't right. It was in a barrel when I heard his voice. I want to hear that beautiful voice again.

Laters,
O.

P.S. No sign of Quick...
P.S.S. Not that I've been thinking about him or anything

P.S.S.S. Maybe just a bit...

I survey the camp spots. Was she here, in this very spot when she wrote the journal entry? Am I walking on the same sand? This is like time travel, same place, different time, same journey.

Mom, I'm learning.

I put away the letter, knowing she wanted me to find him. That must be the reason behind all this. But if I do find him, then what? All's forgiven even though he abandoned us?

Back in Texas, that other surfer dude called me a natural. Talented. It must've been obvious to her way back then, but still she didn't tell me. She didn't share this side of her life with me. Maybe because she knew that I would ask more questions about my father. There has to be a reason why she didn't tell me. That's what still worries me.

I get to my feet. I want to try the longboard at some point today. And I want to know what a soul arch is.

But first thing's first. I grab my board, the one that Sam bought me. Before I run into the water, the girls ride up to intercept me.

"Too many people now," Sam says. "Let's move off a bit so that we can do more training without getting harassed by others."

She's right. There are a lot of people in the water now, and this crowd is a bit more aggressive. Even here at this calm beach, I feel the pressure. I don't want to mess up and embarrass myself.

The three of us paddle past where the waves break. The waves are smaller but good enough. A young girl, maybe six or seven, and her brother, who can't be more than nine, are in the same spot. My earlier achievement suddenly seems like not much of an achievement after all.

"You've been killin' it, Shep," Carmen says, contradicting my thoughts. "You're also moving at a fast pace. So this may be too much too fast. Honestly, the hardest part you have down. Timing, balance, a sense for the waves. What you need to learn now is how to maneuver the board."

"Adjust, react," Sam adds.

"Which means you'll need to learn how to do weight transfer, which is how we maneuver the board."

"The good news is that you'll use a lot of skills you already have: core strength and instinct."

"Exactly," Carmen adds. "Here's the deal: weight transfer is done at the foot and board level. Directional movement is primarily done by your legs."

"But I've seen you guys do sweeping movements with your arms, like windmills when you're cutting up the waves," I say.

"Some of that will come naturally, but you're right, arm movement aids in the more aggressive maneuvers because it's all about weight transfer. Don't worry about that just yet. The thing to know is that the way you move the board is you transfer weight from toes onto your heel. From your front foot to your back foot, and vice versa."

"This is how you'll surf along the wave not just get pushed down to the sand," Sam says.

"What's awesome is that this weight transfer is almost done instinctively. But if you keep it simple and realize that where you look is where you'll go, your body will respond in kind and so will your board."

I'm trying to keep all these things in my head. "My head's gonna blow up. Let's just do it."

They glance at each other. They don't feel confident.

"It's like skateboarding, right?" I add. "I have to shift the weight from toes to heels and vice versa."

They shrug.

"Maybe he does get it," Sam says. "Let's go for it."

I WAS SO sure I got it. Instead, I'm laid out on the sand, exhausted. Sam is sitting next to me.

"What's wrong?"

"I suck."

"You're trying too much, too fast," she says. "Typically when I teach someone, the student practices the initial steps for a few sessions before they move to this stage."

I am disappointed at myself. I thought I had this. Every sport I've picked up, it's been easy. Not this one. "I look like any tourist who tries surfing and ends up looking like a poser."

She's silent. I glance at her. "Well? Aren't you going to say something to make me feel better?"

She shrugs. "I don't like you when you moan," she says.

"That definitely doesn't make me feel better," I say and sit up.

"I'm proud of you. Carmen is proud of you. That's all that should count."

I glance at Carmen who's ripping it out there. "I think she's glad I stopped trying."

"Yeah, probably. You did stink it up out there."

I glare at her. "But you said—"

She punches my arm. "Just pulling your leash."

I watch the water and the sky that's slowly darkening. "I want to take the longboard and place my mom's ashes into the sea."

She hops to her feet. "Let's do it."

———

BOTH ON LONGBOARDS, we sit and wait. We don't say much to each other. Just point at possible waves. The ocean doesn't drag it out.

We both paddle and latch onto a decent right-breaking wave. I don't try anything out of the ordinary. I just take the wave and go down with the energy of the movement. I glance to my left and see Sam on her board, very close to mine.

I straighten slightly and dig the bottle out of my pocket. The board rattles and I almost mishandle the vial.

"Bend your knees," Sam says.

I do, then pop the bottle open.

Love you, Mom.

I tip the bottle to my right and watch as the ash flies away. I take a deep breath, hoping for something, anything. No aberrations, no voice. Just the ocean.

I ride the wave a bit more until it loses its energy. I lower myself to the board and Sam shows up next to me. "Give me the vial," Sam says.

I hand it to her. She turns away, then rides a little wave to the shore. I wait and watch as she runs to the camper, deposits her board, then runs back into the water.

I wait for her as she swims up to me.

"Let's have some fun," she says.

Together on one board, we paddle out. She's at the tail of the board, me near the center.

"Is this safe?" I ask as we prepare for a wave.

"Probably," she says, then yells, "paddle, paddle!"

We do.

"To your feet, soldier."

I do.

The board is wobbling. I extend my arms, trying to control the board. She places her hands on my shoulder.

"Good job. Now try to walk up and down the board."

"I can't."

"You can."

So I try.

Turns out I can't.

We both fall into the water. She grabs me from my pits and tugs me up. When I come up for air, she's laughing. That infectious laugh makes me grin.

"We were horrible," she says.

She's inches away from me.

Her arms on my shoulders.

I place mine on her hips.

We're no longer laughing.

We're just staring at each other. Her smile falters. It's happening with her. I can feel it. But I know how this'll end. There is no point in falling for her.

"Again?" she asks.

I nod. So we do it again and again.

PART FOUR

"Out of the water, I am nothing."
~Duke Kahanamoku

THIRTY

DAY 5 - SHEP

I WAKE UP ENERGIZED, ready. We arrive in Laguna Beach at 7:00 a.m. and try to find parking near Brooks Street, but the area is already packed and parking is hard to find. To make matters worse, we don't have a reserved camp site. The plan is to surf here, then find a place to park overnight either here or closer to our next destination. Oh by the way, we don't have a reserved camp site for the next spot either.

As the minutes tick by, I become more anxious.

"A lot of people here," Sam says. "Did you check the surf report?"

"It's a good day. Expect to see top notch surfers here. Including some names," Carmen says.

"Names?" I ask.

"Pros."

This sucks. I have a desperate need to surf again. I need to learn how to make turns like the girls do. I want to get better, or at least good enough for Pismo, but that'll only come with time on the board in the water—not daydreams. I visualized my movements all night and morning. But with so many surfers hitting the beach here, will I even get a chance?

After wasting more than half an hour, we finally find parking, then burn another good fifteen minutes walking, until we reach the beach. One look at the waves and I know I just wasted my time bringing the board with me. These waves are insane. The skill level in the water is scary good—or scary dumb. The number of people in the water and on the sand is staggering. This really sucks.

"Awesome," is what I hear come out of Sam's mouth.

"Let's go rip some."

As the girls run off into the water, I plop on the sand, frustrated. I wanted to surf. I scan up and down the layers of huge waves that collapse on each other. Surfer after surfer gets engulfed and spit out by the waves. It seems that for these surfers, the real quest is survival and a chance at riding these unruly beasts for three to five seconds. Just like bull-riders, they are playing a seriously dangerous game.

I take that back. There's a bald guy who's killing it out there. I stare at his movements, at the way he fearlessly takes on the challenge. Maybe one day that'll be me. Maybe my dad was like him, too.

My dad.

I open my bag and take out Mom's next letter.

July 14, 2000 — Day 5

When we first got here, we thought we were going to have a slow day, so we smoked weed before heading out. By 8:00 a.m. the weather turned and the waves got nasty.

Here's the situation: Rocky bottom + low tide = surf at your own risk.

Stoned & drunk = what risk?

So I surfed at my own risk and loved the challenge.

Beyond the waves, the people here have an attitude. It's okay, so do I.

A fight broke out in the water. While the others watched to see how it would end, I stole a wave and smoked it!

I can say (since I'm mostly sober) that wave wanted to destroy me. It was coming for me, wanting to crush me. I stuck with it until it produced a barrel. A small one, a narrow one, a dangerous one, but for the first time in forever I prayed. I wanted to hear the voice again. I slowed down, to enter the cave, but just then, the barrel collapsed, dragged me and slammed me into the rocky bottom. And all along I listened, but the voice never came.

Laters,
O.

P.S. Day three without seeing him.

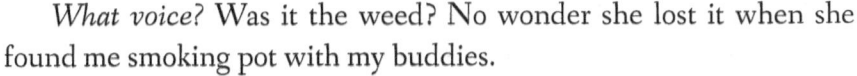

What voice? Was it the weed? No wonder she lost it when she found me smoking pot with my buddies.

I try to slide the letter back into the envelope and it snags. I try again, but it gets caught again. I shove it in and practically crumple the envelope. These letters aren't telling me anything. I'm no closer to answers about my dad. Five days and nothing.

I scan the water. In the sea of bodies, there are a few surfers who are way out of their league. Yet, they still try. Why can't I?

I'M SLAMMED off the board. Again.

I've been slammed off more than I've been on. I look over my shoulder and realize I've barely made a dent toward reaching the lineup. So I push harder, determined to make it. By the time I reach it, I'm exhausted. So I float around, trying to catch my breath and calm my heart rate. The girls see me and paddle over.

"Are you sure you want to do this?" Sam asks.

"I want to try."

They are both worried. "Okay," Carmen says. "Stay between us. We should be able get one from this aggressive bunch."

"But only go when we tell you."

"We'll block for him if we have to," Carmen says.

"What does that mean?" I ask.

"It means be ready and when you go, go all out." Sam comes right next to me. "These are the type of waves that will hold you down for a bit. Hold your breath and don't get nervous. Protect your head and don't panic if it happens to you. Be peaceful. It'll pass."

Now I'm scared. I'm not ready for this.

"Get ready," Carmen says.

I want to just swim back to the beach.

"It's coming," Sam says. "When we say go, you paddle your ass off."

"Got it," I attempt to say but my mouth has gone dry.

The water morphs, then transforms. It roars then takes the shape of a mountain. A giant that may be my death.

"Now!" Carmen yells and all three of us paddle. A few other surfers also try to get it, but Sam gets in the way of one. I can hear him yelling, but I focus on the wave.

My face is pelted by the beast's spittle. I paddle fast. I keep my focus on the wave as it begins to take the shape I've been waiting for.

Before I know it, a force unlike anything I've ever felt grabs my board and accelerates me down the face. I leap to my feet. A perfect landing.

This is fast. Too fast.

The board vibrates hard against the water, like wood on wet

cement. The gyration is heavy and persistent. I'm trying to control the board and control the fear that's choking the air out of my lungs. The wave is behind and to the right of me. I'm going left bound and another wave is breaking toward me. I'll be sandwiched.

I don't know what to do. I decide to attempt a turn so that I can go perpendicular to the sand. I turn my head and arms in that direction. My feet do their thing.

Then the ocean does its thing.

I don't even know where it comes from, but when it hits me, it takes me under, hard and fast. Submerged, an invisible hand grabs my board and drags me around. I try to swim in the opposite direction of the pull.

I'm not strong enough. I can't control this.

The wave drags me, bouncing me off the ocean floor. My vision is replaced with thousands of bubbles from the air escaping my lungs, and the explosion of displaced sand.

Fear kicks in. I want to yell. I want to breathe. I didn't get a chance to take a deep breath before I was taken under.

I want to swim up, but I can't even tell which way is up.

I'm panicking, kicking, reaching for nothing.

Just like when I was a kid, the ocean has found me. It wanted me back then, but Mom saved me. Who now?

Then a slash of light breaks through from beneath me. I must be upside down. I struggle against the current to get myself upright again.

I hear her voice: *Hold your breath and don't get nervous. Protect your head and be peaceful.*

But it's not Sam's voice. It's Mom's.

I trust the voice, close my eyes and allow the moments to pass.

Open your eyes.

I pop them open and I see the surface. I reach, kick and break through.

I'm gasping for air, and my eyes are burning from the salt water. But I have no time to lick my wounds. The waves are collapsing all around me. More nasty ones are coming my way. I need to get my board and ride it to shore like a boogie board.

I spin around and find the board, slide on it, then paddle, all the while looking over both left and right shoulders to assure another one won't get me.

A couple of small breakers reach me, but all they do is help me get to land.

Once there, I grab the board and limp my way to where we had left our bags and towels. I drop my board, unfasten the leash, then drop to the sand.

I'm trying to breathe again, moderate my heartbeat.

"Are you okay?" Carmen's worried voice brings me back.

They both reach me. "Did you hurt yourself?" Sam asks.

"I see a few cuts," Carmen says, but I don't care. I'm on land. Safe.

Both have dropped on the sand next to me, observing me.

"I'm fine," I say.

"We should've told you to head back," Carmen says. "This is not for beginners."

"Get the vial," I tell Carmen. "This one's yours."

I tried, Mom. The ocean won.

A COUPLE of hours have passed and the girls are back in the water. They're insane. Truth be told, I'm jealous. They asked if I'd film them. I wanted to say no, because I don't want to feel insulted. Hey, look at me. Look how easy it is.

I pull the camera out of the bag and train it on them. Turns out, with a camera in hand, it's not as creepy to stare at Sam. Okay, it's still sort of creepy, but it's because I'm in awe. After nearly one hour of footage, I realize I'm transfixed on her and how she takes the waves. Technically, Carmen is better. I can't put it in words, but Carmen rides the waves like a bullet. Reminds me of the snowboarders Mom and I watched during the winter Olympics. She does tricks, performs sharp cuts, and generally leaves most of the surfers staring at her.

Sam on the other hand has an ease about her. She glides. She cuts and all that stuff, but she's graceful. Almost like she's interested in the dance with the wave, not the domination.

I zoom in and out on her. She's so beautiful and powerful. I eventually stop filming because the storage ends. I rewind some of the recording and check out my handiwork. I realize two things: One, I could watch her forever and two it seems like ninety-percent of the recording is Sam. I hope Carmen doesn't watch this recording anytime soon. I hide the storage disk deep in the bag.

I glance at Sam again. I want to surf like her.

What type of surfer was Mom, I wonder? Was she a bit of both? The aggressive ripper and the graceful longboarder?

And my dad? Was he even a surfer? Or some loser? Am I chasing ghosts?

THIRTY-ONE

DAY 5 - SHEP

A COLD FRONT forces us to leave the beach earlier than planned. By the time we reach the RV, we're all shivering. I crank the engine and blast the heater. We're huddled around the heat vents. They're still talking and I'm still pretending like I'm listening. I need alone time. Back on the ranch, I could get lost in work and collect my thoughts. Here, I'm always with them. I mean, they're awesome and all, but still. I need some downtime.

"We can eat something at the club," Carmen says, which tunes me back to them.

"What club?" I ask.

They both sigh audibly.

"If I was a horse I'd get more respect," Sam says.

I grin. "Possibly."

"We're going to a club tonight to dance," Carmen says. "We got the deets from someone at the beach."

I stare at them. "Why would we want to go dancing exactly?"

"Are we the only ones paying attention here?" Sam asks Carmen, then turns to me. "Because you have a challenge to complete. *Dance from when the sun sets to when the sun rises. We* better wash up and get all beautiful. We need to start dancing before the sun sets."

This is starting to feel like another half-baked idea.

WE DRIVE to the resort that's hosting the event. I drive through what looks like a Roman archway. This place is gigantic. The path to the resort is pristine. I drive past Maseratis and Ferraris and a couple of Lamborghinis. When I roll the camper to the valet desk, the porters look at us like we've made a mistake. I tend to agree.

The girls explain our situation. These two can charm a snake to eat an apple. The valet directs us to an appropriate parking spot and instructs us on how to get to the venue.

A couple of smiles later, we've parked and everyone's taking a turn bathing in the RV. I finish first and step outside, taking in the beautiful night. The late afternoon air smells of the ocean and expensive meals from the resort's many restaurants.

I adjust my hat and find that I'm a bit annoyed. I wanted to go off on my own tonight, just decompress. Instead we're going to a night-club. I don't want to dance... Primarily because I don't know how to dance. Also, I don't have anything appropriate to wear.

To me, those are all legitimate excuses. But I didn't even bother trying them on the girls. They would just nod, smile, and tell me to get ready for the dance. Might as well cut out the middle man.

When Sam steps out of the RV, I know I have no choice but to go with them. The sun has found its match. She looks stunning. Then to make matters worse, Carmen saunters out, looking just like my mom. Beautiful and fiery.

Even if I wanted to sit it out, the way they look, guys would be drawn to them like sand to beach.

"Perfect," Sam declares as she checks my clothes. "Jeans, button-down shirt, boots, and a cowboy hat. If we were going to the rodeo you'd be the talk of the event."

I grunt.

"Don't listen to her. You look perfect." Carmen steps up to me and slips her arm through the crook of my elbow. "Let's go."

"Me too! Me too!" Sam runs to my other side and slides her arm in.

"This is a bad idea," I mumble as we skip toward the music.

WE FIND THE EVENT EASILY. That's the good news. Said event is packed with older people who appear to know what they're doing on the dance floor. That's the bad news. The worst news is that this isn't a typical night club. It's all Latin music with beats that I can't even pretend to understand or know how to follow.

"This is *our* music," Carmen proclaims.

"Our island," Sam adds.

We both stare at her.

"What? I'm practically Puerto Rican."

With that, we get on the dance floor.

To say that we stand out is an understatement. The girls are awesome. They dance the way they surf: Carmen is aggressive, on fire; Sam is smooth and in the moment. I'm a giant ogre with a cowboy hat, standing in between them like a banana tree in the Sahara Desert.

"Shake your hips," Sam instructs.

"Feel the music," Carmen pleads.

I try my best and I guess my best isn't horrible because no one is laughing. The girls sing songs in Spanish that I can almost make out. Mom insisted I take Spanish in school and she always listened to Latin music at home. So I can sort of pretend.

An energetic old man, maybe in his seventies, has been dancing with his wife near us. When his wife steps off the dance floor, he extends his hand to Carmen, who does not hesitate. He's a hoot.

Laughing and spinning Carmen around. He wears an oversized belt buckle and cowboy boots. He's my sort of people.

While my attention is diverted, someone asks Sam to dance, but she declines and moves in closer to me.

Sam raises her arms above her head, her eyes closed. She moves breathlessly to the music. I want to have her freedom, her energy and passion for life.

I want to dance with her the way she dances with the water.

A Marc Anthony song I recognize thrums through the speakers. Like him, I want to *Vivir Mi Vida*, live my life. But what I'm living is not mine. My life is because of things that have happened to me, not by me.

I'm about to get down on myself, but realize that although this request of the road trip was Mom's, the decision was mine. What we do here and how we do it, is all us. Maybe this was Mom's plan all along. Live my life by walking in her footsteps.

Another thought dawns on me. Mom's words about dancing.

One day you'll find the girl who'll replace me. On that day, I want you to dance until the sun excuses the moon, and the day starts anew.

I stare at Sam. No one will ever replace Mom. But is Sam the one who'll help me move past the grief?

She opens her eyes and smiles.

I smile back.

AT PAST THREE in the morning, we're back inside the RV. The three of us danced until they closed the place and we danced through the meandering pathways until we reached our mobile home. We're waiting for the sun to rise. At this point I don't know if we can call it dancing. It's closer to standing while swinging the hips and once in a while shifting our feet. But at least our hearts are sincere.

Finally, at exactly 4:39 a.m., we see the twilight. Without

exchanging another word, I drop on the couch and girls pass out on the bed.

Challenge complete. But can I leave the RV parked here at the resort or are they expecting us to leave? I decide that until we're asked to leave, we'll stay. It's not like we have a camp location for tonight.

I flop sideways and switch off.

THIRTY-TWO

DAY 6 - SAMANTHA

"OH CRAP!" Carmen yells right into my ear. Something large falls, shaking the RV.

This better not be about my snoring again.

"What now? What happened?" My voice isn't quite there yet. I turn toward Carmen and force my eyes open. Her hair is parted in the back like an elephant sneezed on her head.

"It's late," she says. "It's so late!"

I flop back into bed.

"What's wrong?" I hear Shep ask. He must've been what fell.

"We're going to miss the window at The Wedge," Carmen says. "Blackball hours are from 10:00 a.m. to 5:00 p.m."

"Which means?" Shep asks.

"No surfing during blackball hours."

"What time is it?" I ask in a yawn.

"Eight-thirty!"

I don't bother to move. "It's too late. By the time we change, get something to eat then find a spot to park, it'll be way past the window."

"Crap," Carmen says through greeted teeth. "I really wanted to surf it."

"We can boogie board there when we arrive and surf after five."

I glance toward Shep, hoping to get his support, but he's not there anymore. I sit up in bed and catch him making friends with the sofa.

"Shep agrees," I say.

He moans something.

"Crap," Carmen adds.

THE THREE OF us are on the sand, in awe of the massive cluster that is the Wedge.

"What the...?" Shep says. "This would be the equivalent of my high school football team going up against the Pittsburgh Steelers."

"Your analogy means nothing to me," I say.

He eyes me. "How's this for a translation? Are you freaking insane? Some of those waves are at least ten feet tall."

"That one's a good twelver," Carmen says.

"Badass," I say.

"This'll be epic," Carmen adds. "Check out the fast drops. It's nearly a free fall. These waves are hollow and fast. Which means powerful and ruthless."

"You two are nut jobs."

"These are legendary waves," Sam says. "Soon you'll see the cameras piling up on the sand, waiting for the damage that will be inflicted on the daring boogie boarders and the late noon surfers."

"Why even bother?" he asks.

"Didn't you hear what I said?" I ask. "Legendary waves, son."

Shep's been searching something on his phone. He chuckles. "Check out what this site says about The Wedge. Skill level needed is pro or kamikaze only."

"Awesome," I say. I marvel at the wedge-shaped waves. All of this the direct result of the long rock jetty on the north end of the

Newport Harbor. A manmade effect that brings out the best and the worst surfers.

"How does someone even start here?" he asks.

"First lesson is don't be a kook," Carmen says.

"English translation," he says.

"Don't be a newbie who thinks he knows better. Also, watch the waves, the surfers, and the others in the water. Listen to what the experienced surfers are telling you. Learn from them. And above all, don't expect the lifeguard to save you. It'll be another surfer who will come to your rescue. So if you piss 'em off, you're on your own."

"You're right, Sam. This is awesome. Maybe it'll be best if we find someone suicidal, pay him a few bucks, and ask him to release my mom's ashes."

Carmen smiles. "You already have us," she says.

"We got this," I say. "We just have to burn some time until the waves are open to surfers."

THIRTY-THREE
DAY 6 - SHEP

THE GIRLS ARE BODYSURFING CLOSE to the shore. They're always on, always active. I'm still recovering from my near-death experience in the ocean. To think I actually wanted to surf at the memorial event in Pismo.

I plant myself in the sand because I have reading to take care of. Day six pokes its head out of my bag so I tear the envelope open.

———— ⌒ ⌒ ⌒ ⌒ ⌒ ————

July 15, 2000 — Day 6

He is here!

Sorry, let me back up and go in order. I only have a few minutes before we head off. So here goes!

The Wedge was amazing. Scary as hell, but amazing. I got my butt kicked many times. A thirty-footer nearly destroyed me. I was told later that it may have been closer to fifteen than thirty, but the way I was manhandled, I think it's more appropriate to call it a fifty-footer...

Anyway, at one point I was on a roll. Wave after wave. So I did an insane move when I knew I was about to eat it. I walked to the tip of the board just before I was crushed. I walked a shortboard. You read it right. I walked a shortboard. But before I became a permanent member of the sandbar, I pulled—you guessed it—a soul arch! It lasted at best a second. But that may have cemented my awesomeness at The Wedge. I will forever be a fixture here.

Note to self: check back in a year to confirm a plaque has been installed honoring me.

Anyway, when I got out of the water, someone tapped my shoulder and said, "I should've known that was you."

I faced him. Quick, with his glorious smile.

I felt like the sixteen-year-old me at that moment. Butterflies, insecurity, head-over-heels. He was about to say something else, I think, but I didn't give him a chance. I hugged him like he and I were twins separated at birth.

I'm dead tired, but I had to write this down because I want to capture the awesomeness before I forget. He and I surfed at night. Later on we were on the sand, just talking about life, catching up, wondering why we lost touch. We talked about surfing, college, the future. We kissed. The best one. Ever.

Then he gave me my new nickname which will forever be my new name: Soul Arch Goddess. Yes, it's a long nickname, but man, it feels so right.

Also, I get to cross out another one off my list: Fall in love. Technically I had been in love with him two summers ago. But I am back in love. Completely.

O Out

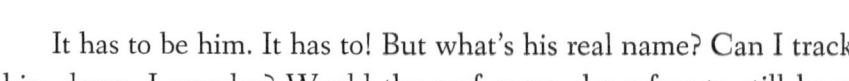

It has to be him. It has to! But what's his real name? Can I track him down, I wonder? Would the surf camp she refers to still have records from some twenty years ago?

This by far is the best letter. But also the worst, because it's a tease. I read it again.

She was so vibrant. A sense of humor that I only glimpsed when she was alive. I wish I had known this Olivia. In a way, I guess I'm meeting her now.

Sam and Carmen join me on the sand and tear open the sandwich bags. I shove the letter back in my bag.

"What's a soul arch?" I ask.

Sam's head swivels. "Where did you hear that term?" she asks, looking very intrigued.

Maybe it's time I come clean about the letters. "The envelopes I received are not just random notes from my mom," I say. They both freeze, hanging on my words. "They are pages from her diary during the fifteen-day surf trip. I am, in effect, reading what happened to her each of those days."

"Oh wow," Carmen says.

"So in today's entry, she has mentioned pulling off the soul arch here."

Sam's brows go up. "She did a soul arch here? At The Wedge?"

"On a shortboard."

"No way," Sam says in admiration. "It's a longboard thing. And even then..."

I shrug. "That's what she said she did. What is it exactly?"

Sam doesn't respond, so Carmen steps in. "Wannabes call it old school, but for those who get it, it's a serious badass longboard maneuver. Doing it right takes style, grace, and balance."

"Big time balance," Sam adds. "Some people do a sloppy version, but when done right, it's magical. It's the one thing that I have tried over and over again, but fail over and over again."

"What is it?" I ask.

"Have you heard of the terms hang five or hang ten?" Carmen asks.

I shake my head.

"Hang five is when the longboarder steps up to the nose of the board and places one foot over the tip. Five toes hang over the tip."

"Hang ten is when both feet are at the tip," Carmen adds.

I can't even imagine the physics.

"Here's the kicker," Carmen continues, "to do a soul arch, you first have to nail a hang ten, then arc your back and raise your hands wide open." Carmen displays the move by extending her arms out to her sides, a bit overhead.

"Like in Titanic," I say.

They both cringe. "Okay, yeah," Sam says, "but no one yells 'I'm the king of the world,' when surfing. It's more like you're throwing you hands to the heavens, at nature's mercy. For those watching the surfer... well it's a thing of beauty."

We're all silent for a few moments.

"So my tía knew how to do soul arches," Carmen says more to herself.

I can hear the awe in her voice. "Someone called her the Soul Arch Goddess."

Both girls stare at me, their mouths slightly open.

My mom was awesome.

THE GIRLS GO BACK into the water while I stroll along the coast. Finally, I get my alone time—with a few hundred beach dwellers surrounding me, but hey, I'll take what I can get.

The ocean inhales, producing an animal-like reverberation, then shouts, altering the shape of the gigantic waves. This place legitimately scares me.

From my peripheral vision, something catches my eye. I turn and see a boogie boarder launch into space. His legs fly in different directions and his foot fins make him look like a frog. He falls hard in the water. He pops out looking like someone who spent a few rounds in the octagon. Yes, these people have a death wish.

My mom, and possibly the man who is my father, surfed these same waters. The patch of sand I'm walking on could've been the same path they walked together.

Another boogie boarder going full out carves a beauty. But when he rides up the face of the wave, he is sent into a spiraling motion—out of control.

That's when I notice the young boy bodysurfing nearby.

As the boogie boarder slams into the water, his legs cross-swipe the boy. The waves and thick foam immediately cover the kid.

I stop, focus on where he was.

The boogie boarder rises from the water and snaps his long hair. He paddles back into the depth, but I don't see the boy.

I look around, hoping someone else has noticed it, too. But no one seems one bit concerned or maybe they're not aware of what just happened.

I spin back to the water. I catch something floating. I remember me, more than a decade ago at Pirates Beach in Galveston.

I run all out. My hat flies off and I yell. I don't know what I'm yelling or what I'm trying to achieve, but my instincts have taken over.

I hit the cold water and pump my legs higher and wider against the pulling water current. Like the best defensive ends trying to slow me down, the waves are trying to stop me.

I see him clearly now. He's not moving. Like seaweed, he's just there, at the mercy of the ocean's movement.

I'm knee-high, only ten yards to go when I dive in and extend my arms, grabbing and cutting through the water. Left, right, air. Left, right, air. I kick my feet harder and harder, open my eyes in the general direction of the boy.

Left, right, I make contact.

I grab him, plant my feet, and turn him, face up. My arm slides through his arm, underneath his neck. I change direction and pull and swim and pump my legs. The current is strong, pulling my feet out from under me.

People are running toward me now.

Two men show up at my side and help me take the kid to the sand. One of them is taller so he has leverage. They're saying something but I can't hear anything. My adrenaline has made me deaf and mute.

They pull ahead and run the kid onto the sand. Another person jumps on the sand across him and starts performing CPR.

I've dragged myself out of the water, stumbling my way.

I reach the mass of people who've now surrounded the kid. I want to see what's happening. I want to see if he's okay. But I can't tell.

"Is he," I start but I can barely breath. I try again. "Is he okay?"

No one responds, but suddenly there's an explosion of cheers.

"He's breathing," someone yells.

"He coughed out water," another one says.

"Thank God," someone next to me says.

I collapse, my knees hit the sand. I don't know why but without reason and without warning, I cry. Relief? Hope? Fear? I don't know. And I don't question the release of energy.

Just as I rise, an older lady rushes me and wraps me in a hug.

"It was you. You saved him," she says in tears. "You saved my boy." I am engulfed in her hug. "Thank you," she says.

"You're welcome," I say.

She pulls away, her eyes red, tears have scarred her cheeks. "God bless you, *hijo. Que Dios te bendiga.*"

"*Gracias,*" I say, extending my Spanish skills to the limit.

"The paramedics are here," someone says and the lady immediately releases me and runs toward her child.

I stare at them as they do their thing, checking his eyes, asking about neck movement, and taking his pulse. All along, random people are slapping me on the shoulder.

My hat magically plops on my head. I turn to find Carmen and Sam, dripping wet behind me.

"Did you just do what I think you did?" Carmen asks.

I nod.

Sam just hugs me.

AT MINUTES BEFORE FIVE, the avalanche of surfers explodes into the water. So much for respecting time. The lifeguards seem to be using the same clock because no one says anything. It just happens.

Carmen and Sam don't react. They're sitting next to me on the sand.

I pull out the vial and hold it out.

Carmen takes it and rises. Sam follows suit.

Carmen looks down at me. "What was the fourth challenge on Tía's list?"

"Surf naked," I say. "Not happening."

Sam smirks then breathes, "Dag nabbit!"

"That's not it. Maybe it was the fifth?" Carmen asks.

I think about it. "Something about changing someone else's life forever."

She nods. "Congrats, cuz. You just knocked another one off the list."

I glance at her.

"Big time," Sam says and highfives Carmen. "He's going to own the list," I hear Sam say to Carmen as they march off toward the vicious waves. Then, though faint, I hear her say, "We just need him to surf naked."

"Never," I yell.

Sam looks at me over her shoulder and sends me a wink that travels through time and space, through my eyes, down my legs.

This girl will be the end of me.

I pull out my phone and notice a new message from Billy. He wants me to call him. The last thing I want to do is get pulled back into whatever it is that's going on back home. But I can't just ignore him either.

So I call.

"He lives," Billy yells. "Already forgot your peeps now that you're hanging out with Beverly Hills honeys?"

"Was trying to forget, but you have this annoying habit of not getting the hint."

He laughs his infamous hyena laugh.

"So, talk to me, what's going on?" I ask.

He clears his throat. "The D.A. is asking for anyone that may have information to step forward and help the case."

Crap, crap, crap!

"Why? I thought they had everything they needed."

"Well, that's the thing, the trial starts in what, eleven or twelve days? The boys have some badass attorneys on their team now. This thing is getting a lot of press now. If you've turned on any news channels, they're talking about this. So these dudes are floating stories about her. Between us, pretty bad ones."

I drop my head. I've been so lost in this trip that I haven't even bothered to check the news.

"Basically, what you're saying is that the D.A. realizes that he's out-gunned so he needs more evidence."

"You got it. He wants eye witnesses. Anyone who was at the party. They're even asking for pictures. I hear they're scouring insta-gram and whatever to find pictures of who was there and when."

I ask the question that I don't have to ask. "So why are you telling me this?"

"Well," he starts, then pauses. "Thought it was obvious. Your name is all over the place. Especially after that way-awesome one-handed catch at the Dodger's game, you're sort of hard to miss."

THIRTY-FOUR
DAY 7 - SHEP

I WAKE up to the sound of the waves. I'm not annoyed by it. I actually enjoy it. If not for that relaxing melody, I probably would've never fallen asleep. I stared at my phone all day, expecting a call from the district attorney. But the call never came. Don't know what to do other than just get on with life.

I unzip my sleeping bag then hop out of the tent, into the camper. Carmen is asleep but Sam is awake typing away on her phone.

When she sees me, she turns off the phone. "Good morning," she says.

"G'mornin'." I point to her phone. "Everything okay?"

"Fine. All's fine," she says, but I can see she doesn't want to talk about it.

I won't press it. "Do you think it'll be rough today at the beach?"

"Don't worry, we'll get you out there. The surf is much more decent here. Perfect for starters."

Carmen squeals like Chewbacca. "What time is it?" she asks/yawns.

"Five-ish," I say.

She scoots forward out of the bed. "Awesome, let's go surf."

"You may want to eat breakfast first," I say.

"And brush your teeth," Sam adds.

"You guys have a warped sense of priorities," she says, then staggers into the bathroom.

"I'll make eggs," I say.

"I'll put on a bikini," Sam says.

I pause.

"*After* you leave," she says.

The red-hot heat of my stupidity overcomes my ability to speak. So I just step out as gracefully as I can muster.

"SURF CITY," Carmen says. "Another historic spot."

Boards in our clutches, we march down the sand, alongside the pier.

"Stay with us the entire time," Sam says. "Don't go wandering off to the south side of the pier."

"Sharks?" I ask.

She glares at me. "No. The currents can sometimes pull you toward the pier, right into the pilings. For a newbie like you, that means mucho trouble-o."

Carmen eyes Sam. "After two years of Spanish with señora, that's all you learned?"

Sam shrugs. "Sorry-o?"

Carmen shakes her head, then faces me. "The other problem down there are all the fish lines. I've seen a few surfers get hooked." She pauses. "Get it? Hooked?"

"That was horrible," Sam says.

"Oh, sorry-o is fine but mine isn't?"

They get into it for a few moments.

"Guys, seriously. I read something about shark sightings. Anything I need to worry about?"

Neither speaks.

"Hello. I asked a question."

Sam grimaces. "It's best that you don't think about these things."

"Because...?" I ask.

"All it'll do is distract you," Carmen says.

"C'mon," Sam says and runs into the water, her board under her arm.

Carmen follows, sprinting to the water.

I get a better hold of my hybrid board and follow them. But as I pass the lifeguard shack, a yellow sign catches my eye.

I'm no expert, but the image is clear. The black silhouette of a shark.

AFTER THIRTY MINUTES in the water, I stop worrying. The only saving grace is that there are plenty of options a shark could go after. Why me? I mean what are the chances?

I catch a few smaller waves, but each time I try to maneuver the board, I lose control and fall backward or forward in the water. This has been my first time trying to directionally control the board in a couple of days. I must be spazzing and forgetting some key steps, I'm sure. Either that or my mind is on the wildfires burning some fifteen-hundred miles away.

Carmen paddles next to me. "Stop thinking about shifting your weight and moving your arms and looking at where you're going."

"Forget everything you guys taught me?"

"Not everything. Just forget the paint by number stuff I fed you."

Sam nods, vigorously.

"Go with your instinct. Surfing is not about mathematical formulas. It's about respecting the wave you get and riding it."

"Preach on!" Sam says.

"Just go for it. You have innate skills. Use those."

I nod. "Okay."

After a couple of minutes of waiting, Sam calls it. "Here comes the set."

We all paddle for a better spot. The girls are so smooth in how they get around, while I look like I'm swimming in honey.

A beauty forms yards away.

"It's yours, Shep."

I paddle slowly, then pick up the speed. I catch it, or more accurately, it catches me. I'm on my feet in an instant. My mind wants to go down the checklist of steps, but I push that out.

Instead, I focus on the wave that drives me to the right. Like I would with my skateboard, I gently lower myself and feel the water beneath my board. I lean back a bit then toward the wave and I have the distinct, nearly imperceptible impression that the board has adjusted with the wave. I'm giddy because I'm hanging with the wave.

I'm separating again. I repeat the movement and again, the tip of the board moves toward the wave, extending the ride for a bit longer.

The wave alters and its energy separates me more drastically. This time, although I repeat the same move, I decide to lean more toward the wave. The board responds taking me up the face of the wave faster than I anticipated. I'm about to fly up and over the wave, but just then I swivel my eyes 180 degrees, throw my hands in that same direction and snap the board around.

I didn't fly off! I'm actually going back down the wave.

Did I really do that?

Did I spray?

I turn my head around, swiveling, hoping the girls saw what I did.

But my investigation comes to an immediate end when I somehow go airborne upside down, then drop into the water.

I resurface, grab my board and immediately slide back on.

The girls reach me.

"That was perfect," Carmen says.

"Up until you acted like a complete newbie."

They're both laughing.

"Did I snap?" I ask.

"Yeah, Cuz. You even showed some fins."

I have no idea what that means, but it brings me unparalleled joy.

AFTER THAT, I was able to catch a few more. I fell more than I caught but it doesn't matter. I'm getting the hang of it. More importantly, I get it now. The addiction.

I want more of those.

I want to get better.

I've been so focused on surfing and improving that it wasn't until Carmen asked if I wanted to spread my mom's ashes that I realized I hadn't even read today's letter.

I decide to release her remains this time—on my own. The girls watch me from the sand as I successfully leave a portion of Mom in Huntington. All the while I eagerly think of the letter that awaits me. I need to focus on why I'm here in the first place. Closure.

The last letter was the hope I had been looking for. It's time to see if I get more clues about my father and why he abandoned us.

By the time we head back to the RV the air has turned cold. It is when they go to shower that I pull out the letter and tear into it. But it's short. Too short.

July 16, 2000 — Day 7

He didn't come.
He said he'd try.
I thought that meant he would. After the beautiful evening we had together, I was sure of it.
But nothing.
Nothing!

O.

I feel dejected. Completely. After an amazing day of surfing, this is not what I was expecting. What does she mean with a "beautiful evening?" Is she talking about the long talk they had and the kiss they exchanged on the beach or did something else happen?

I scan the letter again. Not even a mention of the surfing. It's like he has taken over everything.

A new insight dawns on me. Let me see if I can interpret the story: they did the deed, he promised he'd be back, and he left her high and dry. And that's how she became pregnant.

Awesome. Romantic.

Where's the Hallmark Channel? I have a script for you.

THIRTY-FIVE
DAY 8 - SAMANTHA

AN UNFAMILIAR SOUND jars me out of sleep. I glance at Carmen, but it's not her, nor does she hear it because she has her ear plugs shoved in. I glance at my phone. It's nearly one in the morning.

I listen intently and I hear it again.

Wind?

No, not the wind, but definitely coming from outside.

I scoot out of bed, consider changing out of my cotton shorts, but instead decide to wear a hoodie to keep me warm. I step out of the camper and look into the tent through the mesh. At that instant, I hear the sound.

It's Shep.

He's moaning and thrashing around. A nightmare?

I unzip the tent, step in, then close it up again. I slide next him and hold him tight.

"Shh," I say. "It's okay. It's just a dream."

He stops thrashing, but his breathing is still heavy.

"I'm here," I say again and squeeze him harder.

His breathing stabilizes. After a couple of minutes he's fully calm. I consider leaving, but decide to stay. I slide inside his sleeping bag, drape my arm around him, and squeeze my face into his back.

I hope I don't snore, I think as I drift.

I WAKE up as the sun's rays creep into the tent. I sit up but don't see Shep around. He's left me a note.

I walked to the beach.

I step out and gooseflesh immediately attack my bare legs. I go in the camper, slip on jeans and head out to the beach.

The sand is cool, pleasant. I scan around but initially don't see him. Then I spot him knee deep in the water.

He's wearing jeans, no top. His arms dangle at his side, his eyes trained on the distant horizon.

Underneath my hoodie, I'm wearing a sports bra. That will have to do. I toss my jacket on the sand and follow him in.

The surf is soft, but the water bites, it's so cold. When I reach him I place my hand on his back. He turns slowly and studies me, as if he was expecting me. We just stare at each other without exchanging words for a few moments.

"Thank you," he says.

I give him a small smile. "Was it a nightmare?" I ask.

He nods. "I saw my mom, surfing. She was walking the board, like you do. She was so graceful and... young. Then..."

I wait it out, giving him the space he needs.

"As she reached the tip and spread her arms, wide, her hair color changed until it thinned out and her skin—" He doesn't finish the sentence, his face contorts.

When I caress his face he looks up again. His tired eyes penetrate mine.

"She lowered herself on the board, like she was about to sleep. The wave she had ben riding practically guided her into the water. I yelled for her, I think, but just then, the sky transformed to a red hue.

Not scary. Peaceful in fact. But I panicked and tried to run toward where I had last seen her, but I was stuck in the knee-high water. Suddenly, the ocean's surface around me became violent. I dove in and swam as hard and as fast as I could to break through, but I was stuck in place. So I yelled her name, over and over again. It was no use, she was nowhere in sight. I gave up and felt the ocean take me also... but then I heard her voice. Not weak, not frail like she was near the end, but young and strong. Her soothing voice rising from the ocean." His eyes open wide. "I think she's asking me to be brave. To fight for—"

"Be careful," I whisper.

He studies me intently.

"As much fun as dream interpretations may be, you need to live in the here and now. Don't get lost in dreams and what they may or may not mean. What's real is this. We're real. This trip is real. What you're accomplishing is real."

He nods.

"This freezing water is also real."

He chuckles then brings me into his chest, engulfing me completely. A natural, comfortable move that puts me at complete ease. I get lost in his scent, in the feel of his skin against mine.

He softens the embrace, then kisses my forehead, tenderly. He whispers, "Thank you."

The trace of his words from his warm lips on my skin lingers and hums. I'm off balance in a beautiful way. Holding each other, the gentle waves splash around us. His body against mine protects me from the ocean breeze. I feel his warmth.

In that moment, a thought dawns on me and I am prompted to say it—just speak it out—before I overanalyze it and stop myself.

"I know you're struggling with something. I'm here to help you. Not just with this trip, or surfing. But just help."

He hesitates. The moments tick by. Then he takes a deep breath and speaks.

"Here's what else is real—I wasn't a great son. I was too busy with my own crap. Everyone wanted to hang with me. Friends were talking about the pros, not just college, but the next level. Thing is, I wanted all of that, too. I dreamt about it. So I had no time for Mom."

He's not looking at me anymore. His eyes are downcast, avoiding me.

"All of eleventh grade, she kept asking for more quality time, to catch up, and do whatever. Not that I didn't want to, but the alternative was too good to pass up. I stopped going to church, which hurt her, I'm sure. But she didn't fight me. Instead, she gave me more space than I deserved. My junior year was an amazing year, until it wasn't. I didn't even notice the weight loss.

"By that point I was so lost that Mom was the last thing on my mind, until the time I got home and my uncle José was there with her. They broke the news— melanoma. It all went downhill fast after that. Within eight weeks she lost half her weight. She suffered for a few weeks more and then it was over. I lost her forever."

He releases our embrace, then turns away and splashes water onto his face. He takes his time as he runs his wet hands through his hair.

"I should've been with her, but I was partying," he says. He is staring at the distant horizon. "Then when it all imploded it was too late. She had no energy. We couldn't share a pint of ice cream because she couldn't hold it down. No binge-watching Netflix, and no trading notes on the latest book we'd read. But she never called me out for being a selfish prick. Instead she apologized to me. Can you believe it? I was the ass, but she was the one who felt guilty. Those last days she'd fall asleep holding my hand while I sat by her bed. That's all she wanted. My presence."

He takes a deep breath and when he exhales, I hear tremors, not release.

"During this entire trip, I've been trying to make up for lost time. Honor her, in some way. It's silly and wishful, but I'm trying to make up for my screw-ups."

"It's not silly. And I don't think it's wishful. I think she's aware and is cheering you on."

He smiles.

"Just like I'm cheering you on and so is Carmen. I'm so honored that I'm a part of your journey with your mom."

His eyes have gone glassy. He nods, then swallows. There's more —I'm sure of it, but I won't push because I can feel it, any second now, a tear will dig a path down his cheek. So I hug him, giving him the freedom to cry without an audience. We stay that way until I no longer feel the turbulence roaring in his chest.

THIRTY-SIX

DAY 8 - SHEP

WE ARRIVE IN EL PORTO, Manhattan Beach at seven in the morning. My conversation with Sam is still replaying in my head, because there is more to tell. Even so, I shared too much. That is private and embarrassing. And when I think of Mom in those last days, the way she was, it's not meant to be shared with anyone. I should've kept it inside, deep inside.

I'm thankful for Sam though. I was raw and exposed. Glad I was able to get some of what's been gnawing at me off my chest. I know Sam and Carmen are trying to be helpful, and they definitely are in may ways, but now, more than ever, I need privacy and space.

Instead, I go with the plan. I hope today's letter is better than yesterday's. We are more than halfway through now. I need to know that we're closer to answers.

The El Porto beach looks laid back, but Carmen tells me there is some localization going on. Whatever that means.

"Just don't get into it with the locals. I've never had problems, but friends of mine have," she says.

"The forecast looks good," Sam says, "so expect the beach to be packed by mid-morning."

The water is downright cold. I'm wearing the wetsuit, but my feet are exposed. I have a nasty sinus headache and feel a bit congested. With my dumb stunt this morning, going into the freezing water and now this, I'd be lucky if I don't get seriously sick.

We've been in the water for a while now. Long enough that more surfers have joined the pack. Everybody is struggling and a bit pissed off, because most of the waves are small. Personally, I have my heart set on a barrel to experience what Mom experienced. I want to hear what she heard. I don't know what I'm supposed to do if I get that lucky.

"I want to catch a barrel," I say out loud.

"Unlikely under these conditions," Sam says. "But sometimes, even with very small barrels, you can ride it like a boogie boarder. Meaning that you don't jump to your feet. You just ride it."

"Or," Carmen gets in, "if you do jump to your feet, you stay low, very low. Like one knee on the board."

"True," Sam says.

"If you really want to catch barrels, we have to go—" but I don't wait for the ending of the sermon. I paddle my heart out because I am drawn to take the wave. It has potential.

Another guy is trying to catch it, too. I don't know if I have the right of way or not, I don't care. I want to experience the barrel because something's going on. I don't know what, but I can't help but feel that maybe, just maybe, I'll hear the voice Mom wrote about. At a minimum I have to try.

Unfortunately, I don't catch the wave. I was too slow. Someone paddles next to me. It's the other guy who I beat out in getting the wave.

"Dude, if you don't know what you're doin' get the hell out of my water."

I stare at him. "This is your water?"

He glares at me. "Listen here you kook, if you want trouble—"

I see Sam and Carmen paddling toward us. They look worried.

"No trouble, dude."

"That was my wave," he says and slaps the water.

I turn my board to paddle away. "Sorry, okay? Didn't see you until I was already there. I'll be more aware next time."

"You do that," he says.

I paddle hard toward the girls because I don't want them involved. Also, if I have to talk to this moron for another second, I may be tempted to slam his empty skull into his surfboard.

"Nothing to see here," I say as I paddle away from them.

They don't look convinced.

"So... the pep talk earlier this morning," Carmen says as she deftly paddles next to me, "you know the thing about not getting into it with the locals... this is sort of what I was talking about."

"Got it," I say. I really don't feel like hearing a lecture. I just want to surf.

I wait and wait and eventually a wave forms.

"It's yours," Carmen calls out.

All manners go out the barn door. I don't have to be told twice, I paddle for it and instantly grab it.

Instinctively, I hop to my feet then realize maybe I shouldn't have. I pump the board then cut close to the wave's shoulder. The wave is groaning in a beast way. I have to go deeper into its mouth.

Like I've seen the girls do, I slow myself by using my hand in the water. It works, I get closer into the mouth. The volume increases, but the barrel is small. I crouch down, like a solider about to be knighted. I want to go deeper.

My board slows and half my body is in.

The sound inside is indescribable. A whoosh, a scream, a moan, an exhilaration from the wave. It's yelling at me. It's spitting at me. It wants me.

I'm being pelted. My board is skidding around now. I won't be able to hold this much longer. Either I have to pull out, or get consumed.

Speak to me. I want to hear you!

Instead, another sound blurs out everything else. A shush. A calming sound so loud and so close that I feel at peace. Safe.

The board skids, spinning me upside down. The monster consumes me and spits me out. The board hits the back of my head. All I see are bubbles before I partially black out. I spin and get pulled in all the wrong directions by the tether on my ankle.

I don't fight it. It will end. One way or another, this will end.

After a few seconds I surface. The pain on my skull is dull, but my vision is all over the place.

"You okay?" a voice I recognize asks, but I'm not sure if it's Carmen or Sam.

I put up a thumbs up, even though I don't feel it.

They help me onto my board and we get onto the sand.

"Did you get hurt?" Carmen asks.

I don't respond. Instead they pull me to a seating position, their fingers running though my hair. "Ouch," I say.

"I see it," Sam says. "A cut behind the ear."

"Do you feel light-headed?" Carmen asks.

I shake my head. Although I feel a bit off, I know it's not a concussion. I've been there before.

They both breathe deep and their shoulders drop.

"Well, you killed it," Sam say.

"Until you ate it."

I smile uncontrollably.

"That's what you get, you punk-ass kook," surfer boy says.

Sam is on her feet, before I can even respond. "Go on, your sister's waiting to wax your board."

"What did you say about my sister?" he takes a step toward her.

"You two make a cute couple."

He drops his board, I'm about to jump to my feet to intervene, but Sam's too fast. She kicks sand in his face, then with her other foot kicks him in the nuts. He's on the ground quicker than I can even blink.

"Let's get the hell out of here," Carmen says.

We grab our things and make for the parking lot. We're not running, but we ain't walking either. I'm a bit dazed from the whole thing, but I think I'm also laughing.

I break my self-imposed oath of silence. "What happened to 'don't get into it with the locals?'" I ask.

"This is my beach!" the dude yells. "My sand. My water!"

Sam's about to yell back something, but Carmen stops her. "Don't make it worse."

We get into the camper. "Get out of here and take a left on Ocean Drive. I'll tell you where to park," Carmen says.

"Let's just leave," I say.

"Your mom's ashes. We have to spread them here."

"Crap," Sam says. "You're right."

Even I forgot about it. What's going on with me?

WE FIND a parking spot in the residential areas, just south of where we started. We decide Carmen is the right person for this since dude-with-missing-testicle will recognize both Sam and me out of any lineup. Carmen, not so much.

I'm in the driver's seat of the RV and Sam is in the passenger seat. She's wearing my hat again. As Carmen runs into the water, I pull out my mom's eighth letter.

July 17, 2000 — Day 8

No sign of him.
Surfing sucked. Got into a fight.
I want to go home. I don't want to do this anymore.

O.

"What the hell?" I say out loud.

"What's wrong?"

I glance at Sam, annoyed at myself for making my frustration public. I don't want to share Mom's mess of a life with anyone.

"You can speak to me," she says. "You know that, right?"

I put the letter back in the envelope, drop it in my bag, then lean back into my chair.

"You're going silent on me now?"

"Look, I just want to stew in this, on my own. I'm not ready to go all new-age and share my feelings."

She stares at me, stunned. Like I just told her that the ocean doesn't really exist.

"Got it," she whispers.

What's the matter with me? She's just trying to help. Everyone's trying to help. But no one can. Not really because this is my life, my mom.

I glance at Sam's profile as she intently watches my cousin take the wave. The truth is that she does matter. More than I'm willing to admit. I should say that. Just blurt it out, let her know. But I don't.

Sam gets to her feet. An effortless move, like everything she does. She returns my hat before stepping out of the camper. I should go after her. Apologize. Share the rest and my frustrations and fears with the letters. But I say nothing.

I'm going nowhere real fast.

But is that really surprising? Of course this is how things would go for me. This is my destiny. Alone. Always.

THIRTY-SEVEN
DAY 9 - SHEP

WORLD-FAMOUS VENICE BEACH. This place is an explosion of sights, sounds, and smells. And not all of it is of the pleasant variety. I've worked with manure. Next to some of the people I'm encountering, cow dung is more pleasant. Not to be judgmental or anything.

I scan the place and it dawns on me that it isn't real. I don't mean that I'm in a dream or that I've accidentally stumbled onto a movie set. What I mean is that this place isn't organic. It's not a natural thing, but a carefully orchestrated location that is designed to attract certain types of people—those who really are bohemian street-dwellers, those who think they are but drive up in seventy-thousand-dollar cars, and those who want to watch those hemp-smoking oddities.

Everything is exaggerated here. From the thousands of items that are on sale in the dozens of shops across the strip, to the varieties of foods, to the amazing model-caliber people that walk the pathways. Some of the street performers are actually talented, others not so much.

And then there's the beach. Sunbathers all over the place. From the drop-dead gorgeous to the outright jailhouse escapee. Men and women so muscular that I wonder how many gallons of steroids stream through their veins.

All shapes and sizes are welcome here. Literally.

"Don't give anyone a dirty look," Carmen says.

"I hope you're talking to Sam," I say and bump Sam's shoulder. She offers a kind smile but nothing more.

I've been trying to break the ice I created yesterday. Carmen is probably aware of how I behaved, but has decided to give me a pass. Unfortunately, no matter what I do, Sam doesn't bite. She's not being mean and she's not giving me the cold shoulder. She's treating me like we're acquaintances. And that's all.

"The surf isn't great," Sam says instead.

"Yeah," Carmen says. "When it's good it's really good, but the swell looks less than stellar. Supposedly it was nice in the morning. Right now it's whatever."

"Let's make the most of it," I say.

Tightly bundled in our wetsuits, we paddle out and wait. And wait.

Sam breaks away and catches a wave that seems unworthy. Four strokes and she's on her feet. Her smooth, effortless way makes me feel both jealous and inept. When Mom enrolled me in a swim program at the Y, I learned the strokes and studied the techniques carefully. Soon enough, I swam well. But there was this guy who seemed to swim as if he was being pulled by a string. His movement was no better than mine, but for some reason he was able to effort-lessly do one lap after another and never look like he was working for it. That's how Sam surfs.

She's on a shortboard, but she's doing what I would expect on a longboard. Like a tap dancer, her feet move up and down the spine of the board. Her arms swing up and down, in smooth arcs like a swing dancer. There is no music that I'm aware of, but she's moving rhyth-mically.

"That's beautiful," I say.

"Sam or what she's doing?" Carmen asks.

I close my eyes for a moment, then find Sam again as she glides further away. I turn to Carmen.

She gets closer and drops her hand on my shoulder, the same way she held me at Mom's funeral. "Sam is making us look bad. We should at least try."

For the next hour we both attempt to pull a "Sam." Even when all I want to do is stand aloft, it's a fail. I'm so conscious of the impending fall that I wobble. I can't find peace.

Carmen is better at it. Sort of. She'll hit the guru stance for a few seconds, but her instinct kicks in and before you know it she's riding low again, trying to cut up the wave that doesn't have enough flesh to cut.

Sam, on the other hand, well... she's effortless and so at peace with her board and the water that in that moment I know what type of surfer I'll never be. She has an inner peace that I can't even imagine. I'm at constant war with my thoughts, my past, my present, and the faint outline of the future.

"A buck for your thoughts," Sam says as she slides next to me.

Just her voice releases some of the tension. "Isn't the saying 'penny for your thoughts?'" I ask.

She stares toward the shore. "This is L.A., son. We don't play small."

"I'm sorry," I say.

She glances at me. "You don't have to be."

"But I am. You've been nothing but good to me and I totally treated you like a random person."

"You did, but I'm not hurt by it. I'm sort of used to it."

I stare at her, unable to speak.

"I don't live with expectations. Each time I have, things have gone bad for me. It's a survival thing, maybe. But I have to get over hurt fast. Carmen and her parents accept me for who I am: decent, but flawed."

"What are you talking about?"

She puts up her hand. "Let's be honest. The reason people want to get near me is because I suppose they think there's something attractive about me."

Understatement of the year.

"But once they get to know me, some figure me for a weirdo. An odd pretty girl. I may be one card short of a full deck, but the cards I do have are the ones I wanted to have in the first place."

I grin. She turns her board to face me. "And this is why I love surfing. When I'm in the water, I don't need my medication. I don't even hear the voices that distract me from the quoteun-quote real world. I say inappropriate things sometimes. I react too quickly at times. I can be defiant. So some people get short with me. But hey, life goes on and I go on. I get my board and visit the ocean because she gets me. Or I go to the pool and swim lap after lap after lap until I drown out the noise. Do you know how Michael Phelps defeated his ADHD? Swimming and faith. I'm not quite there on the faith piece, but man, I have the swimming bit down.

"All I have is this mind," she taps her head, "this body," she taps her chest, "and this board," she lays her hand on her board.

We sway, staring at each other.

"You are amazing," I say.

"I am not. I'm just unwilling to give up or give in. Which is a choice you're facing, I think. We hardly ever get second chances," she says. "Your mom has given you a chance at being with her in an awesome cosmic-time-and-place-displacement type of way. I realize you had expectations and that they're not lining up the way you wanted them to. But it's still your mom who left you the letters. It's still your mom's world you've stepped into. And look at you. You are surfing."

"Poorly," I add.

"Adequately. Not poorly. You are surfing and you have knocked out nine sites and six challenges. Seven, once we visit Muscle Beach."

"I'm still sorry," I say and reach for her.

She stares at my hand. "No need to be," she says and places her hand in mine.

I need to tell her the rest. Somehow, I need to come clean.

———

THE MAN behind the counter is a man-beast. His arms are thicker than my thighs, and my freakin' thighs are big. I'm afraid to see what his legs look like. Wider than my entire upper body, I bet.

"Members only," he tells Carmen.

"Not even for just a few minutes?" Sam asks.

"Sorry." His bald head has half-inch veins that gyrate as he speaks. Even his eyebrows are thick and confronting.

"It's really important that he works out for just one set," Carmen says.

He looks me up and down. "He's in decent shape already. Arms are twigs, but he's better than most."

I self-consciously study my arms. I always thought I had decent guns.

"He's trying to complete a bucket list," Sam says.

The man turns to me. "You dying or something?"

I'm taken aback. "No, I'm fine... I think. It's more like a challenge list."

The man glares at Sam.

She opens her palm in front of my face. "Give me the list," she says.

I pull it out of my bag and hand it to her. She unfolds it in front of *The Incredible Hulk* and points to number twelve. "You see, right there. This was his mom's. She passed away a month ago. He's trying to relive her journey."

"That's heavy, dude," he says. "I dig that."

"She started a fifteen day surf trip down in San Diego. Venice was her ninth stop. So we're sure she was here eighteen years ago."

He eyes me, then back to the list. "Eighteen years ago?" he says.

He rubs his face then his shiny dome. "What was her name?" he asks himself.

"Olivia?" I say, momentarily certain we've hit a goldmine here.

"No," he says.

My heart drops.

"Sherry?" he asks himself. "Shannon?"

I dig through my memory. The excitement causes me to stumble over my memories. "Sharon?"

He slams the table. "That's her, Sharon! She was here with two other hotties."

"One of those hotties was my mom Olivia." That sounded very creepy but I don't care right now.

Sam and Carmen are watching me, eyes wide open. "Who's Sharon?" Carmen asks.

"One of my mom's friends. She came with Sharon and Tracey and Tracey's smelly-ass boyfriend."

The big man's once stoic demeanor is replaced with a smile now. Even his smile is muscular. "Oh man, Sharon. She was so cool. She's the reason I tried pot for the first time and got kicked out of a body-building competition the following weekend when I got randomly tested."

"Well that sucks," Carmen says.

"Nah, it's fine. She was worth it. Which was your mom? Olivia you said?"

"My height," Carmen says. "Puerto Rican, heavily tanned, and—"

His eyes pop open. "The surf goddess? Oh hell yeah! I didn't actually see her surf, but some of the guys were calling her that. We were trying to get her to pay for dinner because we were all calling her a pro surfer."

"Do you recall anything else? Was there another guy with her?" I ask.

"Guy? Guys you mean. She was like a celebrity."

I can feel the girls' stares. They must be wondering where I'm going with this. "No one in particular stood out?" I ask.

He shakes his head. "Sorry, kid. I do remember that night, partying on the beach with Sharon. We never kept in touch. What happened to her?" he asks.

"No idea. I don't even know who she is, or her last name. Anything would help."

"Crap, wish I knew. She was hot. Does that help?"

"No."

He straightens. "Let's go check out the cage." He calls another guy to watch the front desk.

All three of us exchange excited looks.

"Let's move it," Sam says and we all follow our new best friend.

We walk briskly to the cage. "Did my mom work out here?"

"They all did," he says. "Your mom did one arm lat pull-ups on a bench."

"That's a fairly specific workout to remember," Carmen says.

He shrugs. "What can I tell you. She had amazing glutes. Hard to forget." He eyes me. "Sorry kid. No offense."

That was awkward, but I won't let my pride cause my death. He can crush my spine with his nostril. I turn to the girls. "I'll do the same."

I grab a thirty-pound dumbbell. As I'm about to prepare on the bench, the man takes the dumbbell out of my hand like it's a popsicle and replaces it with a fifty-pound dumbbell. "Your mom used, thirty. You can do more."

"Right. Okay."

I grab the dumbbell and almost dislocate my shoulder. Left knee and left arm on the bench, right leg on the floor, while I reach down with my free hand and grab the dumbbell.

"Push out ten," he says.

I'm aiming for one, but don't bother telling him that. I take three deep breaths then grind one up.

"That's it, nine more."

I pull one after another. The beach air is invigorating. The eyeballs on me give me an extra push.

"Seven," he says, but I could've sworn I've done twenty. The amount of blood rushing to my lats has already stiffened the movement.

I eke one more out.

"Come on," he says.

"The list says 'work out,'" Sam says. "No pain, no gain."

I grind out one more. No more. I'm about to drop the weight.

"Don't even think about it," the man says. "Change happens once you hit the wall, but still find the will to break through. Find it in you and get it done."

Man's a freaking philosopher. I breathe deep and shred one more out. I drop the weight and rise, feeling powerful and accomplished. I put up my hand for a high five.

He stares at me. "What are you doing, kid? That was just your right. Let's get ten out of your left arm."

———

THE MAN-BEAST, whose name is Tadeh (which I believe means torture in some ancient Germanic language) doesn't let me end with just that one exercise. He makes me do an entire circuit of exercises. After thirty minutes of serious weightlifting, I'm fairly sure I won't be able to carry my surfboard back to the beach.

"I can't move," I say.

"The pump looks good on you, though," Sam says.

I glare at her.

"Just sayin'."

We walk up to a decent spot on the sand and drop our boards.

"Anything you want to share?" Carmen asks.

I glance at her, unsure what she means.

"You were asking if your mom had been with anyone in particular when she was at Muscle Beach."

"Oh that," I say.

"Yeah that."

They both sit on the sand surrounding me. Carmen's eyes are intense. Sam's are full of empathy.

So I tell them. Then I read them her very first letter I was given back in L.A.

"You'll finally get what you've asked about for years—details about your father," Sam repeats. "But details could be anything. They could be nebulous information. Or it can be FBI analysis like a name, address, and social security number."

"She's right," Carmen says. "Be careful, Cuz."

"She sent me off on this journey for a reason. So I want to give it a legitimate shot," I say. "And if nothing pans out, then nothing gained, but nothing lost." I like the sound of that line, I just wonder if I will really believe it if it all falls apart.

"We'll keep you honest," Carmen says.

I hope they do.

"Okay, we have one more job to do out here. Your mom's ashes. You want to do the honors?" Carmen asks me.

I turn to Sam. "Will you do this one?"

Her smile breaks out. "I'd love to."

"One request: surf like you did earlier. The smooth style."

"Done," she says, grabs the board, takes the vial from Carmen and runs off.

Carmen drops next to me then slides her arm though mine as we watch Sam paddle out. After a few minutes, she gets on a wave and glides around as smooth as an eagle. Carmen places her head on my shoulder.

Neither one of us say anything. We just watch the prettiest girl in town carve her way through melted butter and leave Mom's ashes in her trail.

———

BY NIGHTTIME we reach the Malibu RV Park. But this might as well be a resort. Everything we need is already here. From Wi-Fi to hot showers. I don't want to upset the girls, but this is the most ridiculous rendition of camping I've ever seen. When will they bring around lobster tails? I wonder if someone does camp-side pedicures?

After we set up my tent and eat a hearty meal, I tear open the ninth envelope, hoping whatever happened on the ninth day lifted her spirits.

July 18, 2000 — Day 9

It's 1:00 a.m. I almost forgot to write today. I guess it's really tomorrow already, but better late than never.

Still no sign of him. He knows our schedule. I gave it to him. But still nothing.

At one point I saw someone and thought it was him so I started killing it out there. Turned out it was some other guy. But I surfed well at least. Got a lot of attention afterwards. Some guy claimed to be a sponsor. Had a card and everything. But Sharon said he was checking out my ass when I wasn't looking. So who knows what he really wants...

Anyway...

By afternoon, me and the girls sweet-talked our way into working out on Muscle Beach. One more off the list. We were totally flirting with the bodybuilders that were there. Huge, but honestly not attractive at all.

So I smoked pot, because who cares at this point. I smoked

223

more than I've ever smoked. Then we tried to surf. I was so stoned that the entire time out there, I just floated, straddled to my board. Not sure what happened, but I started shivering. Not because I was cold but because I was scared. I was sure a shark was watching me. Tracey helped me out of the water. Once I was on sand, I threw up. Like everything and all over the place.

You'd think I learned my lesson. Nope, at night, I smoked more. Later on, some of the guys got us beer. A lot of beers. So I was partially stoned and completely wasted. I shouldn't have because it'll screw up my surfing for a couple of days. The other problem is that I lose myself.

I messed around with some dude on the beach. I can't remember most of it. I know we made out. And I know I passed out. I hope that's all I did, because I'm disgusted with myself. Maybe that's why I waited to write this... I hate the choices I've made. I hate the choices I'm still making.

I want this trip to be over.

O.

I slowly put away the letter. I don't know if I should be angry or hurt or sad for her. What if she did more than just kiss that guy on the beach? Here it is again—a possible scenario where she slept with some random guy and little Shep was conceived.

Does she really know who my father was? Can she know?

She was passed out, unable to defend herself.

I run my hands through my hair and imagine my mom helpless, drunk, and vulnerable. I cover my face, finally understanding the reason behind her warnings and advice back home. Her words weren't just coming form her spiritual beliefs. They were coming from personal experience and hurt.

If this is the lesson you wanted me to learn, we can stop now, Mom. I agree with you—I want this trip to be over, too.

PART FIVE

"Surfing's one of the few sports that you look ahead
to see what's behind."
~Laird Hamilton

THIRTY-EIGHT
DAY 10 - SHEP

I WAKE up early and decide to read the letter first. I know this isn't
how I've done it so far, and yes, I am superstitious, but I want to know
what happened on the tenth day.

I stare at the envelope and build up the courage I need.

July 18, 2000 — Day 10

My life has become a cruel joke.

When we arrived at Surfline, who do I see? Quick.

*I tried to avoid him, but he found me in the line up. He was
explaining what happened. And it all sounds real and his eyes
are so honest. It's obvious he's not lying, but I gave him the
cold shoulder anyway, because I can't face him. I'm so embarrassed and disgusted with myself. If I had held off. If I had
remained strong... if!*

In the afternoon he found me again, tried cracking jokes, but how can I laugh when all I want to do is cry? I want to die. I should've trusted my instincts and waited and believed he'd come back. But I didn't because I'm an idiot, always making mistakes at the worst time in the worst way.

He asked me if what we had a few days ago meant nothing. I didn't answer because words would've made me cry. He left without saying goodbye.

I've been crying for the last hour straight. I drank so much I threw up for nearly an hour. I can't even sleep in the van because random people are using our van for quickies. I had to wait till now to get back in there and write.

I'm disgusted with my friends, with my life, with what the future holds.

Sometimes I wish the ocean would take me and finish it off. Once and for all.

O.

Man, she went off the hinges. I'm a bit stunned. Now what? It must all come together again. Right?

Poor Mom. I can't imagine the turmoil she must've gone through just to share these details with me. She said she's not proud of her past, so she must've known there was a risk I'd judge her. But she still went for it. Why?

"Good morning, cowboy," Sam says.

I hadn't even heard the door of the camper opening.

"Hey," I say as I quickly shove the letter back in the envelope.

"Don't worry, I can't read that fast," she says. "Have you made coffee yet?"

"On the stove."

She pours a cup, loads it with sugar, then sips it as she looks toward the ocean.

"Surf's looking good."

"You think it'll be crowded?"

"A bit. But it's the weekday, so it should be better."

The door slams open. Carmen stumbles out, her hair a mess of seismic proportions. "Surf report is looking good. Let's get the hell out of here."

I can always count on the surf.

OUR DESTINATION ISN'T WALKING distance so we drive down to Surfrider in Malibu. As we prepare our boards on the sand, I see why Carmen was so eager to get here. The waves are clean and solid. Powerful, but not in a messy way. They are organized and orchestrated.

"This place will either go down as your favorite day, or your worst," Carmen says.

"No shades in between?" I throw out.

"No, because when the waves are good like these, you will catch so many that you'll forever want to have it again. But when they're this good, the kooks come out in droves. They'll screw up the good waves by getting in the way."

"Are you trying to tell me not to get in the way?" I ask.

"Yes," she says then glances at me. "Meaning don't be a kook. You can get in my way or Sam's. But don't mess it up for the others."

Sam raises her hand. "For the record, I'd like it if he didn't get in my way either."

THE FIRST HOUR WAS FANTASTIC. Since then, it's been frustrating. Too many people.

"Did everyone call in sick or something?" I yell.

"Someone get me a doctor," another guy bobbing in the water calls out. "I'm suffering from where's-my-share-of-the-waves syndrome."

We all laugh, but beneath the laughter there's tension. We all want to be in position to get the next wave. With so many people, it's never easy.

"One more and I'm getting out," Carmen says.

We've barely agreed when she grabs a wave and she scorches a path. We see another wave approaching. It may break for me.

"Paddle, paddle, paddle!" Sam yells.

I do. A two-handed scoop and throw like I've seen Carmen do.

I'm on the wave's shoulder. I hop to my feet. Like jumping on a speeding train, the energy of this combustible flow causes me to skid down its face. I pick up speed, going right.

I hear it first, then I glance at it. The peak of the wave, like an awakening monster, is growing above me quickly. At first I think I'm getting sucked into the vortex, but the living cave behind me is accelerating.

I lower myself, but it's more out of fear because this one's huge. A persistent, ever-changing roar follows me and overtakes everything. Suddenly, I'm inside a barrel.

In an instant, I'm back in the zone.

Hyper-aware.

There. Completely.

I'm aware of the changing landscape beneath me. I'm aware of the surfers in the water. I'm just aware. And then, mixed in the cacophony of noise generated from the rolling ocean, I hear a voice. Like a note being held—no, a melody. A tune that is familiar yet unreachable.

I can hear it. I know it.

But where have I heard it before?

In a blink, the world turns upside down and all that was in front of me is immediately replaced with white bubbles, water, and my flailing arms and legs.

My shoulder scrapes against the rough sandy bottom.

I pop my head out and take a deep breath. The wave continues on its journey, unaware and unconcerned that its passenger is no longer graced by her power.

I lost my focus at the worst time.

I grab my board, climb on it, then catch a small breaker and belly ride it to the sand. I have to ask the girls if they've experienced this before.

I need to catch another good one before the day is over. Listen more carefully. I hope the crowd thins soon so I can go back out. As I grab my board, my shoulder complains. It feels bruised. So much for this being a great surf day.

The girls are already rummaging through the cooler. I open my wetsuit and roll it down to my hips. Turns out this is the best way to avoid rashes.

"I caught a barrel," I say as I collapse on the sand.

"What? When?" Carmen asks.

"Was it the last wave I saw you ride?" Sam asks.

"Yup." They both high-five me. "It was inexplicably amazing, until something happened."

They both lean in.

"I heard a sound, like a melody."

"In the water?" Carmen asks, her brows furrowed.

"Yeah, when I was inside the barrel, I heard a weird orchestra of sounds."

"Like the wind rattling chandeliers?" Sam asks.

My eyes penetrate hers. "Sort of, yeah. Have you heard it?"

She shakes her head. "No, not that exactly, but I've heard others describe it that way. I've also heard some call it violins, or thunder. My favorite though is when one surfer earlier this summer called it a chorus of angels."

My heartbeat is so loud, I'm sure they can hear the hammering in my chest.

"My mom called it a voice," I say. "Do you think this is what she was referring to?"

"It's possible," Carmen says. "Each surfer experiences the ride differently. For me, it's so fast in the barrel that what I hear is a high pitched roar."

"On her list of challenges she had one about hearing God's whisper. What if this is what she meant?"

"Cool," Carmen says.

LESS THAN AN HOUR LATER, I grab the tenth vial, with hopes to release it inside a barrel. We've barely been in for fifteen minutes when Carmen paddles out of the water, Sam next to her. Something's wrong. I ride the waves back to the sand and join Sam who is sitting in front of Carmen.

"What happened?" I ask.

"She twisted her ankle. Took a tumble and hit the ground."

"Do you need to go to the hospital?" I ask.

"No, I'll be fine. I just need to ice it."

From the RV I bring her an ice pack. Sam wraps it around Carmen's ankle.

"Anything I can do for you?" I ask.

"Yes, give me the video camera and then surf. I'll video tape Sam's ass. And if I remember, I'll tape yours too." She offers me a nasty smile.

I freeze. Is she referring to the video I took a few days ago? "What are you talking about?" I ask. I had not been filming Sam's ass. Why would she say that?

"Do you want to watch it with us?" Carmen asks. "We had a grand old time watching the whole thing last night."

"You are a very gifted cinematographer," Sam throws out.

My ears catch fire. Molten lava slithers in my lungs. The once loud beach is suddenly silent. Had I really done that?

"You're just jealous," Sam's voice breaks through.

I can't look at her. I can't make eye contact. This is embarrassing. They both must think I'm a pervert.

"But if you seriously plan to tape my ass," Sam says, "then I should get out of the wetsuit."

———

AFTER A COUPLE of hours of surfing, I grudgingly release Mom's ashes when it becomes obvious a barrel is not in my cards. We join Carmen on the sand. She shows us that she can rotate her ankle, in her own way trying to make us feel like she'll be okay.

I glance at the sun. In an hour or so, it'll sink into the ocean. As much as a sunset would be pretty to witness, it's time we head back to the RV camp.

"We should head back," I say.

"Why don't we eat here, on the beach," Sam says.

I scan the area. It's fine, I suppose, but it doesn't seem very convenient. "Wouldn't it be better if we went back, showered, wrapped up Carmen's ankle and ate in peace?"

Carmen's studying Sam's face. "Are you thinking what I think you're thinking?"

Sam grins. "I'm thinking seven."

"Seven what?" I ask.

Carmen turns to me. "Challenge number seven. Moonlit surfing."

"No way. I am *not* doing that."

"Why? It's amazing," Sam says.

"How the hell do we see where we're going?"

"The wave will tell us and the moon will illuminate plenty. We have a full moon."

"It is an exhilarating experience," Carmen says. "Visibility is rough, but when the fog rolls in and the swells move you up and down without warning, you learn to respect your senses."

"You're doing a horrible job of selling this," I say.

"You will not regret it," Sam says.

Her eyes are bright. Her eyebrows sad, but hopeful. Her mouth parted in such a perfect way, that all I can say is what must be said.

"Okay, fine."

THIRTY-NINE

DAY 10 - SHEP

I DON'T HAVE to test the water to know that it's freezing. The freakin' sand is cold. My spine is already spasming, and my toes are curling in on their own. But when Sam helps me zip up the wetsuit, my everything begins to thaw. I return the favor.

"Are you sure you can't join us?" Sam asks Carmen. "The swelling is all but gone."

I don't know what these two are seeing that I don't. I never saw any swelling. But I leave it alone. Don't want to be accused of mansplaining.

"I don't want to chance it." Carmen turns on a strobing flashlight tower and places it on the beach blanket next to her chair. She will serve as our beacon. "Go. Be gone!" she commands.

I study Sam. She looks into my eyes, smiles, then punches my shoulder. "This is going to be so epic, you'll thank me forever."

"If I survive."

"Oh, you'll be fine." She grabs her board and I grab mine. We walk up to the water line. The first ten or so yards are still visible because of the beach-side street lights, but beyond that it's pitch black. As if the rest of the world has been painted black. When the wave splashes on my feet, my toes curl again.

"Oh crap! This is cold."

"Grow a pair, will you?"

"I'm afraid I may lose a pair."

She laughs then shoulder bumps me.

"I can't see anything," I say through rattling teeth.

"Sure you can." She leans in and points to nothing. "Don't you see the moon's reflection? Slivers of light."

At first I see nothing, then for an instant something lights up. "Was that it?"

"That's a wave, getting lit up. That's what we'll look for, too. Of course, out there, we only have a second to react. But we'll deal with that once we're in."

This is madness. I glare at her. How is it that she's not cold? How come she can take this and I'm convinced I'm about to die?

"Oh and I have this." She points to something she's wrapped to her bicep. When she presses it, it glows. "Battery life sucks, but I will use it when we split apart so that you can find me."

"Cool," I say as I try to control my chattering teeth, because I don't want to look like a complete wuss.

"The only way to do this is to just do it," she says.

Her words have an ominous resemblance to Mom's one-liners. "Right," I say, but before I can ask a question, she runs.

So I chase after her. I can't lose her already. As I give chase, I hear Carmen cheer us on. A few steps in and we both slide onto our boards and paddle out. I'm shivering. Maybe it's the cold water, but mostly the utter and palpable fear I'm experiencing.

"You okay?" she asks.

I glance at her. Even though we're getting further away from the shore, I can still see her. The neon green lines on her wetsuit don't need much light to reflect.

"I'm about to pee myself," I reply.

"Your suit, your board. Your business."

Without notice, a wave is in front of us. She goes above it, but since I'm just slightly behind her pace, I consider if I should duck dive, turtle roll, or—

It doesn't matter what I want. The wave crashes into me and throws me off. Panic sets in as I pull out of the water. Where is she?

"Sam!" I yell. "Turn on the light."

"I'm right here, you doofus."

She's literally a foot to my right. "Sorry, I thought I lost you."

"You won't lose me." She gives me a hand and helps me back on the board. I hold her helping hand longer than necessary.

We paddle out further until she determines we're far enough. We sit on our boards and turn to the shore.

"Can you see her strobe light?" she asks.

"I think so." I point at what looks like a blinking star.

"That's it."

"We're so far out."

"You just think so because you're scared."

"I'm not scared," I say.

She spins to me. "You were just talking about peeing on yourself."

"I'm way beyond the pee stage. I'm about to throw up."

She snorts. "Dork," she says. "I went well past the swell line to make sure we were all good. When we catch a wave, we come back here. You see how Carmen's light is in direct line with the street lamps?"

I nod. Perfect location in fact. You'd almost think they know what they're doing.

"Good. If for some reason you don't see my light, that's another way you'll find our spot again." She places a hand on my shoulder. "Ready?"

"Hell no. But what other choice do I have?"

"None. Let's roll."

I can see better than I thought. Don't get me wrong. The visibility is horrible. I assumed it would be like swimming in a zero-light room. But I can see lines. And I can see her for the most part.

"Here we go," she says and immediately after, she grabs a wave and disappears.

This must mean there's a swell, because waves come in batches. I scan for her, but she's hard to see. Instead I feel for the wave.

I can do this, I think and immediately after, a small, but respectful wave forms by me. I paddle quickly and as if by pure instinct, I catch the wave. I'm on my feet immediately.

I don't do anything fancy. I just ride the wave, adjusting the board to continually ride the face of the wave.

All thoughts vanish.

I hear the sweet sound of a board splashing smoothly on the surface of the wave. I pick up speed. No noise of other people. No sound of beach dwellers yelling and playing. Just me and the board and the wave. And my thrumming heartbeat. Yes, fear is playing a role, but in some bizarre way, it's adding to the sensory overload I'm feeling.

The wave sputters out and I drop in the water gracefully. I'm back on the board and paddling to our starting point. I glance toward the shore and panic.

I don't see the lights. Where the hell are they? I search the water for Sam's light, but nothing.

Don't panic, just keep swimming.

"Sam!" I yell out, unable to keep calm.

"Here," I hear a very faint voice.

Thank God. She's near.

"Marco," she yells.

"Polo?" I reply.

After a few rounds, I find her.

"I can't believe that worked," I say.

"I can't either. We're awesome."

My cheeks hurt. I must be smiling ear to ear, but the fear and exhilaration are jumbling up all my emotions. "That was fairly awesome."

"I saw you blow by. With the metallic shine of your gray wetsuit, you totally looked like the Silver Surfer. With hair, of course."

I freeze. Had I told her about the nickname? I don't think so. "That's what my mom used to call me. Her Silver Surfer."

"You're kidding." Silence. "It's like she knew what you could become."

That's because she had seen my potential from that first time, but Sam doesn't know that part of my history. She doesn't know a lot about me. But I don't have the confidence to tell her and Carmen. Not yet.

"Again," I say.

"You don't have to ask twice," she says and paddles. I follow.

WE'VE BEEN OUT HERE a good forty minutes. At least that's what Sam claims. Neither one of us has a watch so I'm not sure how she knows.

"The stars," she claims.

She's gifted in the art of lying.

"A fog layer is coming through," she says. "Will be a bit harder on the visibility."

"Crap. Maybe one more run?"

"Sure. Let's wait for a good set."

We float next to each other, the tips of our boards just poking out.

"This is nice," I say.

She glances at me then pulls herself right next to me.

"I never, in a million years, would've thought I could do this," I say and I mean it, because this is so outside of anything I could've thought was possible. "Thank you, Sam."

"Deflowering you has been my pleasure," she says, her voice low. Our boards are practically on top of each other we are so close now. "In fact—"

But she doesn't finish because something causes our boards to move vigorously.

My breath catches. "Was that a wave?" I ask.

"No," she says, very gingerly. She turns on her arm light and scans around us.

My heart drops to the bottom of the ocean. "What is it?"

She doesn't say anything. She's still scanning the water, then turns to me.

"Let's pull up our feet and head back to shore."

"What the hell was it?" I ask, as I attempt to do what she recommended, but I am clear about two things: I am downright petrified and my voice has gone up five octaves.

"Not sure, but it feels sharky."

A sound escapes my throat. "What does that even mean?"

"Like we're being watched."

A shark leaps out of the water no more than five feet away.

I yell, like a howling monkey in heat.

It explodes out again, on our other side.

I'm saying things.

Indistinguishable words.

I'm trying to paddle, but my arms are flailing, because I am both trying to paddle to shore and grab Sam's board to save her.

She's saying something, but all sounds are jumbled.

I need to get us to safety.

"It's okay," she yells.

What is she saying? Is she asking me to save myself? Is she insane? "We can make it," I yell back. "Don't give up. We just have to go. Now!"

"They're dolphins," she says. "Not sharks. They're dolphins."

I stare at her. I'm sure my mouth is open. My face is wet, my eyes are stinging. I'm not sure if it's from tears or the water.

She reaches me, grabs my arm, and pulls me closer. She places her hands around my face.

"Are you okay?"

I don't say anything. I should be trembling, vomiting because of the fear, but the proximity to her beautiful face and parted lips eradicates every thought and emotion.

"Sorry, dude," she says.

Golden eyes stare into mine. Her lips inches from mine. All I can think of is the taste of her mouth.

"I should've warned you," she adds. "Are you okay...?" she begins to say, but trails off.

Our eyes are locked, her lips tremble.

A momentary, unspoken agreement and our lips find warmth.

I hear the sound of our boards colliding and scraping, the sounds of the ocean water splashing around us. But most importantly I taste her delicate lips as they merge into mine.

Her lips are soft, her mouth, accepting and warm. The taste of salt water has never been more sweet, more potent than it is right now.

I grab her face, while her fingers travel into my hair. We're tasting each other, exploring the curves of our lips, and the texture of our skins, when her hands drop to my chest and she gently nudges, causing our lips to part.

I stare at her face. She's breathing heavily, her eyes soft. "We can't do this," she says. "This isn't right."

I don't know what she's talking about. "No, this is very right," I say. "That was beyond perfect. This is great—"

"Shep," she says and the sound of sadness is laced in the way she says my name. "I can't go down this path when you hold back so much."

"What are you talking about?"

"Something's been eating you up, but I don't know what. I'm still waiting for you to show me who you really are."

I can't speak.

"I want to see where this'll go. I do. But if this is real, then you need to be real with me. I hope you're close to trusting me. But you're not there yet."

I say nothing.

She lays her hand on my cheek. "Do you understand me?" Her touch should be cold. Instead it sears me. "I like my simple life. That is why I choose to be on my own," she says. "I need real, raw, and honest. I don't do well with half-truths and incomplete stories. That's not how I roll."

I nod. But don't offer more.

"Let's head back."

As she pulls away, I hold her by her arm. She lays her warm eyes on mine.

"I want to tell you," I say. "I just don't know how."

She smiles. "My gut instinct? I don't think you're ready. I'll be here whenever you are."

For how long, I wonder. *And will you understand once I tell you?*

I recall Mom's words to me in her letter that started this trip.

You asked me if I believed you. Of course. My question all along was, do you believe you?

We paddle toward the shore. Carmen's beacon guides us.

"Let's not mention anything about the whole kissing thing to Carmen," she says.

Although I had zero intentions of saying anything to her, because I don't want her to get mad at me, I can't help wonder why Sam wants silence. I thought girls talk about everything.

"Sure," I say between strokes. "Can I ask why?"

"Because she'll hurt you if you break my heart."

I absorb her words.

"You wouldn't do that to me, would you?"

I pause longer than I want. "N-no," I stammer.

She slows down, her eyes locked on mine. "I don't want to be used. You wouldn't play with me, right?"

"Never," I say without hesitation. I would not hurt her on purpose.

"Good," she says and offers her beautiful smile.

"You were right," I say. "Today *was* epic."

She takes my hand and squeezes it. "To more epic days," she says. She releases my hand and paddles away. We both use our boards like boogie boards near the end and glide our way to the sand.

"How was it?" Carmen asks when we approach her.

"Amazing," I say. "The best thing that's ever happened to me."

I force myself to keep my eyes off of Sam, but Carmen's eyes travel to her.

"We had another twofer," she says, quick to not let Carmen get a whiff of anything.

"How so?" she asks.

"Moonlit surfing and survive a shark attack."

Carmen springs to her feet. "What the hell are you talking about? Are you okay?"

"Oh yeah, we're great. Turns out they were dolphins. But let me tell you, the way gunslinger here reacted, he totally experienced the shark attack thing."

"The way I reacted?" I interrupt. "I was a badass. I even tried to save you."

"Yes. Between tears and howls you did try," she says, smiling ear to ear. "Anyway, I think under the circumstances, we should get a check mark next to that one, too."

We both look at Carmen.

"The Russian judge appears to be deliberating," Sam says.

She nods. "Da. That verks for me. Let's head back. We have an early start tomorrow," she says.

I grab the rest of our possessions and as we head to the RV something dawns on me. Carmen isn't limping. I mean not at all.

"How's the ankle?" I ask.

Instantly, she hobbles a bit. "Better," she says, then glances over her shoulder. We hold each other's gaze for a couple of moments.

She knows. And so do I.

FORTY

DAY 11 - SAMANTHA

I CAN FEEL Carmen's mind-reading powers trained on my thoughts. She's going to break me, of this, I'm sure. And she's not even awake yet!

I quietly get out of bed and enter the bathroom. I spend more time than typical for me. I tell myself it's not because I want to look any different for Shep. I am who I am and if he likes me it's for the person that he's known over these past two weeks. I will not take this any deeper until he tells me why there's so much hurt in his eyes. It's not just the passing of his mother. He could've said that last night. He didn't. He went silent instead. I have to be smart.

Wow, that almost sounds convincing.

I ruffle my hair a bit so that it doesn't look like I paid it much attention. I breathe into my palm, like I see people do on T.V. I don't know what you're supposed to smell, but I won't take any chances. In the event Shep suddenly finds his voice and decides to speak, I want my breath to be fresh and perfect. I check my teeth by producing an exaggerated smile. I run my fingers through my hair and shake the strands around.

"Perfect," I say, as I open the door.

"Ah!" I yelp when I find Carmen standing in front of the door.

"What's perfect?" she asks.

"The day. The... surf and weather."

She frowns. "It's windy and cold with the possibility of rain."

"Right." I don't know what to say. "He'll get to experience surfing in the rain which is perfect."

She shrugs. "Whatever."

I squeeze out of the bathroom as she enters then closes the door. I dig through my clean swimwear when I hear her say something.

"What was that?" I ask.

"You used my gargle? Since when do you gargle?"

Cold sweat breaks out. I have to think. Think. Think!

"It's all that coffee we've been drinking. My mouth feels dry or something."

I cover my face. She'll know.

"Yeah, we've been overdoing the coffee. It's Shep's fault. His veins must stream with caffeine."

I drop on the bed. Why am I not telling her? Why not come clean? I sit up, my elbows on my knees, my fingers steepled in front of my face.

I'm not telling her because I don't want to hear what she'll say. Even if she denies it, I know how she really feels. I'm not right for her cousin. I'm not the right type for him. She loves me. But not that much. She knows who I really am. How broken and flawed I am. She claims she loves me because of those reasons. But does she love me enough?

"GOOD MORNING," I say, with all the nonchalance I can muster.

"Hey," he says.

Why does his voice sound so perfect now? What happened to me?

Carmen hops out of the RV. "The weather sucks," she declares. "But we can't control what we can't control."

"So what does that mean?" he asks.

"It means we eat, drive down to Zuma Beach, grab our boards and do the best we can before the twelve o'clock blackball. They're very strict about giving the beach to non-surfers in the afternoon."

"Under normal circumstances, Zuma is awesome," I say. "It's wide, a better crowd than Venice, and sometimes you'll see a movie being shot or a wedding being held."

"How's the surf?" he asks.

"Can be great," Carmen says. "Clear water most of the time, hollow waves which make for great barrels. But the beach can get crowded so..."

"Then grab your bacon and coffee while I load up the camper."

WE PARK on Pacific Coast Highway and grab our gear. I didn't want to put on the wetsuit today, but the air is cold and windy, which means the water will be frigid.

"How's your ankle?" Shep asks Carmen.

"Good as new," she says.

"You had a miraculous recovery," Shep says.

Now that he said it, I realize he's sort of right. "Yeah, what's up with that?"

She shrugs. "Don't know, but I won't complain."

I'm about to question her more when the wind gets aggressive.

"This sucks," Carmen says as she turns her face to protect her eyes from the blowing sand.

"Let's get in the water," I say. "No sand there."

So we do, and a few minutes later when we're in the choppy waters, we're no longer getting sprayed by sand. Now it's the salty water that's pelting us.

FORTY-ONE
DAY 11 - SHEP

I'M NOT good enough to surf in these conditions. The winds and the unpredictable waves have made it nearly impossible for me to do anything decent. But I keep at it.

I glance over at Sam, who's been keeping her distance from me. She takes a wave and disappears below the wave. Carmen catches a nasty-looking wave and rides it for a few seconds before she gets sideswiped.

Do I dare tell them? I sigh. What holds me back is shame.

The wind sprays me with foam. Even nature is spitting at my face!

"Good set coming," some surfer calls out to another.

I glance and for just a moment the water rides me high, giving me a perspective of what's about to come. I can count six maybe seven coming down. If I position myself just right, I may be able to catch a good one.

I paddle next to the others and try to position myself.

The first two come and a bunch of surfers attempt to catch them. A few do. Some don't.

On the next one, Sam, who has sneaked herself back in the

lineup, grabs it, holds on to the wave for dear life and it looks like she rocks it.

A wave appears behind me, ramming through. It's going to peak just ahead of me. I paddle, with both hands sinking and pulling, sinking and pulling. I'm in a good spot, a bit more and—I'm in it!

I slide to my feet and immediately see the drop. A six or eight foot slide greets me. The board and my front feet disconnect momentarily. We hit the water, jarring my skull. I compensate my body position, transferring weight until I have the surf steadily under foot.

I skid the rest of the wave and pull right. The wave is barreling. It's going to be a good one.

I'm wrong, it's a beauty.

I dip low and with my hand, I apply the brakes in the water, adjusting my proximity to the wave. The waterfall above me breaks and I'm inside the barrel.

The blood that streams through my veins cools momentarily. I listen, focusing on what I hear. Like wind chimes and voices and a breathy howl. It's amazing. Beautiful.

The water beneath me froths violently, lifting and gyrating me, throwing me off balance. I fall and hit the board. I'm under.

I'm kept down for a bit, but I don't have the fear I used to have. I hold my breath, wait it out, then paddle up.

I grab my board and paddle back to the lineup.

"Well done. That looked gnarly, dude," another guy says.

"Thanks."

"You got pitted, brah. Wappah, wappah, wappah. But you did well. Props my man."

I have no idea what he just said. "Thanks, dude."

"Word up. Catch ya laters."

He rolls off and positions himself for a new set. Well that guy seemed decent.

A few minutes later, I witness a mass exodus. The surfers are heading back to the shore. It must be surfer-segregation time.

WE PACK our things and head out to Leo Carillo State Park. Another great campground. We're lucky we have a reservation because this place is packed, which reminds me of how helpful Aunt Rosie was in setting up this whole thing. Her daily check-in texts, a reminder that I have a new family.

I often think about them and how much they know. Is it possible that Mom had told them more details near the end? I hope so, because so far the details are sparse and I fear that with four letters to go, there won't be enough.

I park the RV and after I shut off the engine, I consider reading today's letter, but decide to leave it for later. I'm not ready to feel more disappointment.

I join the girls outside, who are visibly cold.

"The clouds are thin, but it feels like rain is on its way," Carmen says.

Sam has wrapped her hands around her arms. "It smells like rain."

"So that's it?" I ask. "We give up and cry ourselves to sleep? Or do we go out there and chance it?"

Carmen and Sam stare at each other and at the same time say, "Longboards."

Even with the weather the way it is, the breaks are awesome— slow rolling and nicely shaped. I finish waxing my mom's longboard and wonder if I'll be able to do the type of moves Sam and my mom did. We have all opted for longboards as our weapon of choice.

"Remember," Carmen says, "offer waves to others. Show respect and it'll be reciprocated."

"Roger, captain."

As they run into the water, my phone rings. It's Uncle José. I quickly answer it because he wouldn't be calling unless it's important.

"Hi José, is everything okay?"

There's a pause. "Well, not sure, to be honest. The district attorney, the same guy I spoke to a couple of months ago, says he needs to speak to you."

My heart lodges itself in my throat. "Did he say why?"

Another pause. "Not exactly. He just said it's urgent."

"Okay," I whisper.

"Listen, I don't know what he wants, but it's really important that you don't call him without an attorney."

My heart skips a beat.

"Your mom suspected you knew more than you shared. Which means we need to be careful. So give me a day or two to get us a good attorney. I'm on it."

We hang up and for a moment I forget where I am and what I'm supposed to be doing. I breathe in, then exhale out.

D.A. Donner is suspecting something, or someone has spoken. With an attorney or not, this is not good. I have to think this out, plan what I'll say and how I'll say it. If he has anything substantial, just like he told my uncle when he met with him just before Mom passed away, he'll force me back there for a testimony. If he knew anything, he wouldn't be asking for a discussion. He would yank my butt back in a hurry. Does he know? Did she say something? I shouldn't be surprised. Why she kept quiet was never clear to me. I guess everyone has a breaking point.

I watch the girls. They're in the lineup, completely stress-free. I need to think. I need to have a clear mind. So I grab my board and run in and for the first time in many years, I pray for answers.

The moment my feet hit the water, all my joints seize up. It's so cold, I think ice will form on my toes. But when the girls stepped in, they didn't even flinch. It's time I woman up.

I join the lineup where there's a good mix of people from our age all the way to forty-somethings. The waves are plentiful and unlike other spots, I don't sense the tension. Carmen and Sam paddle next to me.

"The surfers here are more relaxed," I say, as we bob, waiting for the next set.

"Exactly what I was talking about," Sam says. "When the wave wranglers are all on the same page, the experience is always great."

"It's like cliques," Carmen says. "Sometimes the right people are there to set the tone. Before you know it, everyone is cool, congratulating each other, celebrating. Then at night, they're all sharing joints and a laugh."

I turn to her. "What about—?" I start to ask but both of them take off on a wave I had not been paying attention to.

Carmen is doing a decent job of pretending to be a calm, free spirit, but she's at best a good imitator. Sam is a natural.

Mom would've liked her.

I miss her. All these days, all these experiences, what I would've given to share it with her. If only we had done this together. Then I remember her words to me in her letter: *I will always be there with you. And if you listen—really listen—I promise to whisper to you once in a while.*

Whisper.

I scan around, looking for the next wave. As if conjured by my mere thoughts, one forms yards away from me. I paddle, slide in, and catch the wave.

It breaks with a calm roll. No pressure, no rush. It's just carrying me.

I breathe deep and rise out of the low crouch pose I've been using on the shorter board. I study the wave and wonder when I can try to walk the board.

Speak to me, I think, hoping on a crazy hope that she'll actually tell me, but her voice does not come.

I need your advice, Mom.

I wait for the supernatural, but all I hear is my own voice.

So I decide to feel it and go with instincts. A constant velocity, I decide, is what I need to achieve in order to take a few steps. So I negotiate with the wave, feel it for a couple of seconds, and then I do a four step shuffle. Left forward, right forward, then reverse the pattern back to the starting point.

The board does not wobble, or complain.

I lower my body slightly to pick up speed, adjust to the breaking wave, then prepare again.

Walk the plank, I think and then do. Three steps and my left foot is almost at the nose of the board. I immediately walk it back and get back to starting position.

I almost did a hang five. My toes were inches away.

The wave loses its energy so I drop down then turn the board back toward the lineup. I am close to a breakthrough. I can feel it.

"I SAW YOU, DUDE," Sam says. "You totally did a hang five and even a hang seven."

"Yeah, not my best moment," I say, as we float way past the lineup. "I got greedy, tried to do a hang ten."

"Half your second foot and off you went. But, you're doing it. You really are."

"Had the best teacher," I say. I study her, focus on her lips, then her eyes. I glide toward her, and her eyes pop open—wide open.

"Don't. Carmen will see," she says and at that, the rain showers down on us.

"What the—?" I look up, hardly able to believe it.

"Ahh," she says. "A beautiful summer shower—L.A. style."

I attempt to head to shore, but she holds me back. "Don't leave, this is awesome. Experience it."

So I let go, close my eyes, and tip my face to the sky.

Thousands of baby kisses tap my face. I open my mouth, tasting the rain. The sound of splashing water in the ocean is like a symphony of a million chandeliers and harps and—that's when I hear it.

A voice, thin and faint, yet real. I want to open my eyes, to make sure it's not Sam, but I don't have to. That's not her voice.

I focus in on the voice. The water comes down harder, the sounds crash and compound into each other, producing a music unlike any orchestra has ever created. And the voice, for just an instant whispers, *now*.

I pop open my eyes and swivel around. Sam has her eyes closed, facing the sky, her arms wide open. Like a worshiper in church, she is showing humility. She is showing her frailty and insignificance in this beautiful display of creation.

She opens her eyes. They are red, blood shot. Her face slack.

I paddle toward her. "Are you crying?" I ask.

She nods.

"Why, Sam? What's wrong?"

She shrugs. "I don't know," she says as she wipes at her face. "Sometimes, a strong emotion rolls through me. And all I can do is cry. But it's not a sad cry. It's a good cry."

I think I understand.

I open my arms and she glides into them. "Are we going to get in trouble?" I ask.

"No," she says into my chest. "This is God's doing."

I hold her tight as the rain baptizes us, and the ice-cold ocean turns warm.

FORTY-TWO
DAY 11 - SAMANTHA

THE THREE OF us are on the shore, our boards dug at an angle into the sand like makeshift canopies to protect us from the downpour. The rain transforms into barely a drizzle, but the movement of the water has become very unpredictable. It was as good a time as any to take a break.

We're huddled around our portable mini-fire pit when we first feel them behind us, then hear them.

"Carmen. Sam. Is that you?"

I know that voice. I almost don't want to turn, but Carmen does.

"Kevin?" she asks then rises. "What are you guys doing here?"

I remain seated. I don't have to say hello to her ex. But I can feel Shep's eyes on me, so I lean in and whisper, "Her ex."

He says nothing. He just rises and stands like a sentinel next to Carmen. So I decide to join him, since it's really odd for me to be just sitting there, alone, like a doofus.

Kevin's hair is a bit longer now. His typical cropped hair has a near-surfer look to it. Has he picked up a few shades of color? Is he trying to make himself more desirable to Carmen?

"We were up north driving down when we saw your RV."

Carmen introduces Shep to the three amigos. That's what they call themselves. I don't know why. All of them barely passed Spanish 1. They are the best buds, the 'bros' from the football team.

"Good to finally meet you," Kevin says and they slam their palms together. The others exchange bro hugs with Shep. What is that, anyway? Just hug. What's this half-shake, pull in, awkward hug business?

"Coach said you'll scrimmage with us next week."

"Yeah, looking forward to joining the team."

"Hope coach can get you into the rotation," Kevin says. Something exchanges between Shep and Kevin. Kevin is implying that Shap's not good enough. What a tool. He knows Shep's one of the best seniors in the nation.

"Dude, I saw the video from the Dodgers' game," Jeremy, the sidekick says. "That was cool. So what are you guys up to?"

"We've been on a surf trip," Carmen says. "What's today?" she turns to Shep.

"Day eleven."

"Wow," Matt, the running back of the team, says. "Eleven days with them?"

They all chuckle, but Shep just gives a polite smile. "It's been pretty awesome, actually," he says, which makes me grin.

"It sure has," I say and slip my arm through the crook of his elbow. How you like them apples?

"Ditto," says Carmen and grabs his other arm.

A few moments pass.

"Carmen, can we talk for a minute?" Kevin asks.

She shakes her head. "We already are, Kevin."

"I mean in private."

"You can say whatever you want to say right here. I hide nothing from Sam and Shep."

Kevin's jaw muscles tighten. Yes, asshat, that means we know what you tried to do to her. But I don't say that out loud.

He nods. "It's cool. Not that important. Anyway, we best get going. We're going to a party if you're interested."

"We're good, thanks," Carmen says.

He nods then glances at his friends. "Let's go guys. The party can't start without us."

They make a show of movement, but at the last instant Kevin faces Shep. "What's with that mess in Houston? "

"Mess?" I ask.

"Yeah, you know, the scandal with the whole sexual assault thing."

My heart stops beating and my mind explodes into a trillion pieces. But I show nothing to him.

"Those are some of your ex-teammates, right?" Kevin asks. "Lucky you're not there."

"Yeah," Shep says, his energy noticeably lower. "They were my—"

"That's old news," Carmen interrupts. "Glad to see you concern yourself with that stuff, Kevin."

Kevin's face turns red. She's bluffing. She doesn't know anything about this. She would've told me. Whatever this really is, she's handling it like a champ. I, on the other hand, am channeling all the peace and grace I can find.

"Have a good time at the party," I say, still holding onto Shep's arm. I hope they get the message.

They leave with their bravado tucked between their scrawny butts. But I'm still reeling.

"You can let go now," Shep says.

I've been squeezing his arm so tight, I've left a trace of my fingers around his bicep.

We're all silent. None of us are making eye contact.

"I better take Olivia's ashes to the surf," Carmen says. Her voice is strained. I don't detect anger, just defeat.

IN SILENCE, we head back to our camper, shower, and change. During dinner it's all small talk. We're all pretending nothing has changed. But we all know something has.

"I love the sound of rain," Carmen says.

We enjoy the silence for a few minutes.

"The guest house Mom and I lived in had a tin roof," he says. "We'd prepare coffee, sit on the covered porch and just listen to the *tap tap tapping*. Sometimes, the rain poured down so hard, that it sounded like the world's largest drum-line was performing a concert just for us."

He leans into his chair, lost in the memory. Carmen and I glance at each other. I can practically read her mind. Should we say something?

But in that moment, he digs into his bag and pulls out one of the letters from his Mom.

He doesn't spend more than a minute on it before his face turns red and his jaw muscles pulsate.

"What's wrong?" I ask, knowing he may go silent on me again.

He shakes his head, then grunts. "Here," he says, holding out the letter, then pulls the rest of the letters from his bag and hands it to Carmen. "Go ahead, read them. Maybe you'll see something I don't."

He walks toward the camper. "I'll prepare coffee."

With that we start from the first letter all the way through today's.

July 19, 2000 — Day 11

I am exhausted. I detest myself, my life, and my friends. I can't count on anything or anyone. Only my surfboards are true to me.

I told the girls that I want to go back home. I'm done. They're urging me to stay. Why? Why do they care? All they do is

screw, surf, and get hammered. And when they do it...
Anyway, I've lowered myself to their level. I've messed myself
up so much that it takes very little for me to lose my balance
and direction. Also, the freaking urge to throw up is non-stop.
Just before writing this, the smell of sex on Tracey and her
boyfriend almost made me gag again. Again!

I have nothing here. This is not for me. This is not who I am.
It's time I leave.

Against my better judgment, I've decided to give it one more
day. Someone told us swells showed up at Rincon. That is
totally unexpected. If true, it means no one else will know
about it. It will be all ours.

I pray that I find peace there. I don't want to feel ill anymore. I
want to feel like myself.
O.

As we put away the last letter, we look at each other. Carmen
leans in. "What do you think?"

"Not sure what to think. These letters are raising a lot of questions that I don't think he's considered."

Carmen nods, sagely. "And what about what Kevin said?"

I take a deep breath. "I think—" but I don't get to finish my
sentence, because Shep drops on the chair in front of us.

"Done?" he asks.

"Yeah," Carmen says, her voice subdued.

"What do you think of my *perfect* mom now?"

"Don't do that," I say.

He stares at me. "Don't do what?"

"Judge her. She was our age. People do a lot of dumb things when they don't know better."

His face turns yellow then drops his gaze to the ground for a few moments. Something I said has hit home with him.

"Also, it's unfair to judge her when she can't defend herself," Carmen says.

He goes silent just as the rain picks up in intensity. Puddles are forming on the camp ground. The sound reaches a steady roar.

Shep grabs the coffee pot and tops off his mug.

"You may want to get some, too," he says. "I owe you a story."

FORTY-THREE

DAY 11 - SHEP

I STARE at the steam that plays off the surface of my coffee. A dance caused by the invisible. I glance up at them. It's time.

"Kevin was right. Weeks after the championship football season, our athletic program got hammered because of sexual assault claims. It happened after a typical, big—slightly out-of-control—party."

"Were you there?" Carmen asks.

I take a sip and relive what I've tried to forget. "Yeah, I was there."

"What kind of party are we talking about?" Sam asks.

"The type of party where girls are ready to hook up and where the guys are expecting it."

Carmen breathes out. "Oh boy."

"Are you saying you assaulted someone, too?" Sam's voice is dry, hard.

"No."

"Then what?" Sam asks, her tone is confused now.

I find a tattered thread of courage and continue. "On the day of the incident, Jill told me to look her up once I got to the party. I'd liked her from the first day of high school. She was a year older—

always stunning, always unattainable. But suddenly, there she was, interested in me."

I make eye contact with the girls. They appear sad and conflicted.

"Is she the one who was assaulted?" Sam asks.

I rub my face and put up my hand, asking for patience. This is hard enough as it is.

"The smell of beer and marijuana slammed me the moment I walked in the party. I remember my eyes getting a bit teary from it. But before I'd even grabbed a drink or tracked down Jill, Mom rang my cell. I didn't want her to know where I was, so I ducked into one of the bedrooms. Three people were going at it. I was about to rush back out, but..." I close my eyes and the images come to me like a damaged, but vivid movie reel. "I remember a lot of bare skin, limbs, laughter... and her. Jill. With my *teammates*. She faced me and her eyes went wide, in shock. My vision went blurry. Heat, anger, disgust —all of the above. But as one of the guys turned to me, I ran out and shut the door."

I take a deep breath and speak the truth. "I was angry. On so many levels. Why was she with them? Why were *they* with *her*? They knew I liked her. My gut kept yelling at me to go back in there and say something. Anything. To just make a scene. Instead, I decided to get drunk and wait for her. I was going to let her know what I really thought of her.

"A while later, the guys came out, clearly drunk, highfiving each other. It took a whole-lotta self-control not to go after them. I waited a bit for her, but got so disgusted with the whole situation that I left the party. I was done with them. All of them. But by the next afternoon, word spread. She had accused those guys of rape."

"Oh man," Sam whispers.

"But..." Carmen starts and pauses. "Is that what you saw?"

I get to my feet and run my hands through my hair. "Carmen, I've asked myself that question dozens, if not hundreds of times. Time alters memory. Sometimes, denial does a better job. When she faced me, I thought the shock on her face was because I had caught her in the act. But maybe it was fear. Or maybe hope that someone would save her. Then again, I heard laughter. But did I hear her voice mixed in there too, or was it just the guys? I tried to relive those few moments because either she was the victim or my teammates were.

"There was one fact I returned to over and over again: I doubted the guys dragged her to the room in front of so many people. In other words, she put herself in that room. So my conclusion was that at worst she had done more than she had planned to and felt guilty. Or maybe she regretted being with *those* guys. Or she got in trouble and needed a scapegoat. Either way, I decided I would not get involved."

Both Carmen and Sam appear defeated. I slump back down.

"I felt justified, even righteous. But by Monday, my conviction lost some of its fire."

"She confronted you?" Carmen asks.

"No, the assistant coach called me to his office... to explain things."

"Disgusting," Sam hisses.

"He reminded me that I had a bright future. That my scholarship was well-deserved. After all, not everyone from the ranches made it to that school. He reminded me that my mom was loved at the school, too. He explained that in one year I'd be at the college of my choice. I'd make something of my life—no more tin roofs. He also reminded me that those types of girls tended to make things up—particularly when they were drunk. All I had to do was deny her version of the story."

They are both stunned, silent.

"Mom heard about Jill and asked me what I knew. I totally denied being at the party or even knowing her. Mom was visibly shaken and at every turn tried to defend Jill even though she didn't know the girl. Within days, people were calling Jill a whore, a liar, you name it.

"By the second week, as things got more intense, my teammates visited me at the ranch. No threats, just explaining that sometimes in

264

the heat of the moment things get out of hand. The classic 'He said, she said.' A misunderstanding. An unfortunate confusion."

The girls look dejected.

"And then what happened?" Sam asks.

I shrug. "The district attorney interviewed a bunch of people who were on the team and at the party. The D.A. had enough to move forward so there was no point in me getting involved. And anyway, soon after, Mom got ill."

She shakes something off. "I don't want to sound disrespectful or anything, but... so what?"

My body jerks involuntarily. "What's that supposed to mean?"

"Listen. Your Mom got ill. But why would that, in any way, stop you from giving your testimony? Doesn't the prosecution need that type of information?"

"Or did they have sufficient physical evidence that they didn't need your story?" Carmen asks.

"So what?" Sam repeats. "Even if they do have physical evidence —which makes me sick just thinking about it—why wouldn't the D.A. want everything they can get their hands on to bury those bastards?" She lands her eyes on mine. "Did you tell the D.A. anything? Do they even know?"

"They know I was at the party."

"That's not what I'm asking. Does the D.A. know what you saw?"

I run a hand over my face, then shake my head. "No," I whisper.

She slams the table. "Unreal! Shep, you've got to be kidding me."

"Calm down, Sam," Carmen says, then turns to me. "Explain, Shep. Why not?"

I rise. "Look, I don't know what I saw. I saw three people having sex. Yes, that sort of stuff happened all the time. I don't know if Jill was a willing participant or a victim. So how could I honestly say what I saw?

"Carmen you asked if I saw rape. I. Don't. Know! Maybe. Maybe not. I mean who am I to say who is telling the truth and who isn't?"

"That's not on you. The jury does that," Sam says.

"Your job is to say what you saw. The rest is on the lawyers, the judge, the system," Carmen says, her voice soft, but measured. There's silence for a few moments. "What's really happening, Shep?"

I can't say what stopped me. I can't.

"Look, I get it," Sam says, her voice still firm, but softer now. "Life has just tossed you a granade that will explode in your hands one way or the other. But let's speak honestly: if you shut your mouth, you are in effect testifying against her, because those criminals may get away with it; if you say something, you are testifying against your team-mates. Game over. Literally. You are worried that no high school team will want you."

A string breaks in my gut. I nod and hold back my emotions. "No high school team means no scholarship because no college will want my type of cancer. No future. No nothing." I wipe at a renegade tear. "Then what happens to me? Everything I worked for is all gone because of someone else. This is not my problem. Why am I in the middle of all this? For all we know those guys will still be found guilty. I don't have to sacrifice myself."

Carmen drops a hand on my shoulder. "Then why do I get the sense that you suspect they will get away with it?"

The tears come uncontrollably. I can't stop it, I can't breathe. My throat constricts, my chest heaves. I cover my face and for the first time the dam breaks.

The girls huddle around me and hold me tight. They say things to soothe me, but there's no way to calm this explosion in my chest. No matter how I look at it I lose. Either I have to live for the rest of my life knowing that I helped two guys get away with rape, or live my life wondering what could've been if only I had focused on my career, my future.

The minutes pass by in silence. Eventually, I find my voice again. "Mom suspected all along. Each time something new came up, she'd ask me if there was anything I wanted to tell her. But I couldn't. When the assistant coach gave me the speech, alarms in my gut were blaring. I knew this was wrong, and ugly, and dirty. When the guys came to me, it smelled of desperation. But couldn't honest people do desperate things to fight off a false accusation? Here's what kills me: in all of this, Jill didn't come after me. She didn't threaten me, or explain things to me. She could have, because she saw me there, but she decided to keep me out, to not drag me in.

"She was giving me a lifeline. That's how I saw it. Jill doesn't want me to lose everything. I'm sure of it."

"You can't know that."

"Why not? Maybe she gets my world—my tiny little world. Maybe she gets that I hate being poor. I hated having to beg for people to give us a roof. I hated not belonging. I don't want that life. I have a chance now. On the shoulders of my own abilities, to make something of myself. No more handouts from anyone else. Did she get that? Maybe."

More silence.

"If you truly believe that, then why are you so torn up? How strong is the case against the guys?" Carmen asks.

I shrug. "Before I left, it was very strong. But... I hear they have brought on big time attorneys. And... the district attorney is looking for eye witnesses."

Both Sam and Carmen take a deep breath and when they exhale there is heaviness to it.

"When's the trial?" Sam asks.

"August 1st," I say.

"Then you have less than a week to decide what you're willing to live with for the rest of your life," Sam says.

FORTY-FOUR

DAY 12 - SHEP

"RINCON DOES NOT BREAK in the summer," Carmen says.

I glance at her in the rearview mirror. She and Sam are on the bench in the camper, yawning, as I drive us north. As hard it is to imagine, since our conversation last night, I feel lighter. Not because the answer is clear, but because there are no more lies between me and the girls. To their credit, they've been decent with me. Not browbeating me or giving me lectures. They're giving me space. Space to think.

"Therefore what?" I ask. "What does that mean?"

"Therefore, don't expect to actually surf. We'll float in cold water."

That's disappointing, but it also means something else. No crowds. After last night's confessional, I could use some uninterrupted sleep time on the beach. I may have one day or two before Uncle José's attorney gets in touch with me. Then what? I don't know.

"We can use the rest," Sam says, reading my mind again, "But at least Shep will have visited this legendary spot. If we came during the regular season when it does break, he'd be frustrated. Everyone and their uncle flock there when it breaks."

We exit the *101 Freeway* and find our way to *Highway 1*.

"Hardly any campers in the camp parking area," Carmen says. "And I bet most of them are just road-trippers, not surfers. Because Rincon does not break in the summer."

Is she gonna say that all day?

We find a great spot, facing the ocean, then step out. The remnants of the previous day's rain has left the sand wet and has brought a lot of seaweed on the beach. But if there's seaweed there, something must have pushed it up to the sand.

"Are you sure it doesn't break?" I ask.

"Yup," Carmen says. "Never."

"Well, something dragged all this kelp and seaweed onto the shore," Sam says. I love how we think alike.

Carmen studies the beach. "Hmm. Although I said never, there are those that claim once in a while, some weird weather patterns bring swells to Rincon, even in the summer."

"So when you say never, you sort of mean what exactly?" I ask, fully aware that I'm being a smart ass.

"Just suit up and let's see what happens."

Fifteen minutes later, we're done waxing our boards. The three of us, fully draped in wetsuits, step into the frigid water then paddle out and wait.

And wait.

And wait some more.

"I told you," Carmen says, "it never breaks here."

"Stop with all the weather forecasting already," Sam says. "You need to believe."

"I believe," I say.

Sam eyes me. Now that she knows my past, will she still be interested? I want to believe we can still have a chance at something together.

"Fine, you two keep believing while I go back to the shore and get warm."

Carmen paddles away.

"She has no patience," Sam says.

"You'd think the Caribbean blood would've made her calm," I say.

"She's just a poser. She's not a legit islander like me."

Carmen reaches the shore, grabs her board, and walks onto the sand. She turns and waves at us, but after a half-hearted wave she stops, dead. She grabs her board and runs back into the water.

"What's the matter with her?" I ask.

Sam spins her board around. "No freakin' way," she says. "Swells!"

WE SURF for three hours straight. One beauty after another. The beach is ours, the waves are ours. When we're finally back by our camper to get food and rest, I realize my cheeks hurt... from smiling so much.

"This is the most amazing beach ever," I say. "They've all had their awesomeness, but the fact that it's just us, in this beautiful corner, makes me feel like someone's looking out for us."

I don't know where those words came from, but as soon as I speak them, I think of Mom and wonder if she's behind it. Is it because I came clean? Can those who've moved on affect the world we're in? Mom always suspected that I knew more about the party, but by then she was so weak. Was this trip her way of keeping me away from what she knew would eventually come? The thought gives me chills, which is then replaced with hope. What if Mom is really here?

"I'm getting back in," I say.

"Relax a bit," Sam says. "You need to recover."

"I want to take care of my mom's ashes while the swells are so perfect." I zip up my wetsuit and grab my board.

"Shep, rest up. Get warm," Carmen says. "Staying in that water for too long will not do you good."

"I'm a Texan," I say. "I worked on a ranch under hail and thunderstorms. I can take this and more."

TWO HOURS after I went back into the water, a batch of local surfers showed up. Thirty minutes after that, dozens of surfers, all in black wetsuits attacked the water.

By the time I get out, the damage has been done. I'm exhausted, I'm freezing... and it appears that I have a cold.

I'm inside the camper, splayed out on the couch that they converted into a bed for me. I am shivering and my head is spinning.

"*I'm a Texan,* he said." Carmen imitates my voice. "*I can handle it,* he promised."

"To be accurate," Sam says, "he said, I can take this and more. I shepherd cows and buffalos."

"You two are being mean to me," I say then sneeze.

"Oh great," Carmen says. "Now he's spraying the news."

"Don't worry," I say. "I have the constitution of a horse. By tomorrow I'll be all good."

"Constitution of a horse and the sensibility of a mule," she mumbles.

"Hey, I heard that."

Carmen smiles an evil smile. "The only way to solve this problem is by giving Shep an enema."

"True," Sam says.

"An enema? That does nothing for a cold," I say.

"But it'll do wonders for my disposition."

I WAKE up in a cold sweat. I search for a clock and read the time. 12:37 a.m. I need water.

I stumble my way to the pack of water bottles and guzzle one down. I'm feeling stronger already. I told them, I'm Texas strong! Practically.

I notice my bag and realize that in the excitement of it all, I forgot to read the next letter.

July 20, 2000 — Day 12

The swells were amazing at Rincon. Yes, you read it right. We had amazing swells in Rincon during summer.

I was finally able to shut it all out and focus on the waves again. This was therapeutic and completely unexpected. I came here fully expecting it to be crap. I was going to tell the guys to call it quits, but when we arrived, the waves were crashing in beautiful formation. One after the other. I felt like I was five again on Christmas morning.

I'm glad I came. Even though I was off, I felt that this stop started to clean out all the crap I've been taking in over the last few days.

More than ever, I realize that I want to be in the water all the time because at least when I'm there, it's just me and the waves. Completely lost and present in the moment. I'm present in the present.

Unfortunately, when I'm out of the water, I remember him. I betrayed him. No point in pretending. I betrayed the person I want to tell everything. The good, the bad and the downright shameful. But he's not with me because of choices I made.

I just hope I can find him again to at least try to clean it up.

Laters,
O.

Hopeful. Finally, this is hopeful and the way she talks about him, it's clear that she's in love with him. Has been for years. I'm sure she found him. But then what happened? Did he turn out to be a complete jerk? Is that why they didn't stay together?

I read the letter again.

He's the person I want to tell everything. The good, the bad and the downright shameful.

If she did find him, did she tell him everything? Is that what broke them apart? The shameful overpowered the love?

Only three letters left. Three days in Pismo.

I grin.

Let's see what you have planned for me, Mom.

PART SIX

"You can't stop the waves,
but you can learn to surf."
~John Kabat-Zinn

FORTY-FIVE

DAY 13 - SHEP

"SHEP, WAKE UP," a groggy voice says. "We're here."

I open my eyes and not only is the voice off, but so is the face. Then I realize, I'm the one with the vision and hearing issues.

"Where are we?" I ask.

"At the hotel." I can now make out Sam's face.

I slide up, feeling weak, but not horrible. "We're staying at a hotel?"

"Yeah, that's what Rosie had rented for the last three days in Pismo. They'll arrive tomorrow night."

The RV door opens and Carmen pops her head in. "All set. Got the keys."

As I drag my body across the parking lot to the rooms, I read the signage: *Pismo Lighthouse Suites*. Place looks fairly nice. Above the parking lot is a play area. Some kids are running around and a few others are playing table tennis.

Our room is on the first floor. As I step in, I instantly feel at home. A large, but simple room with an oversized couch, coffee table, and a TV. Sam draws the shades open and exposes the balcony with an amazing view of the ocean.

"Oh man," they both say, as Sam opens the sliding door to the balcony. Coastal air flows in with vigor. The crashing waves sing their primal chants.

The girls step outside. I follow.

The hotel is perched above the bluffs, probably fifty feet high. The ocean roars at us and the birds sing their hoarse demands. The Pismo Pier is off to the south, maybe a mile away.

The balcony faces a common passageway that appears to connect the different hotels. We open the balcony's gate and approach the main gate that keeps people from falling down the bluffs. There are worse places to die.

"This is awesome," Carmen says.

"I wonder if we can get to the beach from here," Sam says.

They scan around and find an older couple strolling nearby. We ask and get confirmation that it's a short walk south until we reach a wooden stairwell that goes all the way down to the beach. From there we can march toward the pier if we want.

I breathe in the air and smile uncontrollably. "I think I understand why Mom stayed here the last three days."

"No doubt," Carmen says.

Sam tugs me back toward the room. "Let's get you in so you can rest some more. You're still a bit pale like cheap wax."

We stroll back in, but the air has already done me good. Carmen opens the sofa bed. I don't feel like sleeping. I want to explore this place.

"What time is it?" I ask.

"Ten-ish," Sam says.

"Oh no, we missed the morning surf," I say.

They both grin. "This is not the same cowboy we met on day one of this trip," Carmen says.

AFTER A BADLY—VERY badly— needed warm shower, we decide

to eat late breakfast/early lunch in Downtown Pismo. I'm feeling pretty good. I need to make sure that I'm back at full-strength for the memorial in a couple of days.

The stores and streets give me the impression that this place hasn't changed much since the fifties or sixties. Everything has a vintage feel to it. That's what makes this place different. It's quaint and cool. Like only the simple things are important. And by important, it's clear surfing is front and center in this town.

At the 50s style diner I order a burger, chili, salad, and a chocolate shake. I feel like I haven't eaten in days. I need to refuel to recover fully.

Stuffed, we head down to the pier. There are a handful of surf shops and a lot of surfing references throughout the place. At the pier, down the stairs that take you beneath the walkway, two mounted surfboards remind us we're in Pismo. Near the showers, board racks are featured in plain sight. I wonder if the tourists realize that this beach has a surf culture that has lasted decades.

We walk down onto the sand and stroll to the shoreline. People are surfing. The waves are decent, but the beach isn't very crowded.

Sam turns to Carmen. "What do you think?"

"Definitely."

I'm unable to track their dialogue. "What's going on?"

"Sit and rest. Get some down time while we go do what we do best," Sam says.

With that speech, they leave me on the beach while they go back to fetch their boards.

I admit, I feel left out, but there's no way I can get out there in my condition. I do need to rest. I guess this is the alone time I'd been looking for.

So I lay on the sand and watch the ocean, the waves, and the sights of the beach. The waves break in mind-altering patterns. They are majestic, beautiful, scary, peaceful, and evil.

A text from Uncle José interrupts the moment of peace. "We have a lawyer. Let's chat tonight when we arrive there."

Yes, sir. Life can come in may unique ways. Time to see what came into Mom's life here. I pull out her letter from her first day at Pismo.

July 21, 2000 — Day 13

Lucky thirteen lived up to its name. He was here. He came for me.

After yesterday's amazing day, I decided to finish the trip as planned. I had just started to wax my board when I heard his deep voice from behind me.

Yes, it was a sappy moment. It was a total cliché, but when I heard his voice, I forgot about all my reservations, all my concerns. I jumped to my feet and hugged him.

We strolled the beach, ate in downtown, and caught our share of waves. I'm at home when I'm with him. Like he's the person I'm meant to be with. I'm going to tell my van-mates that I want to stay in Pismo for the rest of the trip. He'll be here all three days. I want to spend every minute with him.

They said no at first. So I told them to go on without me. An hour later they changed their mind and agreed to stay. It really didn't matter. I was going to stay.

I wasn't going to do it. I didn't want to hurt him, but my insides were going haywire. I tried to fight it, but it was like I was fighting gravity. I told him what happened—what I did when he didn't come back. I told him how I messed up. He was hurt, but forgave me, completely. Is this guy for real?

He did go all papa-bear on me because of my health. At one point I got all light-headed and almost threw up. I told him about the alcohol and weed use, but I also explained that I've cut it out. Two days clean. This seemed to calm him a bit. He worries too much. He also wants to know what I'm writing about. He keeps looking over my shoulder. I promised one day he will definitely, most likely, some possible day, see some elements, that may or may not be from this diary. He's giving me a quizzical look, unsure if he should be happy or upset. Yeah, he's awesome.

I spent the whole day and night with him. I told him about Texas, which completely and utterly threw him into panic mode. We agreed that we'll find a way. We also agreed that unlike last time, this time we'll commit to seeing each other. Back then we didn't have email. Technology may just save us.

Dear Quick: if you see this without my permission, first know that you're in trouble. And second, I love you.

Life is good,
O.

I put away the letter, as a sense of comfort embeds itself in my chest. They found each other and for that day they were happy. Mom was happy. A moment in time before everything went wrong.

Clearly, everything went wrong.

I bundle up my bag in the form of a pillow, tuck it behind my head, then cover my face with my hat. I can rest with the knowledge that at this beach, some eighteen years ago, she was whole and complete.

FORTY-SIX
DAY 13 - SAMANTHA

SHEP SPENT some time with José. Apparently he has a lawyer now, but doesn't know what he's going to tell the lawyer. I don't want to push. No, that's not true. I want to push, I want to shove. He can't see it, but I know this as clearly as I know anything. If he doesn't come clean, this will eat him alive forever. He will never get over this.

For now, Carmen and I have decided to back off and let him finish this fifteen-day journey. After that, we'll have to raise it again. Not only for Jill's sake, but for his also.

We're in our balcony, past midnight, enjoying the concussive cadence of the waves. It's dark, so we can't see the ocean, but I can feel its presence; its power resonates though my body.

As Carmen and I read the diary entries for the last two days, we eye each other. Then ask Shep to let us read the previous ones again. Although he's confused over the request, he does as asked. We silently point to words and passages that catch our attention.

When we are done, we put the letters back in their envelopes, trying to delay the question that is on both our minds. I'm a chicken, I admit, so I wait for Carmen.

"Shep," she starts, "there's something that Sam and I noticed."

He looks at us. "What?"

Carmen hesitates so I speak up, knowing that she's searching for the right words. "The state of her health," I say. "It raises questions."

He frowns. "What questions?"

Carmen touches my knee. She doesn't want me to be in the firing lane. Silently, I thank her.

"Shep, what Sam's saying is that maybe her health problems weren't because she was drinking a lot or smoking a joint or two."

His eyes narrow, like our science lab teacher, trying to understand what we're up to. "Go on," he whispers.

There's silence. I'm sure it's only for a few moments, but to me it feels like minutes pass as one wave after another crashes against the rocks and boulders beneath the bluffs.

She swallows visibly. Then speaks the words that we know he needs to hear. "Maybe she was already pregnant."

After a momentary hesitation, he shakes his head, tries to smile, but it doesn't work. His face changes, contorts. "No. Of course not. She got pregnant during this trip."

"Do we know that for sure?" Carmen asks.

He pauses. "Everyone knows that. Even your dad said so."

"That's the story we've all come to believe," Carmen says. "But there are clues here that we shouldn't overlook."

"Mom would not have been smoking and drinking if she had known she was pregnant. There is no indication in her letters that she suspected."

"Exactly," Sam says. "She may not have realized it herself."

He freezes.

"Shep, some girls feel the symptoms as early as two or three weeks after doing the deed. She could've gotten pregnant just before she went on this trip and not even know it. She does mention a rough end to the school year at the very start of her letters. She mentions some guy, Tom twice."

His face goes slack.

"This is just a theory," Carmen quickly adds. "All we're

suggesting is that the answer you've been searching for may not get delivered in a nicely-wrapped name. Just don't want you to get hurt again."

He looks derailed. Without a word, he walks off, opens our balcony gate and marches onto the trail we had taken earlier that leads to the beach. I rise, wanting to follow him, but I hesitate, staring at Carmen.

"Go," Carmen says.

"You sure?" I whisper.

"He needs you more than he needs me."

Does she suspect? It doesn't matter now.

I go after him.

FORTY-SEVEN
DAY 13 - SHEP

ALL THE SURFING, the searching, the hoping, dead in one instant. I walk, then stride, then break into a run. This can't be how it happened.

But it's possible.

They're wrong. These are conspiracy theories. They don't know who they're talking about.

But it sounds rational.

Mom was not promiscuous. She didn't just sleep around.

Mom was not the same person back then.

She wanted me to respect women, remain pure. Be different. This wasn't just about protecting girls. She also didn't want me to become one of those guys who pursued sex, but abandoned their responsibilities when the relationship became inconvenient.

This can't be what she wanted me to discover.

Or maybe this is exactly what she wanted.

Why do it like this? Imply the possibility of answers only to be left with more questions? The truth is that even she didn't know who my real father was.

A journey without answers.

I run down the steps, almost lose my footing a couple of times because the only question left in my mind is, why? To what end?

To chase after a ghost.

I come to a stop once I reach the sand. Number thirteen on her list. Lucky thirteen was, "Find a ghost."

I'm frozen in place, trapped with nowhere to go.

From behind, strong arms wrap themselves around me. My shoulders slump and she turns me to face her.

"Shep," she whispers, her eyes inches away from mine. Her lips are parted, her breathing hard. The glare from the hotel windows above cast a beam that drapes her in a hazy glow. A misty spray covers her face and hair with tiny droplets. A manifestation of an angel.

"What we said is a theory. We have two more letters, right? Two more days. Your mom orchestrated this. So let's not give up."

I sigh. "I'm exhausted, Sam. I'd grieved her. I had come to a stable understanding. I was moving on, only to be slapped with this."

"It hasn't been all a waste, right?" she asks.

I smile. "No, of course not." I lean close to her lips. "These two weeks have been the best I've ever had."

"I don't want to take all the credit for—" she starts with a smile.

"You're the best thing that's ever happened to me," I say.

The waves don't stop pounding, the mist doesn't pause to listen to what will happen next. The water is as wet and the sand is as thick and heavy as before I uttered those words. But her eyes have grown.

"Me?" she starts, hesitates, then asks, "Why?"

I laugh, but her question is sincere. In that instant, I know, without a doubt she'll be the reason I survive this. My mouth crushes into hers. She doesn't resist. She melts in my arms and all the frustration I'd been feeling just a minute ago disappears. I am hyper-focused on this wave right now. The one I've been given.

I'll deal with the mess called 'my life' later.

FORTY-EIGHT
DAY 13 - SAMANTHA

BY THE TIME we return to the room, I'm entirely wet, so is he. My lips feel swollen. My heart may never beat the same again. It's still erratic. Honestly, I could've stayed out there forever, but I didn't want Carmen to worry or get suspicious.

He reaches for the sliding door. We walk in silently because only the accent lights are on. Carmen must be in bed.

"Go dry up," he whispers.

"You too," I say.

He kisses me on the lips, then another on the tip of my nose, lands a warm one on my forehead, and finishes it off with a lingering kiss on the inside of my wrist.

I peel myself away from him. "Go. Sleep."

I enter the room in ninja mode. Carmen's tucked in, her back to me. *Good. One less conversation.*

I tiptoe to my bag and pull out undies, sweats, and a t-shirt. In the bathroom, I shed all my wet clothes, then change.

Much better.

I dry my hair one more time then slide into bed, under the sheets. I prep the pillow, close my eyes and smile. Just then, there's movement on the bed. I open my eyes to find Carmen staring at me. Literally inches away.

"Is he okay?" she asks.

"I think he'll be okay."

She doesn't move. A beat.

"Straight out," she says, "I need to know the deal."

"The deal?" I ask, fully unprepared for how I'm going to handle this. What will I say? How best to couch it? What if—?

"Do you feel something for him?" she asks.

I try to control my mouth. I try to activate the filter. Instead, I smile and the words slip out. "Yeah. Definitely something. I don't know what, but is it weird that I want to lock in a commitment from him for prom from now?"

Her mouth parts.

I cringe. "Crap. You're not happy."

Her eyes remain stern. I wait for the other shoe to drop, but instead she grins. "I knew you two would hit it off. I'm an amazing matchmaker!"

"All right, don't go giving yourself an award just yet. But... what I do know is that I really, really, really-really like him. A lot." I pause, think some more, then add, "A lot."

Carmen drops back on the pillow, a huge smile plastered on her face.

"How do we get him to do the right thing?" I ask.

She glances at me. "We don't. He needs to come to that conclusion on his own. It's the only way he'll own it and not have resentment toward us if his life doesn't turn out."

I stare at her. What if he doesn't do the right thing? What then?

FORTY-NINE
DAY 14 - SHEP

LAST NIGHT I BARELY SLEPT. Hard to when I'm both annoyed and hopeful.

Hopeful because there's still time. The next letters may have the answers I've been searching for. That's the only 'hope' I have left to hang my hat on.

Annoyed because she made promises in her letter to me. I'll learn the truth, I'll get answers, even details about my father. She even said that if I listen, she'll speak to me.

I'm not sure this was the *truth* I was looking for. Truth is Shep, we don't know what the heck happened.

I'm also annoyed that I didn't see the signs in her letters. She was getting sick all the time. Did I not want to see it? I allowed this trip to become about finding my elusive father. And elusive he remains.

And what was that crap about listening for her voice? Sorry, Mom. I don't hear nothing.

I have to be okay with the possibility that it'll all end like this: a misdirection.

I hate my mindset. I can feel the match that wants to burst the oxygen in my chest into flames. I'm ready to snap, but I can't do that to the only people in my life who know everything about me, and still accept me. They are the only good things I have left in my life. Literally. I have nothing else.

I decide it's time to ride Mom's honeybee board. Not sure why, but I feel I'm finally ready. No more starter board for me. And no longboards either. All evening, as I visualized my time in the water, all I saw was wave cutting. So I'll honor my instinct.

As we wax our boards, the girls talk about the waves, the tides and the current. I'm lost in my own world. No, I don't think of anything specific. Instead I see phrases from her letters.

Find a ghost.

Hear God's whisper.

I messed up.

Learn the truth.

All words that are at best dangling carrots.

Carmen bumps my shoulder with hers. I glance at her. She darts her eyes toward Sam, who's walking on her own toward the water.

"She's cute," Carmen says.

My thoughts vanish. "What?"

"Sam. She's cute," Carmen says. "Don't you think?"

A smile almost breaks on my face. I may complain about wanting time to myself, but I'm glad I'm with these two. "Yeah, I suppose. If you're into good-looking, athletic, strong, badass, sharp, funny, and a bit of a nut-job."

She leans into my ear. "I can vouch for her."

She stares deep into my eyes. Wow. This is like the godfather giving her blessing. I can practically hear the theme music.

"What about all that snoring?" I ask.

She shrugs. "No one's perfect, Shep."

Some of us are perfectly imperfect. I should know.

We grab our boards and run toward Sam. She turns, her long hair spins, revealing a beautiful face, an honest smile, and eyes that see the good in all situations. "It's about time," she says.

"Let's shred some," I say and with that we splash into the water.

THE WAVE HOLDS ME DOWN, then spins me around like a rag doll before it allows me to kick back up to the surface. It's been doing that all morning. Like it's taunting me, daring me to try to play above my level.

I'm game, buddy.

I slide onto my board and paddle back to the line up.

"Let's take a break," Carmen says, looking spent.

"I agree," Sam says.

I don't, but I decide to go with the flow. The honeybee board is harder to control. Things that worked on the hybrid are not as easy to pull off on this one. Either that, or the ocean has a personal grudge against me.

Once on the sand, my mind drifts. I'm reliving the last few weeks. It seems clear now that I did this to myself. Weeks back I declared who I was, a lone wolf. Then when the letter gave me hope, I went after it, because deep down I knew I didn't want to be alone.

I was so sure I'd find my father. I would march up to him, yell or something, and he'd give me a sincere explanation and we'd be fine. I'd find the man who would now and forever be in my life. I would not be alone anymore.

But I should've known better. Nothing good lasts. Something grows in the pit of my stomach. An emptiness, a rush of sadness.

"Did you bring today's letter?" Sam asks.

"Yeah," I say, but I dread what may be written. More twists? I pull out the envelope and decide to read it out loud.

July 22, 2000 — Day 14

He told me he loves me.

I cried. I know, it's stupid. It's weak. I don't even know why, but I did.

Last night we completed another one of my challenges. We danced from sunset to sunrise. We should've been exhausted this morning, but we didn't miss a beat. We spent our time in the water, on the sand, sleeping in each other's arms. I don't ever want to be away from him. The thought that we only have two days is killing me. How do we do this?

This is not the best plan, but for now it's as good as it'll get. We agreed that on December 26, we'll meet here. He has a cousin in Pismo. So this beach is our home base.

We did throw crazy ideas around, but reality sank in. I have to go to college and he has some amazing opportunities lined up. He'll be going to Baja, Hawaii, Australia. This is his career.

I'll put in a transfer to San Louis Obispo if we decide to stay up here, or Santa Barbara or USC. I don't care. We just have to agree on a spot and call it home.

I've never been more excited about the future.

Tonight, we spend the night together. I'm nervous. Excited. Scared. Luckiest girl in town.

O.

I stare at the letter.

"Wow," Sam says. "Imagine if they'd had today's technology. They could've used Skype, Snapchat, FaceTime, you name it. It's so sad that back then they had so few options."

Carmen says nothing. She's looking at her toes in the sand.

"What happened, I wonder?" Sam says. "I wonder if the last letter will give us any more clues." We're all silent, but she adds, "Do we know if she came back here in December?"

"She would've been more than halfway through her pregnancy. Probably showing," Carmen says.

I carefully return the page to the envelope and slip it back into my bag. My heart feels compressed and my scalp feels warm. She was in love. Deeply. When she found out she was pregnant, did she tell him I was his and he didn't believe her? Or did they do a test and it turned out he wasn't the father? So many possibilities. All of them make me feel a bit more ill.

"Quick Silver," Sam says absently, as she grabs a fistful of sand and drizzles it over her thighs. "And your mom used to call you Silver Surfer..." She nods then wipes the sand off her hands. "If you ask me, there's a connection between Quick Silver and Silver Surfer. Too close for coincidence."

"So you're saying her Quick Silver became Silver Surfer?" Carmen asks.

I see the connection that she's making, but if he's not my father, then what gives? "Nicknaming me after this Quick Silver surfer guy is only meaningful and relevant if he was my father."

They look at each other and shrug. "Yeah, you're right," Sam says.

"It would've been a touching way of showing her love for him and his role in your lives."

"Let's be clear," I say and rise. "He had *no* role."

Maybe if I had a father in my life, I would've made better decisions when my world imploded in Houston. Maybe.

I grab my board and march into the water.

I'VE BEEN at it for an hour. I'm exhausted beyond measure. I was already low on energy and I also know that if I push myself I might get sick again. I've barely recovered, but I can't leave because I need a breakthrough here and now.

Over the last week there've been times when I thought I heard or experienced something: when I was in a barrel or when I thought I was drowning; in dreams and when the rain showered down on me.

I was close then. I need to try again. Now.

I paddle back to the lineup. Thankfully the surfers haven't shown up in droves. It's full, but I can pretty much catch waves without worrying that I'll get into a collision with kooks.

I bark out a laugh. Now I'm calling others kooks?

A beauty comes. I am the closest to the peak, so I take it. *Hop*, I encourage my legs. I take the wave and follow the break. I lower my body, pump the board then steer up the face of the wave, snap it back, carving back down, knowing I've sprayed a load. I do it again. Another solid hit. I push my luck and accelerate even more. Up the face and when I prepare to snap back down, my legs give up on me and the wave implodes at the same time.

My board and I fly, above and behind the wave. I crash into the water hard. The impact knocks the wind out of me.

I resurface, get on the board then paddle back. Sam shows up next to me.

"You're fighting the waves," she says and rests her hand on my arm. "You have to be calm—"

"Sam," I almost snap, but control myself. "I need to do this," I say and paddle away, creating space. How can I explain that I feel like I need to confront my emotions, right here, right now, in this way? And that I need to do this on my own.

I turn my board and watch the swells.

You said if I listened you'd speak to me. Those were your words.

A breaker shows up. I hop and catch her. No, she catches me.

Mom, I'm listening. Give me something.

I carve, climb, and snap.

Anything.

I take another one, and as I cut back down, the wave behind me almost knocks me off. Almost. I pump, accelerating, creating space.

Who was he, Mom? Is it Quick? Was it someone else? I did what you asked. What did you really want me to find out?

I go up vertical and execute a cut-back, rotating my hips as violently as I can, throwing my arms around to bring my board back to the water.

Where are you, Mom? I'm listening.

"I'm"—I snap the board—"listening!" I yell.

I over spin, my board goes into the wave that's been chasing me. I try to compensate, but I'm too slow, the wave shuts down, swallows me, swirls me, then spits me out, causing me to hit the sand hard. But he's not done, he puts his foot down on my chest, keeping me down, reminding me who he is and what I am. Insignificant.

My foot, which was being pulled violently by the leash a second ago releases the tension and so does the wave.

I pop out of the water, out of breath and search for my mom's board. I see the yellow and black board to my left. I swim toward it, but as I reach for it, I see something from my peripheral vision. The board is also to my right.

I pull the board while I try to make sense of what I'm seeing.

It hits me.

Her board broke.

I snapped Mom's board.

I can't move. I can't send any message to the rest of my body.

The nose of the board, all two feet of it, is floating away.

I watch it leave me.

I hear voices. Not my mom. It's the girls.

I can't face them. I can't face myself.

In the blurry world I'm trapped in, I see a surfer reach down and grab it, then paddle toward me. Another arm lands on my shoulder.

The world becomes a blur.

FIFTY

DAY 14 - SHEP

WE'RE ALL on our knees, on the sand staring at the pieces of my mom's board.

I didn't listen to Sam. She was trying to protect me. But I went ahead and destroyed my most-valued possession from Mom.

Carmen must be devastated. She had been in awe of Mom's board for all these years.

My uncle will be here tonight. What will I tell him?

And my mom... who had left this for me.

"We can repair it," Carmen says. "I've broken boards before."

I stare at her, my face numb.

"You probably won't be able to tell the difference when you ride it," she adds.

"Will you please stop trying to protect me? We all know I messed up. Even the strangers who are watching us know. So please, don't minimize this."

She stares at me, looking mildly stunned.

Sam scoots over and drapes her arm around my shoulder. "If you've surfed long enough, this'll happen. Don't think of it as damaged. You've added your mark to the legacy of this board. The amazing story that goes with this board hasn't ended."

I shrug off her arm and rise. "The story of a stupid kid who tried to find his dad but instead destroyed his mother's gift."

Sam's face hardens. She jumps to her feet and steps into me. "Let's be clear about what happened: the board snapped. That's all it is. You're creating an entire Shakespearean tragedy around a snapped board. You're not suddenly condemned for the rest of your life and no, your mom is not disgusted by you. So get over yourself."

I stare at her. I know she's right. But right now, I want a fight. I'm about to say something I know I'll regret when a lady walks up to us.

"Looks like the wave won this round," she says in a Jamaican accent.

I gaze at the middle-aged woman with her majestic silver dreadlocks. Her radiant smile diffuses the situation. The lady kneels down, studying the break point.

"In the hands of the right person, you won't see the repair line."

"Will it be the same again?" I ask.

"Probably not," she says.

I look at Sam and Carmen, in their eyes I see the dejection. They wanted her to say I didn't mess up. That the board will be just fine. But the truth is different.

"There are three reasons to repair a board: sentimental reasons, to have a backup board, or if it costs less to repair than to buy another one. What's your reason?"

"Sentimental," I say. "This was my late Mom's board."

She produces an empathetic smile. "Then honor her. Get this repaired by someone who respects boards. Then keep this board as a reminder of her life on the water. Most importantly, move on from under her shadow and find yourself a board that fits your style and personality."

I stare at her.

"I abso-freakin'-lutely love that! And I love you," Sam says to the lady. "Can you be my friend?"

"I usually like to know my friend's names first."

The three of them laugh, but I'm lost at sea. I'm processing her recommendation, her advice, and her wisdom.

"Who can fix it? Do you know anyone?"

She nods. "Only one man within 100 miles I'd recommend. And his shop is two blocks from the pier."

WE HEAD out to the most ridiculously-named surf shop ever: Bodacious Badass Boards.

With the broken nose in Carmen's hand and the rest of the board inside a protective bag, we traverse the streets until we see the store.

Each word is individually nailed to gigantic wooden longboards. Three longboards, three words.

The boards are highly glossed and the oversized windows promise more beautiful boards and beach attire inside. We accept the invitation and enter the store.

My eyes are immediately drawn upward to the ceiling, adorned with dozens of surfboards, of different sizes and colors and shapes. I find myself scanning the entire store, just appreciating the unique boards that await a surfer.

A surfer like me.

"'Sup?" a white guy with medium-length blond dreadlocks asks Carmen.

"Who can we talk to about repairing a broken board?" she asks.

"That'd be the boss," he says, then turns and yells, "Silver! Customers!"

I stare at Dreadlocks then eye Sam. "Silver?" I mouth.

She shrugs, then glances at Carmen, who's frozen.

A bald man steps out. He's a bit shorter than me, but with well-defined, exposed shoulders. He's wearing a tank top, board shorts displaying lean leg muscles, and flip flops that announce each of his steps with a pronounced smack of his heels.

He walks toward us, wide smile, white teeth, aqua blue eyes.

"Nice hat, champ," he tells me.

Self-consciously, I touch it.

"Oh, a broken board," he says. "Bring it over here." He points to a wide table, clear of obstacles.

"Is your name Silver?" Sam asks.

He glances at her as he taps the table, asking us to put the covered board on it.

"Yeah, my surfing nickname for years. Some claim it's because of this," he taps his shiny bald head. "Or possibly because I was fairly decent in my days. They called me Silver Surfer, so it stuck."

I'm not moving. I'm stuck, motionless, unable to breathe or think.

Sam spins to me, then snaps to Carmen. Her mouth is open.

"Let's see what you did," he says to Carmen because she has the broken nose.

"I did it," I say, surprising myself that words came out of my mouth.

Silver glances at the nose in Carmen's hand and his head tilts slightly.

"That's an interesting design," he says then turns his attention to the covered portion of the board. Silver proceeds to open it.

"Here we go," he says as he slides it out, momentarily focused on the break point. "That's not too bad..." he begins then he scans the length of the board and he freezes. His eyes go wide as he studies it again, up and down.

He looks up at me, then Sam, and finally Carmen.

He pulls the cover off, allowing it to drop to the floor. He runs his hand over his face then his head. "Where—?" he starts but abruptly stops, collects himself then asks. "Where did you get this board?" he asks. He attempts to sound calm, but there is a tremor in his voice.

I can't answer him. I don't know what to say.

"It was my aunt's board," Carmen says.

Silver turns to her, his eyes ablaze. He is studying her: the features, skin tone, lips, hair color. All so similar to my mom's.

301

"Olivia?" he asks, and the bottom falls out from under me.

IN A CORNER of the café next door, we huddle on a small table and squeeze in four chairs. I swallow, studying his features. Do I look like him? We're both white. Is that enough? All other similarities require a lot of imagination.

"How's Olivia?" he says. "I haven't seen her in..." he is lost in thought for a moment. "I don't know, two decades probably. Is she still in Texas?"

Carmen looks at me. It's time I grew a pair.

"Sir," I start.

"Call me Scotty."

"Scotty, Olivia is my mom."

His eyes go wide, his face goes slack. "So you're her child."

He knew about me? So many questions try to surface, but I remain focused. "Less than two months ago," I start and immediately his eyes turn crimson.

"Oh God, no," he says.

I nod. "Cancer," I utter, not having the ability to produce complete sentences.

He covers his face and breaks down.

So do I. And so do Carmen and Sam.

MINUTES LATER, silence has draped our table.

"Scotty, are you Quick Silver?" Carmen asks.

His bright blue eyes flash on her. He smiles. "That's what she insisted on calling me, even though my professional nickname was Silver. But she was persistent."

"That's Mom," I say.

He smiles with empathy. "When I finally agreed, she changed her mind again and decided my original nickname was better."

"What happened?" Sam blurts out. "I mean... we've read her diary. You guys seemed so perfect."

He takes a deep breath. "Man, this is a lot to take in, but I need to step back because I don't want to be unfair to Shep."

"To me?" I'm stunned.

"We were going to meet here in the winter when she came back from college. But she never came. We had been emailing each other for a good month or so after she left Pismo, but then she stopped responding. December came and went and not only did she not come here, but she just refused to reply. Then in January or maybe it was February, I received an email from her. She apologized and said that what she had to do, she couldn't do with me. That I needed to focus on my future and career.

"I wrote back immediately. A long email, saying some really sappy things like comparing her to the waves and the ocean and a bunch of really bad analogies. But I did the best I could. I explained my heart in words, then hit send.

"A couple of days passed and then I got another email. I'm pregnant, she wrote. I need to be fair to the child and the child's father."

My heart tears into pieces. A blunt force shreds it, then steps on it and smears what's left. The sounds in the café fade and a burning sensation scorches my face. Scotty is not my dad.

"I had suspected something was going on. She had morning sickness and vomiting. Honestly though, I didn't give a rip. I replied immediately. Told her if the father is a jerk, even if he's not a jerk but she loves me more, if she ever needs help, if anything, I'd be there for her... and you. I hit the send button and waited. In a matter of seconds, I got an automated reply email. 'This email account no longer exists.'

"I Googled her, tried to find her friends, contacted the University of Texas, hoping they'd give me something. Nothing. She had disappeared. I kept returning here every December 26, just in case, but clearly she never came back. In the end, I liked this place so much that after I retired, I decided this would be home."

He's not my dad. Then why did she make me come here? Why did she put me through all this?

"I can't believe she's gone." He dabs at his eye. "She was so alive, so full of joy. And oh my God, what an amazing surfer. I could watch her forever. I bet many people fell in love with her just by watching her."

I think of how I felt watching Sam.

"She was fearless with an unparalleled instinct for the wave. She could've gone pro. She would've gotten sponsors with no problem. She had the attitude, the skills, and the looks. She was the whole package."

Now what? I think. Where do I go from here?

"Come to my shop. Two things I want to show you guys."

I drag my body and we follow him. He takes us to his office. Hanging on the wall is a replica of my mom's board.

"I built it a decade ago. She's been my good luck charm."

I step up to it and touch its glossy finish.

"It's a perfect replica," Sam says.

"I'll do the same thing for Olivia's original. It'll look perfect. But... maybe you should just save it and not use it anymore."

"Okay," I say.

"How did you make such a perfect replica?" Carmen asks.

"That was the other thing I wanted to show you guys." He turns on the T.V. then scrolls through videos. My heartbeat accelerates. "Here she is," he says and presses play.

My mom, in Technicolor, surfing. She's graceful, a gliding goddess. She maneuvers her board like it's attached to her. Like they are part of each other—a symbiotic relationship. I watch her young face, and long black hair. The cancer that would eventually reshape her full cheeks and steal her hair was nearly two decades away.

The clip ends.

"Can I have a copy?" I ask.

"Absolutely."

"Scotty, we need your help on one more thing," Carmen says.

"Anything. Everything."

"Shep needs a board. He's riding in the Remembrance tournament tomorrow."

He snaps to me. "So am I. I'm riding to honor one of my buddies. Yeah, I'll hook you up. Let's find something that's right for you."

I don't have the heart to say I don't have any money, but we march after him, scanning the room. I didn't find my dad, but I found the man she loved for a brief period of time. *We* found the man she loved. Me and my posse. That has to count for something.

"Shep, I will kick your ass," Sam says.

I turn to her. "Why? What did I do?"

"This is my gift to you. And if you disagree, Carmen will hold you down, while I kick your ass."

I shake my head. "Sam, thank you. Really. But I'll need to pay for this." How is a different question. I'll have to borrow from Carmen for now, then sell the truck.

"This is non-negotiable. I have to buy it. I must."

"But why?" I ask.

She steps up to me, drapes her hands around my neck. "Because each time you surf, I want you to remember me."

"Why would I forget you?" I ask.

"Because things happen in life. People change their minds. People hurt each other. They make poor choices. But once a surfer, always a surfer. The stories you make with that board will stay with you forever. And my connection will stay with you forever."

FIFTY-ONE

DAY 15 - SHEP

SAM, Carmen, and I are huddled around my phone, watching the clock. It's stupid. At this point, we can open up the last letter and move on. We don't have to observe the commitment we made at the beginning. It's done. We already know all that was meant to be shared. Yet, we wait.

We're in our balcony, wrapped in blankets because it's very cold, holding cups of hot coffee on the porch table.

"Moment of truth," Sam says.

12:00 a.m.

I pop the envelope open, slide out the letter, and read out loud.

July 23, 2000 — Day 15

I write this as we head back home. I spent the night with him. I could've spent eternity in his arms. Someday soon, we will. He is everything I don't deserve. But I will take him and hold on to him.

I told him he will forget me when I'm gone.
He said he'd marry me on the spot.
I almost said yes.

To think that if I hadn't been given the permission to go on this
trip, I would've never met the man that I will one day marry.
Of this, I have no doubt. He's the one.

He wants to move to Texas. He said he'll learn how to milk a
cow and count eggs. That alone shows me that this is real. A
divine gift. We'll do anything for each other. None of that will
be necessary, of course. I'll transfer to a school somewhere
along the coast. We'll get married after I get my degree. He'll
continue to grow as a respected surfer and later, we'll have
little Silver Surfers.

That's what's going to happen.
We're committed to each other.
We just have to stay focused.
I'm also looking forward to getting healthy again!

Life is good. Always.

Laters,
O.

I look up to the girls, both are sniffling.

"Shep," Sam says, her voice hoarse and soft. "She must've put you on this journey because she thought he was your father."

I study her. "Why do you say that?"

"She set up all these things so that you'd find him. She was sure you'd put it all together. Silver Surfer. Quick Silver. Three days in

Pismo. The memorial tournament. She must have known he was in Pismo. She must have been following his life and career."

I'm motionless, listening to her words.

"But she told Scotty he wasn't the father," I say.

Sam doesn't like that bit of fact.

Carmen pipes up. "What if she was playing with words? What if she was being a bit elusive. Didn't she say something like she 'needs to be fair to the kid and the kid's father?' That does not mean the kid's father is someone else. She wanted to be fair to Scotty."

I'm staring at her, trying to buy her logic, but it's a leap.

"We can't know what she really meant," Sam says, "but I feel strongly that in her heart, she didn't think she was lying to you. She thought you would find your dad and that you'd have a life with him. She loved him so much, she wanted to believe he was your father."

"She's right, little Cuz," Carmen says. "Olivia must have thought he was the guy. In a way, you've found something more important than your biological father. You found the person your mom would've married. The person she loved so much that she didn't want to get in his way. Wouldn't you want to have a real relationship with that man? Even if he's not your real dad?"

I STUDY my uncle and aunt. They seem lost for words. I've been speaking for over an hour, telling them about everything I've discovered. Recounting our conversation with Scotty, mom's pregnancy, and what this all means.

"I don't like to be negative," José says, "particularly about my sister, but let's face it: she did the wrong thing."

Aunt Rosie nods, but I'm not sure what he's talking about. Getting drunk, getting pregnant, or something else? "What do you mean?" I ask.

"She should've told Scotty."

"But we now know he wasn't my father," I say.

"Doesn't matter. At the time she thought he was the father. By that decision she denied Scotty a family that he wanted and denied you a father that you desperately needed."

I don't say anything, I just digest this insight.

"To be fair," Aunt Rosie says, "she did it out of love for him. She didn't want to ruin his career, his future."

"Yes, fine," he says, "but still, that should not have been her call. She thought she was doing the right thing, while doing the wrong thing. If she had opened her mouth, tests would've shown he wasn't the father. Then maybe the right person would've entered their life. Now we can't know, because disguised in what in her mind was the right thing, she set off a chain of events that feels wrong."

My heart is hammering away and my lungs are taking in shallow amounts of air. Is this what Mom wanted me to understand? Is this it? Is this why she sent me on this journey? I snap to my feet.

She tried to save his career, his future by doing the wrong thing. I've been trying to save my career, my future by doing the wrong thing. She wanted me to see it, to break the cycle.

I hug my uncle and kiss my aunt. "I have to go," I say.

"Are you okay?" she asks.

"Yes, I think so. I need to go and wake up the girls."

As I open the door, he calls out, "It's 2:00 a.m. Can it wait?"

"No, it can't."

"SAM, WAKE UP," I say. She doesn't respond, nor does Carmen. "Sam, Carmen, I need your help." I shake her.

"Wha... what the dealio?" she mumbles.

"I need help," I say.

"Shep, we can get you a psychologist later," Carmen says. "Can you let us sleep for now?"

"Guys, this is important."

They both sit up and stare at me.

"Here's what's going to happen: the lawyers will ask why I was at the party in the first place? Was it true that I had plans of hooking up with her? Wasn't hooking up, just code for irresponsible sex? Wasn't she just embarrassed that I had caught her? Wasn't she doing exactly what everyone expected? And isn't that why I didn't stop the quote-un-quote rape? And what was the reason I took months to speak up? Then they'll find names of girls that I've been with. Girls that I may not even remember. They'll question my credibility. They'll show that I am in fact one of 'those' guys. They'll try to destroy me."

Carmen and Sam are locked onto my eyes.

"I don't want them to destroy everything I've done. But I think Mom wants me to lay it out there, no matter what happens. I'm being honest with you two—I'm worried. Scared. But I have to do it, so here's the big ask—will you two come with me to Houston next week? I need to tell the district attorney everything I saw. I need to do it in person, but I really need you guys there with me."

Sam's eyes glisten and a tear rips down the side of her cheek. She's crying, but smiling ear to ear. Carmen leaps from her seated position and hugs me so hard that air whooshes out of my lungs.

Sam reaches out and joins the group hug. "Surfers take care of their own," she says.

"I'm scared," I whisper.

"Whatever happens, happens," Carmen says. "You took on your fears and owned them. We can handle lies. Your mom put us up to this for a reason."

An idea pops in my head. "I have one more favor to ask of you two."

"Shoot," Carmen says.

"I need to have one more challenge taken care of," I say.

Sam's eyes brighten. "Finally! He's going to surf naked!"

I glare at her. "Not that challenge."

"What then?" she asks.

"Shave my hair," I say.

A few minutes later, I'm in the bathroom, a towel wrapped around my neck. They're using shears from the camper to trim my hair down. My once-awesome hair is now horrible, the ugliest thing possible, but it's also perfect.

Once it's short enough, they lather some soap and apply it to my head. Carmen applies the cream while Sam studies my head, her disposable razor at hand.

"Don't cut me," I say.

"You forget my nerves of steel when I extracted your mom's picture after Carmen broke the picture frame."

"Um... you broke the frame," I say.

"Now you're just being mean."

I close my eyes. "Just do it."

The first stroke is the scariest, but with each successive slide-slide-slide of the razor, I feel more at ease. They apply more cream, more cuts.

"Can I open my eyes?" I ask.

"Almost," Carmen says.

Sam takes my arm. "Get up and walk over to the shower."

I do.

"I'm going to wash it down," she says. "Bend your head."

The warm water sprays over my scalp. I love the feel of the smooth surface and how the water slides right over it.

She cuts off the water. I open my eyes and straighten. She throws a towel on my head and dries it.

"Let's see," she says, as she unveils the new me. She nods. "Not bad at all."

"Well done," Carmen adds.

I step around her and stare at my vision. My scalp is pale compared to the shades I've picked up over the last couple of weeks. That'll be addressed soon enough when we hit the beach.

As I stare at my reflection, I remind myself of when Mom asked me to shave off her hair. The chemo was already causing her hair to fall. She didn't want the nurses to do it, so she asked me.

I feel it appropriate to be just like her when she passed on the day I honor her life.

FIFTY-TWO

DAY 15 - SHEP

THE WEATHER HAS OPENED UP. It's perfect in fact. It's California beach weather. It's what I didn't understand or appreciate two weeks ago, but it's what I can't get enough of now. I thought about how my mom kept herself away from both Scotty and the ocean all these years. I thought about how she was able to do that. Then I remembered what she had written.

We'll do anything for each other.

She'd do anything for me. Including put everything else on hold. Everything that mattered to her because I became her priority.

We find our way around to the check-in table. There are two dozen surfers. All of them are much older than me.

When I see Scotty, I go up to him.

"Good morning," I say.

When he sees me, he at first doesn't recognize me because of my hair. But then it clicks. "Love the do, Shep," he says. "You guys have been on my mind. Are the ladies here?"

"Yeah," I say and wave them down. My uncle and the others come as well. They have not met each other formally. There will be time for that later.

After they shake hands, Scotty pulls out his tablet from a rucksack. "Here's another video."

"Of Olivia?" Carmen asks.

"Yes, one of her best clips."

My uncle shoves his way around to see the screen.

He presses play and a low quality clip plays. My beautiful mother is on a longboard. She paddles, slides to her feet and just glides that board around. She is poetry in motion. She is legitimately dancing on the board, spinning around, tapping one foot into the water. She controls the board then quickly, but smoothly walks up to it, hangs her ten toes over the edge, then arcs her back, so much so that you'd think she'll fall backward. Instead, her arms go up, and she faces the sky above. She looks like an angel ready for flight.

She holds it for two seconds. Maybe a bit more, but the image burns itself into my heart.

The wave loses its velocity and Mom maneuvers the board around, before she lowers herself then turns it around and paddles back to the lineup.

The clip ends.

"Can I have a copy?" I ask. "Please."

"You can have anything you want, Shep."

I stare into his blue eyes, nothing at all like mine. I study the honest face of a man who never gave up on his one love. Then I dig into my bag and pull out the blue vial, the same color as his eyes. The thirteenth vial. Lucky thirteen. I hold it out in front of him.

I can't see the looks on my uncle's face or my aunt's. But I can feel the energy from Carmen and Sam.

"This is the last of my mom's ashes," I say, my voice breaks.

His eyes go red.

"I'd be honored if you'd release her ashes into the water."

He's nodding, his jaw pulsating, trying his best to not cry. He doesn't use words, he grabs me and pulls me into a hug unlike anything I've ever experienced. The type of hug a father would give his son.

I PADDLE PATIENTLY to the lineup. My mom's longboard promises me a good ride. I have no doubt. From where I am, it's hard to make out the people on the shore, but because Sam's wearing my hat and a hot yellow bikini, it doesn't take too much effort to triangulate on her.

Scotty's next to me, waiting patiently. He arranged it with the organization for us to be in the same lineup.

He's riding the replica of my mom's board he'd shown us the day before.

"Here comes the set," Scotty says.

"It's yours," I say, and he takes it without hesitation.

He immediately catches the wave, as if the wave was just waiting for him. He rips the waves, one after another. Even though the crowds are far away, I can hear them cheering. He's so good. He may be forty, but to me, he lives up to his namesake.

I take a wave and do my best to be smooth and calm. I don't want to mess up. I take a couple of steps back and forth and I tell myself people are cheering, although I think the sound I'm hearing are the waves, cheering me on.

I return to the lineup and we take a couple of more waves.

"For the Soul Arch Goddess," Scotty says, winks at me and takes the wave. He's on his feet so fast, that I convince myself he was never down in the first place. He takes a wide turn, so quick that I nearly get whiplash watching him. I catch him sliding the vial out of his pocket just as he turns the board back up the face of the wave. He's building up more speed. He lowers himself to the board, grabs one of the rails and he flies up the wave. He performs a 360 and comes back down the face of the wave. The white foam surrounds him. He's going to eat it. Instead he pumps the board, accelerates and pulls through. His arm raised high, the vial most likely emptied out when he did the aerial move.

No pressure.

How do I follow that one?

It doesn't take me long to know what I want to do. I just have to let go and let it happen. What did Mom use to tell me? *Let go and let God.* I'll try.

I catch a small wave with good energy. I adjust direction and velocity. For just a moment I visualize it then calmly take a few steps up and get one foot to the edge of the board. I hesitate.

Now, I hear in my mind. Clear. Crisp. With authority.

I slide my back foot next to the other one. My first official hang ten.

I close my eyes, remember my beautiful mother and lift my arms up.

I don't know if it looks right. I don't know if my back is arched. I don't even care if a shark is about to attack me. All I know is that on this board, in this water, I am with Mom. And I can always be with her each time I surf.

SCOTTY AND I finish our set and ride the waves back to shore. As we grab our boards and jog onto the sand, my family surrounds me. From the corner of my eye, I see a handful of people approach Scotty and speak to him. For an instant I think I see the Jamaican lady who told us about Scotty. Smiling and applauding. But just as quickly, she disappears behind the crowd.

Sam goes up to Scotty and says something. My uncle is speaking to me, but I only listen haphazardly. I see Scotty place the vial in Sam's hand. She thanks him then walks up to us.

Carmen hugs me. "What you did out there was beautiful."

A couple of feet away, I notice Sam kneeling on the sand.

What is she doing? I'm about to ask her when Scotty walks up to me, drops both hands on my shoulders and smiles, ear to ear. "Your mom is smiling down on you, Shep. You honored her. Angels are singing, because you did great for one of their own."

FIFTY-THREE
DAY 15 - SHEP

SCOTTY INVITES us to his shop for a little celebration event. Many local surfers, some YouTubers and surf bloggers are also there. My uncle and aunt have gone back home already. José walked away with a couple of video clips of his sister. He is the happiest man alive today. He's also concerned, because I told him what I saw the night of the incident. Although he fully supports my decision to tell the whole story, he wants our attorney there just in case.

Carmen and I are hanging out together in silence. Sam hasn't joined us yet. She had to "take care of business." I didn't question her. She's had that adorable smile on her face all afternoon. She also refuses to return my hat. I'm not complaining, just making an observation that my hat has suddenly become her hat.

I study Scotty, who is charismatic and funny and decent. A good guy. What I would've given to have a father like him in my life.

"Where you at?" Carmen asks.

I glance at her. "I'm thinking."

"Excellent idea. Nothing like using that thing once in a while."

I rise.

"What now?"

"I'm done thinking," I say, and walk up to Scotty who's in mid-conversation with a young guy whose easy way of being tells me he's a pro surfer.

"Can we chat for a second?" I ask.

"Of course," he says and motions me to follow him.

We enter his repair shop. Wall to wall are containers of chemicals, tools, benches, partially finished boards and raw boards, stickers and silk-screening tools. It's chaos, but I am certain for him it all makes sense.

"What's on your mind?" he asks.

I hand him Mom's letter. The one that kicked off this journey.

He studies the paper and the words on the paper. He's not reading it yet. He's analyzing what's in his hand. He brings the paper closer and reads. I stand next to him, reading along.

He finishes, but instead of speaking to me, his eyes drift to a corner of the shop. He comes to when I take the letter out of his hand.

"This part," I say and read the passage.

"And in the process, you'll finally get what you've asked about for years—details about your father."

He's studying me. "Was she talking about me?" he asks, genuinely confused. "Did she think I was your father?"

I nod. "I think she did."

He drops onto a high back stool. "But... are you saying you never met your dad?"

I shake my head. "No clue who he is. She never told me. This trip was my only hope." He's studying me intently. "We still don't know. She may have been pregnant even before her trip began."

"Because of the vomiting..." he adds.

"Right."

He's in deep thought. "We can do a test."

"Or..." I take a deep breath. "We take Mom's word for it and roll with the wave she gave us."

I'm afraid of the results. That's the truth. Because if he's not my father, over time, there'll be no reason to stay in touch with me. But while the possibility exists, we'll remain connected. Maybe forever.

He's trying to understand what I just offered. His eyes go wide. "Are you saying, we just assume she was right?"

"We both loved the same person. And she loved us."

He rises. "So, what does that mean? How do we do this?"

"I have no idea," I say. "But I guess we just... you know. Start."

WE STROLL BACK to the party. I have decided to tell him about the Houston testimony later. I don't want to scare him off too quickly.

Sam is back. She's waving at us.

"Is she your girl?" he asks.

"Yeah."

"I approve," he whispers.

Sam walks right up to us, a wrapped narrow box in her hand. "I got this for you," she says and hands me the box. It's heavy.

"Another gift?" I ask.

"Open it," she says. She's fidgeting.

I flip the edges and carefully tear the wrapping. I first see a corner, then the rest of the shadow box. The wrapping paper drops from my hand.

"Came out perfect," Carmen says.

"Ah man. That's primo stuff," Scotty says.

"Well?" Sam asks. "Do you like it?"

I study the thirteen blue vials, each numbered and labeled with the associated beach location. A brass label at the top reads, "Fifteen Days, Fifteen Beaches, Three Friends, An Epic Story."

In each vial she has trapped the sand from the beaches we visited. Like a movie on replay, I remember each time she took the vials from us. She'd been planning it all along.

"You're freaking me out," Sam says. "Do you hate it?"

Like Mom, I went on a trip with friends and came back with so much more.

"What can I tell you?" I say.

"You can say you love it."

I hand the shadowbox to Carmen and hug Sam so hard I practically feel her ribs crack. The smell of sunscreen and sand and salt emanates off her. It's like she's bathed in nature's tonic.

"I love it," I whisper in her ear.

What do you think, Mom? Do you approve?

I feel warmth travel from the nape of my neck to the small of my back. It's probably nothing. Just my imagination. Or possibly, it's a promise kept.

FIFTY-FOUR

DAY 15 - SAMANTHA

CARMEN and I are observing Silver Surfer Junior and Senior from behind. They're talking to some random people, but we don't really care what they're talking about. We're studying them.

"No," Carmen finally says.

"Then you're blind."

She glares at me. "You're totally reaching. Just stop."

"They have the same exact skull."

"That's because they're both bald." She eyes me. "Let it be. He's in a good place."

"Fine," I mumble, but something keeps kicking me in the shin.

Then it happens.

Silver Surfer Senior rubs the back of his head.

His fingers.

A pinky that from here looks nearly as long as his middle finger.

Amazing Grace

"Amazing grace! How sweet the sound
That saved a wretch like me.
I once was lost, but now am found,
Was blind but now I see."

Amazing Grace — John Newton, 1779

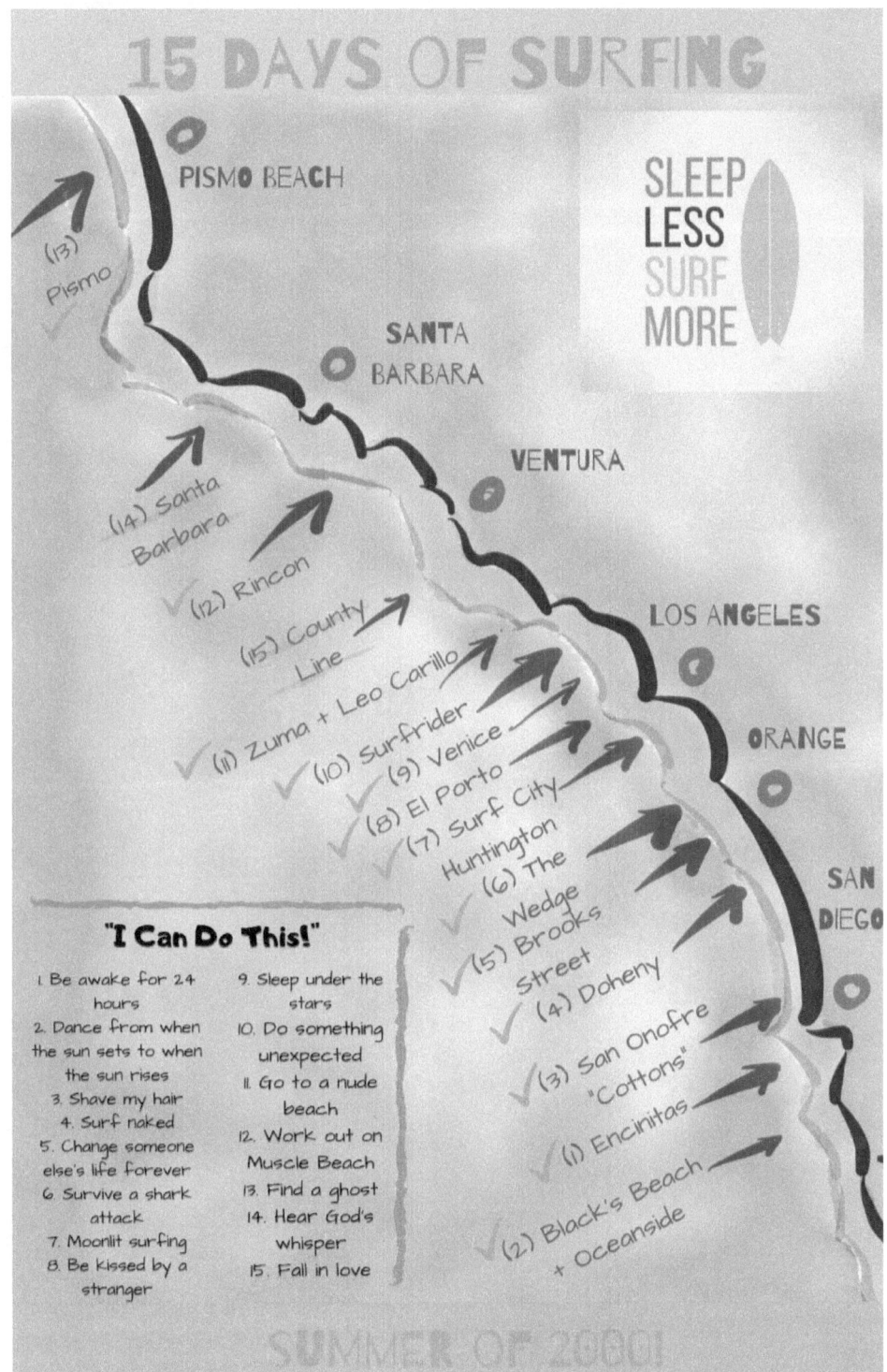

15 DAYS OF SURFING

PISMO BEACH

SANTA BARBARA

VENTURA

LOS ANGELES

ORANGE

SAN DIEGO

SLEEP LESS SURF MORE

(13) Pismo

(14) Santa Barbara

(12) Rincon

(15) County Line

(11) Zuma + Leo Carillo

(10) Surfrider

(9) Venice

(8) El Porto

(7) Surf City Huntington

(6) The Wedge

(5) Brooks Street

(4) Doheny

(3) San Onofre "Cottons"

(1) Encinitas

(2) Black's Beach + Oceanside

"I Can Do This!"

1. Be awake for 24 hours
2. Dance from when the sun sets to when the sun rises
3. Shave my hair
4. Surf naked
5. Change someone else's life forever
6. Survive a shark attack
7. Moonlit surfing
8. Be kissed by a stranger
9. Sleep under the stars
10. Do something unexpected
11. Go to a nude beach
12. Work out on Muscle Beach
13. Find a ghost
14. Hear God's whisper
15. Fall in love

SUMMER OF 2000

Map Designed by Ara Grigorian ©2019

PLEASE LEAVE A REVIEW!

If you enjoyed this book, you can make a big difference by leaving a review.

Although I can't afford to run a thirty-second commercial during prime time to get the attention of readers, I can ask my loyal readers for help. Honest reviews of my books help bring them to the attention of other readers.

To leave a review, return to the retailer's website, search for 15 DAYS WITH YOU, and leave an honest review.

Thank you!

V.I.P. CLUB

Join my VIP Club to receive a free behind the scenes content to my novel's world.

Members are always the first to hear about my new books, events, and special announcements.

It's completely free to sign up and you will never be spammed by me: you can opt out easily at any time.

Click to Join my VIP Club:
www.AraGrigorian.com

AUTHOR'S NOTES

In the Summer of 1987, my brother and his friends decided to go on a multi-beach odyssey. I had just graduated 11th grade so I was no longer the snot-nosed kid brother who always wanted to go wherever his big brother went. Okay, that's not completely true, but that's not the point of this story.

We had a romanticized notion of what those trips would look like. We would visit one awesome beach after another. We'd meet people. We'd have fun and we'd have an unforgettable summer. At one point we got stranded in La Jolla, but let's not get all negative. We even considered creating different personas for the people we were bound to meet. I think I recommended speaking like Arnold Schwarzenegger — "Bring down the chopper!" — they probably regretted allowing me to join them after that one...

Anyway, we did just that. We hit the road and had a blast.

In many ways, that summer was a turning point for me. Maybe it was those beach visits and hanging out with college-age guys. Maybe it was something about the ocean that called me to appreciate that beautiful, melodious cacophony of sounds that only the ocean can produce. Whatever it was, those trips, or what those trips promised, stayed with me. That summer was a turning point for me. I entered 12th grade different.

Nearly thirty Years Later, in the Spring of 2016, my friend Norm Thoeming (who writes brilliant thrillers under the pen name of August Norman — go check him out now!) and I were eating at Portos in Burbank. I don't know why it came up, but I told him about that summer. When I was done, he said, "You know, that story of yours needs to be a novel." Two thoughts flashed into my head. Thought #1 — Why? I'm so boring. There are so many more interesting things that have happened to other people. Thought #2 — I write fiction. I'm a professional liar. I can take out all the boring parts and make it really fun.

How, I was not sure, but I knew I had to try.

I prayed and meditated and prayed some more. I really wanted this story to be different. I didn't know what type of story I wanted to tell, but like all my other novels, I knew it would be a story of second chances. An obvious idea dropped into my head — I had to write a young adult novel, it had to a be a road trip story, and of course, a coming of age story. A story of teenagers on the cusp of tasting adulthood.

So why surfing? Shortly after I had been meditating on the story, a Beach Boys song came on. Coincidence? Me thinks not! I had always observed surfers with a fascination. In my first novel, *Game of Love*, I have a scene where Andre explains to Gemma why he loves surfers and the different mindset of some of the surfers that grace the waters (if you want to know what he said, please check out the book. It's really good — it won awards and stuff!).

In my heart I knew I needed to tie these amazing aquatic athletes and dancers into this story. There is something about those who dare to be on the other side of the sand. They sit in waiting, listening for the roar of the ocean, ready to accept the challenge to dance with her one more time.

So surfing it was. A sport that's reserved for the brave. A journey for an orphan kid that was lost in the sea of loneliness who desperately needed to learn to brave the truth that he was about to unravel. All I had to do was get out of the way of my characters and let them tell the story.

I hope you enjoy the ride. And if you decide to give surfing a try as a result of reading this book, do let me know. Because that would be really cool!

ACKNOWLEDGMENTS

Anyone who takes on a dangerous task needs to have a team with specialized skills. A diver needs his dive buddy. A climber of the Himalayan mountains needs his sherpa. A pencil needs an eraser. An author is no different. In fact, this author needed an entire army.

Stacey Donaghy, who is more than an agent. She is a friend, practically family. If this was the mafia, she'd be a "friend of ours." An untouchable. Thank you for all your guidance.

My first reader: Delia, my wife. I so married up! Thank you for your (sometimes painfully) honest feedback when the first draft is fit for a trash liner.

My beta readers who read multiple versions of the manuscript: Andreh Anderson, Norm Thoeming, and Janis Thomas. You guys are the best. I don't know how I got this lucky. But I won't argue.

Janis Thomas — I value our friendship, our partnership as teachers, and your heart for telling a true story, no matter how hard it may be to execute. You help me write better.

Norm Thoeming (who writes as August Norman), thanks to our lunch sessions at Portos in Burbank, this story received its heart beat. You are a force for good. Your grit encourages me. Thank you, my friend.

Friend, author, unrelenting supporter, Demetra Brodsky — Thank you for who you are and your resilience. You are an inspiration.

Jean Jenkins... this editor's superpower is making all stories better. All writers need someone like her (or her specifically) in their circle of friends. Once you're one of her writers, you are forever blessed.

Jennifer Silva Redmond is genetically designed to be helpful. She is a editor professional through and through. Also, I am nearly certain that when they came up with the term "eagle eyes," they had her in mind. Above all, she's just a good good person.

Michael Steven Gregory for seeing what I didn't. The story is better because of your insight.

I got a lot of insight into the minds of surfers from amazing people who willingly step into the water, knowing that there are sharks in those waters! Jay Yow for connecting me with the right people. Mike Takahashi for being the master at introductions. Who needs LinkedIn when people like you exist? Thank you, sir! And now, the people who helped me feel the waves: Silicon Beach Surfers, Allen Avanesian, Cristina Behrens, Dr. Lena Dicken, Patrick Eli, Roni Eshel, Tom Geck, Rick Geist, Christina LoFranco, Reyn Murphy, Dale H Rhodes, Fred Sookiasian, Nolan Starczak, Jesse Timm.

Last but not least Laura Woods and Sean Woods. You guys gave me gold. I am not kidding. Gold, time and time again. Special thank you to Robin Ruel for introducing me to you. Please check out Sean's instagram account — he's an inspiration (@seanwoodzy).

My cover designer, Tracy Van Dolder of Virtually Possible

Designs. Thank you for tapping into my mind and finding the emotion I wanted to create with this book.

The magicians who made me look marginally human — my friend, Armen Melik-Abramians, and his partner in photographic crime, Alan Falcioni, from FlashCube Photography — thank you!

My sisters of the NAC, we connected in 2015 and you are still a critical part of my tribe: Missy Belote, Marnee Blake, Diana Gardin, Sophia Henry, Jamie Howard, Kate Lynn, Marie Meyer, Sribindu Pisupati, Jessica Ruddick, Meredith Tate Servello, Laura Steven, and Amanda Rae Stogsdill — I hope you ladies never find out I'm not worthy to be in your company!

My wolfpack: Norm Thoeming, Trey Dowell, and Chase Moore. Always there, always supporting me, always the best.

The conferences that give me time with my people and the opportunity to teach in alphabetic order: Santa Barbara Writers Conference and Southern California Writers' Conference (Irvine and San Diego) . I look forward to my days with you guys. From the staff, to the volunteers, and the workshop leaders — you make me better.

My Second Chancers — My sincerest gratitude to this secret street team. Your joy and enthusiasm is contagious.

My friends and family: I love you. There, it has been said!

To my fans. I write for you. You keep me going. All your emails, messages, posts, and telepathic thoughts are like oxygen. Don't stop :) You are the best. Thank you.

Finally, don't forget to fight the good fight!

ALSO BY ARA GRIGORIAN

<u>GAME OF LOVE (2015)</u>

Game of Love is set in the high-stakes world of professional women's tennis where fortune and fame can be decided by a single point. In the Game of Love, winner takes all.

- **WINNER** - Outstanding "Romance" in the 2016 IAN Book of the Year awards
- **WINNER** - Readers' Favorite 2015 International Book Award — GOLD - Sports Category
- **FINALIST** - 2015 USA Book News & USA Best Book Awards — Romance
- **FINALIST** - 2016 International Book Awards — Romance

<u>TEN YEAR DANCE (2017)</u>

Best friends since sixth grade. A ten-year high school reunion. A truth they've danced around for a decade...

"Ten Year Dance is a delightful and engaging romance about two best friends. Like When Harry Met Sally, you will root for Pete and Sophie to find each other before it's too late!"

ABOUT THE AUTHOR

© 2014 *FlashCube Photography*

Ara Grigorian is the international award-winning author of GAME OF LOVE and bestselling author of TEN YEAR DANCE. He is a technology executive in the entertainment industry. He earned his Masters in Business Administration from University of Southern California where he specialized in marketing and entrepreneurship. True to the Hollywood life, Ara wrote for a children's television pilot that could've made him rich (but didn't) and nearly sold a video game to a publisher (who closed shop days later). Fascinated by the human species, Ara writes about choices, relationships, and second chances.

Ara is the co-founder of the popular Novel Intensive seminar. He is also a workshop leader for various writers' conferences in Southern California. Ara is a member of the Romance Writers of America and its Los Angeles chapter. He is represented by Stacey Donaghy of the Donaghy Literary Group.

www.AraGrigorian.com

PERMISSIONS

The epigraphs at the start of each part are quotes that were carefully curated by Cristina Costea who wrote a blog post for Book Surf Camps (www.BookSurfCamps.com). Thank you to Cristina for doing the hard work of finding these perfect quotes from the public domain. A special thank you to the marketing team at Tripaneer.com. The original blog post is "10 Famous Surfing Quotes to Inspire You in 2018."

Author's photo courtesy of FlashCube Photography © 2014